WILL McINTOSH

BURNING MIDNIGHT

MACMILLAN

First published 2016 in the US by Delacorte Press

First published 2016 in the UK by Macmillan Children's Books
an imprint of Pan Macmillan
20 New Wharf Road, London N1 9RR
Associated companies throughout the world
www.panmacmillan.com

ISBN 978-1-5098-0356-9

1 3 5 7 9 8 6 4 2

A CIP catalogue record for this book is available from
the British Library.

Book design by Stephanie Moss
Printed and bound by CPI Group (UK) Ltd, Croydon CR0 4YY

To the Fredericks family:
Donna, George, Sarah and Tim

CHAPTER 1

Sully pulled the thin wad of bills from his pocket and counted. Thirteen bucks. He'd hauled his butt out of bed at six a.m. on a Saturday to make thirteen bucks in seven hours. He couldn't work out how much that was per hour, but he knew Dom made more stacking yogurt and cream cheese at Price Chopper.

The flea market was depressingly empty. Most of the other vendors were parked on lawn chairs, their feet propped on tables. Sully spent enough time sitting in school, so he was standing, arms folded.

The timing of this epically bad payday couldn't be worse. It would have given his mom a lift, for Sully to hand her a hundred bucks to put towards the rent or groceries.

He still couldn't believe Exile Music had closed. Nine and a half years, Mom had worked there. By the end she'd been their manager, their accountant, their everything. But she had no accounting degree; she didn't even have a high school diploma. Where was she going to find another job that paid half of what she'd been making?

Sully took a deep, sighing breath and stared down the long aisle.

A girl around Sully's age turned the corner and headed in his direction. He watched her walk, head down, beat-up backpack slung over one shoulder. There was a swagger to her walk, a little attitude. Or maybe the combat boots, the black gloves with the fingertips cut off, the mass of dark braids bouncing off her back like coils of rope provided the attitude.

As she drew closer, Sully looked at his phone instead of staring. It was hard not to stare.

To Sully's surprise, she slowed when she reached his stall. She eyed the orbs he kept locked under glass, running her tongue over her teeth. She was wearing loose-fitting cargo trousers and zero make-up. Her brown angular face was striking, her take-no-shit scowl a little intimidating. Not your usual flea market customer.

He cleared his throat. 'Anything I can help you with?'

She studied him, squinted, as if he was slightly out of focus. She unslung the bag on her shoulder and knelt out of sight in front of his table.

When she reappeared she was clutching a sphere – a Forest Green. Enhanced sense of smell. Sully didn't have to consult the book to know it scored a three out of ten on the rarity chart. Retail, he could easily get six hundred for it.

'How much?' she asked, holding it up.

His heart was hammering. This one deal could make his whole weekend. 'Wow. You find that in the wild?' She didn't strike him as a collector or an investor.

She nodded. 'It was caked in mud. I thought it was an Army Green.' Which was a big fat one on the rarity chart.

Resistance to the common cold. Sixty bucks.

'Man, you must have died when you cleaned it off.'

'How much?' she repeated, with the slightest of nods to acknowledge his comment.

Sully tried to remember how much cash he had on him. Two fifty? Maybe two seventy. Usually that was more than enough, because who brought a Forest Green to a flea market?

His gaze flicked between the Forest Green and the girl's face. 'Two fifty?' His voice rose at the last minute, making it sound more like a question.

The girl chuckled, bent to pick up her pack. 'I can get three twenty-five from Holliday's.'

Sully flinched when she said 'Holliday's', but to her credit, she said it like it hurt her mouth.

'Hang on. I can go to three fifty, but I can't get you the last hundred till tomorrow.' He'd have to borrow it from Dom.

The girl put a hand on her hip. 'I'm sorry. Did I give you the impression I thought three twenty-five was a fair price? Let me rephrase: even the bastards over at Holliday's would give me three twenty-five.'

Sully laughed in spite of himself. They *were* bastards. The brand-new store they'd opened in Yonkers was a big part of why Sully's earnings had taken a nosedive. And Alex Holliday himself was more than a bastard. Sully squelched any thought of Holliday before that particular train of thought could start running down the track.

He did some quick calculations. This girl could list the Forest Green on eBay and get at least four fifty. Minus eBay's cut, that would leave her with about four hundred.

'OK. Four twenty-five.' Two hundred dollars profit. He

could definitely dance to that tune.

The girl scowled, opened her mouth to counter. Sully raised his hand. 'Don't even try to tell me that's not a fair offer.' He looked her in the eye. 'We both know it is.'

She held her scowl a second longer, then broke into a smile. It was a terrific smile, complete with dimples. 'You got me. Four twenty-five.'

He pulled the cash from his pocket, started counting it out. 'Like I said, I can give you two fifty now, the rest next Saturday.'

The girl's eyebrows came together. 'I hope you're not thinking I'm going to give you this marble now. If you'll have the cash next week, I'll come back with the marble then.'

Sully licked his lips, which were dry as hell. If she left, there was always a chance she wouldn't come back. It had happened before; it was never a good idea to give people time to find a better offer.

'Look, I'll give you a receipt. I'm good for it; I'm here every weekend.' Sully spotted Neal across the aisle, unpacking used DVDs from a cardboard box. 'Neal!'

Neal lifted his head. He was wearing Ron Jon sunglasses despite being indoors, in a cavernous room that was not particularly well lit.

'Can she trust me?' Sully asked, holding his palms out.

Neal stabbed a finger in Sully's direction. 'You can trust that man with your life.'

From the next booth over, Samantha shouted, 'And that's the truth!' and crossed herself. Samantha was Neal's wife, so her testimonial was somewhat redundant, but the girl with the Forest Green didn't need to know that.

Sully turned back to the girl. She folded her arms. 'I wouldn't trust my *grandma* with that kind of money.'

'Hey, Sully?' Sully hadn't noticed the kid hovering at the corner of his booth. He was twelve or thirteen, Indian, holding a replica sphere – a Cherry Red. 'Would you sign this?'

'Sure.' Sully reached for the replica and a Sharpie the kid offered, feeling a flush of pleasure that the girl was there to witness this.

'You sure you can trust me with this?' Sully asked as he signed.

The kid laughed.

Sully blew the ink dry, tossed the kid the Cherry Red, said, 'Thanks, man. Thanks for asking.'

'What was that about?' the girl asked, motioning towards the kid, who was disappearing around a corner.

Sully held out his hand. 'David Sullivan.' When the girl only looked at his hand, he added, 'I'm the guy who found the Cherry Red.'

'I know who David Sullivan is.' She sounded annoyed. 'A millionaire for ten minutes, until Alex Holliday's lawyers stopped payment on the cheque. Tiny Tim ripped off by New York's favourite billionaire.'

The words stung like hot sauce on a wound, but Sully couldn't deny she was just stating the facts without any sugar-coating.

She held the Forest Green by her ear like a shot-putter. 'Moving on. We got a deal? I'll see you Saturday?'

'Tell you what.' Still trying to shake off her words, Sully took out his key ring, unlocked the display case, and pulled out his two most valuable spheres – a Lemon Yellow (grow an inch) and a Slate Grey (singing ability). Both were rarity level two; together they were worth about two sixty. 'Take these as collateral. They're worth way more than one seventy-five. I'll trust *you*.'

She considered, looking down at the spheres, then back up at Sully. She scooped the spheres out of his hand and stashed them in her pack. After exchanging numbers in case one of them couldn't make it next week, Sully counted the cash out on the table. She stuffed it in her back pocket and, finally, pressed the cool Forest Green sphere into his slightly sweaty palm.

'See you next Saturday,' she said, and turned away.

Sully watched her go, her wrists flicking as she walked.

'Hey,' he called after her.

She turned.

'What's your name?'

She smiled. 'Hunter.'

'As in, marble hunter?'

She pointed at him. 'You got it.'

'Maybe we'll do more business in the future, then?'

Hunter nodded. 'Works for me if your offers are straight.'

Sully nodded. 'See you Saturday.'

When Hunter was out of sight, he held the Forest Green up, rotated it, admiring.

'She's a beauty,' Neal called over. His buzz cut always seemed wrong to Sully; his bright, open face just cried out for long, surfer-dude hair.

'I nearly choked when she pulled it out. I've never had a Forest Green before.'

'I wasn't talking about the marble,' Neal said, laughing.

Sully grinned but said nothing. She was fine, no doubt about it, but not his type. Too serious. Sully liked to laugh.

'I met my first wife at a flea market.' Neal put his hand on top of his head. 'She was . . . dazzling. Long auburn hair, freckles dusted across her cheeks.'

'You do know I can hear you, right?' Samantha called from behind her table, which was covered in tarot cards, crystals, incense.

Neal acted like he'd been jolted out of a trance. 'Sorry.' He grinned at Sully. 'Did I say dazzling? I meant frumpy. Face like a Mack truck. Anyway, back then I was selling Grateful Dead memorabilia—'

'And pirated concert tapes,' Samantha interjected.

Sully laughed. 'The Grateful *who*?'

Neal didn't take the bait. He knew Sully knew who the Grateful Dead were, because he'd lent Sully one of their CDs. He also knew they put Sully to sleep.

Samantha crossed the aisle and, without a word, set a sandwich wrapped in tinfoil on Sully's table. She always made an extra for him.

'Thanks, Samantha.'

She patted Sully's shoulder as she passed.

Sully munched on a homemade meat loaf hero as Neal went on with his story. Sully wouldn't want to trade places with Neal, but he had to admit the guy had led an interesting life. Well into his sixties, he'd never had a real job with a steady pay cheque. He and Samantha lived in a little camper that Sully knew well from the many times they'd invited him to hang out after the flea market closed.

After ten years of sharing an apartment with his mom,

Sully'd had more than enough of living in cramped spaces. As of last Tuesday, they were in danger of losing even that. If something didn't give, by summer they'd be living in the basement of his weird uncle Ian's house in Pittsburgh. That couldn't happen. It just couldn't. Sully's friends were in Yonkers; his life was in Yonkers.

He tossed the Forest Green in the air and caught it, relishing the hard, perfect smoothness as the sphere slapped his palm. It was a start. Later, he'd call a few of his regular customers and see if anyone was interested in it. If not, he'd put it in the display case. It wouldn't be hard to sell. The values on the rarer spheres just kept rising, and Sully kept his prices ten or fifteen per cent below the big retailers'.

They'd get through this; they'd keep the apartment. In two years he'd graduate from Yonkers High with Dom by his side.

CHAPTER 2

Sully slid one of the huge, flaccid, greasy fries off Dom's plate and bit it in half. Normally he wouldn't go near the ode to grease and swine parts that was the school cafeteria's hot dog platter, but he was starving. He'd forgotten his lunch, and couldn't bring himself to blow half of yesterday's paltry earnings on a chicken sandwich and a Coke. He turned in his seat, eyed the wrapped sandwiches and steaming steel serving bins. He was sorely tempted to get something. He couldn't afford to buy school lunch, though. He and his mom might not be able to afford anything if Dom didn't loan him money for the Forest Green, unless he sold it before Saturday. Sully hated selling in a panic; it would mean knocking fifty, even a hundred off the price.

Dom was talking to Rob Dalton, his sleeves rolled up to show off his impressive biceps. Sully tapped him on the shoulder. In profile you could mistake Dom for a tough guy, with his thick eyebrows, meaty lips, and boxer's nose, the big jawline. But once he turned those open, friendly eyes your way, the illusion was shattered.

'I want to show you something.' Sully unzipped his pack, which was on the floor between his knees, and pulled the Forest Green halfway out so Dom could see it.

Dom leaned closer, tilted his head, trying to see the colour. 'Is that a Forest Green?'

'Yup.'

'Holy crap.' Dom grinned at him, squinting. 'A Forest Green? Where did you get that?'

'Someone brought it to my table at the flea market.'

Dom set his hot dog down, wiped his hands on his trousers. 'Can I see it?'

Sully handed it to him under the table. 'Keep it low – I don't want to get jacked on the way home.'

Dom rotated the sphere under the table. 'How much does one of these go for?'

'Six hundred. Maybe six fifty.' Sully felt slimy about asking for the loan. It was a hell of a lot of money. Dom's parents were pretty well off, but they didn't give Dom crap. Sully took a big breath. 'The thing is, I still owe the girl I bought it from a hundred and seventy-five. I'm supposed to pay her Saturday.'

Dom shrugged. 'I'll spot you.' He handed back the Forest Green, pulled out his phone.

'Really?' Sully was relieved he hadn't had to come right out and ask.

'Sure, no problem.' Dom tapped keys on his phone, looked up. 'Give me your account number.'

'I can pay you back as soon as I sell it. I'll cut you in on some of the profit.'

Dom gave him a look. 'You're not paying me interest. You're like my brother.' He squinted, shook his head. 'Come to think of it, my brother's an asshole. I wouldn't loan him my used gum.' He laughed, clapped Sully on the shoulder.

'I feel bad asking.'

'Don't worry about it.'

Sully felt a warm glow of affection for this guy he'd known since second grade. He could still picture Dom down in his basement, making explosion sounds as their Hulk and Spider-Man action figures stormed a fortress they'd made out of Lego. It would kill Sully if he had to move away.

He didn't like thinking about what life would be like if they moved in with Uncle Ian and his family. It gave him an awful sinking, panicked feeling. He'd have to share a room with his mother, with no privacy except in the bathroom or outside the house. He'd have to go to a new school where he didn't know anyone.

The fire alarm sounded.

Sully was halfway out of his seat before he realized it was one of the kids at the spoiled brats' table, showing off his Tangerine-driven ability to mimic sounds. Again. A couple of weeks back, the lunch attendant had evacuated the whole cafeteria before figuring out that it was some kid, not the fire alarm.

Mr Boyce, Sully's English teacher, approached the table and stabbed a finger at the kids. 'I hear that again, and I'll put you *all* in detention. It's a felony to cause a false alarm, whether you're pulling a lever or using your mouth.'

As he stormed off, the kids laughed and made obscene gestures behind his back.

'Look at those twerps,' Dom said, shaking his head. 'You can't trust guys who always look like they just got their hair cut. What do they do, get it cut twice a week?'

That got their whole table laughing. Sully had never thought about it before, but Dom was right, their hair always looked freshly cut.

Rob leaned in. 'Have you guys seen Jayla Washburn yet?'

'Have I *seen* her?' Sully asked, confused.

Rob nodded. 'Her parents got her an early Christmas present. A pair of *Cranberries*. You're not going to believe it.'

Cranberry. Better-looking. Rarity *seven*. How did these people afford this stuff? Sully knew you could get twenty-, thirty-year loans from the bank to buy spheres, but he couldn't believe people actually *did* that just so their daughter could be prettier.

'There she is.' Rob pointed towards the cash registers, where Jayla Washburn was paying, her back to them. She lifted her tray and turned.

'Holy –' Dom said.

Results varied when it came to Cranberries. In Jayla's case, she'd hit the jackpot. Her eyes were bigger and brighter, her cheekbones higher, her chin smaller. She'd been OK-looking before; now she almost looked like a model. She was grinning like she'd won the lottery.

The bell rang. As kids grabbed backpacks, Mr Boyce called, 'Buses with blue tags in the window are going to the Hammerstein. Have a good afternoon.'

Sully still couldn't believe they were letting school out early for Alex Holliday. It made him want to puke.

'You guys going?' Rob Dalton made a face. 'I'm going to the mall instead. I need sneakers. You want to come with?'

Sully looked at Dom, who shrugged. 'Why not? I'm sure as

hell not going to the Hammerstein.'

Sully appreciated Rob and Dom not saying Alex Holliday's name. Everyone else in the school, especially the teachers, had been saying almost nothing but Holliday's name for the past week. Big deal, Yonkers was giving its prodigal son some lame award. Was it really so noteworthy that they closed school early? It wasn't the president, or Taylor Swift, or Kanye West. It was a con artist with a lot of money.

No one seemed to understand what it felt like. They'd shaken hands. Alex Holliday had *handed him* a cheque for two and a half million. In that moment when Sully took the check, everything changed. All of his and Mom's money problems had melted away.

Rent? No problem; in fact, they could buy a house, cash.

The old junker Ford he had to share with his mother broken down, again? Buy two new cars.

College tuition for Sully, when he graduated from high school? Paid for.

Then the Cherry Red hadn't done what Alex Holliday expected. It hadn't given him, personally, any new abilities to add to his repertoire. It had only reseeded the entire freaking planet with new spheres – as many spheres as had appeared in the first wave five years earlier.

And, *poof,* the money was gone. Cheque, voided. Next time read the fine print, sucker. There would be no college for David Sullivan.

Holliday had opened that old wound again just this week, mailing Sully a gold-embossed VIP invitation to his appearance. Front-row seats to hear how great Alex Holliday is! Admission to the private reception afterward! What a petty, bush-league move. Cheat a kid, then rub it in. Nice.

Sully hated Alex Holliday. Would throw a party if the man died. Not that he was likely to die any time soon, since he was barely thirty and had burned the entire spectrum of health-boosting spheres, from Aquamarine (quick healing) to Olive (pain control).

Central Avenue was quiet, a cold wind keeping pedestrians inside, traffic cruising along the wet street past the muffler shops and fast-food restaurants.

'Where's Jeannette?' Dom asked Rob as they walked, hands in pockets, chins tucked against the wind.

'She's going to the thing,' Rob said. 'You know. Holliday.' Rob muttered the name.

Dom glanced at Sully, who kept his eyes on the gum-stained sidewalk.

'That asshat,' Dom said.

Holliday. Everywhere Sully went, Holliday. At this very moment, the elite of Yonkers were falling over themselves to kiss Holliday's rich butt. Those without VIP passes would have paid good money for Sully's. He'd torn it into pieces and flushed it.

Everyone knew Holliday had ripped Sully off, ripped off a thirteen-year-old living in the Garden Apartments. No one cared. Success was a whitewash for shitty behaviour.

'I'd like to tell him what a thief he is to his face,' Dom said.

'I guess now's your chance,' Rob said. 'When he asks for questions you could raise your hand and ask why he's such a crook.' He cackled at the idea.

Dom slowed. 'You don't think I would?'

'Come on, Dom,' Rob said.

'Two and a half million dollars. That's how much he owes Sully.'

'I *know*. I'm not saying it's right, I'm just saying you don't have the balls to call Alex Holliday a thief in front of a thousand people.'

Dom slapped Sully's arm. 'Let's go. Come on.'

'No way.' Sully didn't want to see Holliday's smarmy face while everyone clapped. 'All the way into the city for that? No way.' There was no venue in Yonkers swanky enough, so the Yonkers Citizen of Distinction Award was being presented in Manhattan.

He *would* like to hear what Holliday would say if Dom called him out about the Cherry Red, though. The thing was, Dom would probably chicken out.

Although maybe Sully should ask the question himself.

'We're going. "Not only are you a liar and a criminal, you walk like a rooster." That's what I'm gonna say.' Dom shook his head, laughed. 'Oh, man, this is gonna be great.'

He wouldn't do it, though. Dom could talk a blue streak with his buddies, but in class he sat in the back and clammed up. He wasn't much on public speaking. Sully was the talker. He'd have to see how he felt when they got there, but if the mood hit him he might just call Holliday out. What did he have to lose?

'Hang on,' Dom said, 'I have to take a piss.' He cut into a shallow alley beside Addeo and Sons Bakery, which was festooned with Christmas wreaths and garlands. Sully and Rob waited, Rob weaving slightly as he stood, as if he were

15

standing on the deck of a ship at sea, while Dom pissed against a silver rubbish can and chuckled to himself.

A lone figure stood on a portable podium to one side of the Hammerstein Ballroom on Thirty-Fourth Street. He was young, holding a Bible, his polished black shoes pressed tightly together.

'Every time you absorb a pair of those titillating balls, you welcome Satan into your soul. They are Trojan horses, sin in your choice of colours.'

'I've got a Trojan for your balls right here,' a guy shouted as he passed, setting off laughter among his friends.

Ignoring the crack, the preacher opened his Bible to a bookmarked page. 'In the book of Revelation, God warns, "Worthy is the lamb that was slain to receive power, and riches, and wisdom, and strength . . ."' He held up a finger. 'They are the mark of the beast, a sign that the end of days is upon us.'

Sully found it interesting how split religions were on the spheres. The pope thought they were OK, because they didn't go against anything in the Bible and didn't hurt anyone. Some of the evangelists on TV were like this guy on the podium; others claimed the spheres came straight from God. If there was a God, Sully didn't think he had anything to do with the spheres. They weren't angels or devils; they were pretty obviously things, even if no one could explain how they suddenly materialized all over the world or why they gave people enhanced abilities.

'The arrival of the spheres is a sign. Judgement Day is upon us, and Alex Holliday is a servant of Satan. He offers you the mark of the beast!' the guy on the podium shouted as Sully and his friends pushed through the doors.

Sully couldn't argue with the guy's view of Holliday, even if he didn't buy into the Judgement Day stuff. Not that there weren't a lot of non-religious people who were saying the same thing, that the spheres were bad news. It was hard to turn on the TV without hearing some pundit warning about pigs being fattened for the slaughter. Sully only sold spheres – he couldn't afford to burn any – so he figured he didn't have anything to worry about, even if the doomsayers turned out to be right.

There was a huge poster to the left of the ticket window, advertising an Arcade Fire concert in a couple of weeks. All seven band members had finally given in and absorbed Lavender spheres (enhanced musical ability, rarity level two) live on the *Late Show with Stephen Colbert*. Sully was dying to hear their new album. He'd kill to see them live. But no, he was going to see Alex Holliday live instead.

The Hammerstein had a high domed ceiling, plush burgundy seats, four levels of balconies along the sides for VIPs. It was packed. Sully, Dom and Rob nabbed some of the last general-admission tickets reserved for Yonkers High students and found three open seats near the back on the ground level. Holliday was already speaking, backlit by animated slides. A lot of people thought he was good-looking, but Sully thought he looked like a cartoon bandit, his black eyebrows dark and thick, as if drawn in with a fat-tipped Magic Marker, his jaw peppered with black speckles like he needed a shave. The black boots with heels didn't mask that he was short, despite the extra inch or two he'd got by burning a pair of Lemon Yellows. His shirtsleeves were rolled up, exposing muscular forearms. Chocolate spheres, which gave you both enhanced strength and the build to go with it, were rarity level nine. In today's market they would set you back three or four million each at auction, and of course if you wanted to burn them you needed two, which meant six to eight million.

The shoulders of Holliday's tailored white shirt were covered in a rainbow of the pearl-sized brag badges his company had pioneered. They spilled down the front of his shirt in dueling swirls that met at the breastbone. Sully had read that Holliday commissioned fashion designers to stylishly incorporate the badges into his wardrobe.

Sully studied the brag badges, trying to see if there was any colour the guy *hadn't* burned.

Even from a distance Sully could see all of the super-rare ones represented. Besides Chocolate, there was Mustard (high IQ), Cranberry (better-looking – although in Holliday's case the results weren't as striking as they'd been on Jayla), Cream (athleticism), Vermillion (need little sleep), Periwinkle (good with numbers). That was only the tip of the iceberg, though. The guy seemed to have everything. He had all of the enhanced senses (including good old Forest Green), and tons of common, marginally useful stuff like Copper (ambidexterity) and Taupe (artistic ability). There were forty-three sphere colours total, but Sully didn't think he'd be able to count the badges with Holliday moving around . . .

Sully smiled, realizing one brag badge was missing. Cherry Red. Was it because Holliday didn't want to remind people how he'd got it, or because it hadn't provided him, personally, with any benefit?

'Spheres are the only truly magical things in the world that you can hold in your hand,' Holliday said. He was holding an Aquamarine towards the audience. 'You can set them on your shelf and admire them while they appreciate in value more reliably than any stock or bond. You can burn them and gain remarkable abilities for the rest of your life.' He looked around the hall, let that sink in. 'For the rest of your life.' He shrugged. 'They're miracles. That's not to say we don't understand how they work. We do.' He made a sheepish expression. 'Sort of.'

The audience erupted in laughter. They were acting like he was some titan of business, an international celebrity. The truth was, he was a regional player; he had maybe a hundred stores in the North-east, fifty in other parts of the country and none outside the United States. Yes, Holliday's was expanding fast, but he was still nothing compared with Jin Bao, who had something like two thousand Wanmei stores all over the world.

'We know when someone burns a sphere it alters them physiologically. Some spheres alter receptor sites in the brain, some influence glandular secretion, like Lemon Yellow, which stimulates the pituitary gland.' Holliday set the Aquamarine down, spread his arms. 'Not that some of us couldn't use a little more help than they provide.' More laughter. 'Others go right to the source, altering the DNA in our cells.' He shrugged, let the silence build. 'It's still magic. We understand what it's doing, but it's still magic.'

He was slick. Charming. Sully gave him that. But Sully

knew better than anyone what was underneath the thin veneer Holliday showed the public. Seeing him strut around up there made Sully's skin crawl.

'There are no shortcuts to finding spheres. If they were hidden underground, geophysical survey techniques that archaeologists use to find buried artefacts could be used. But most are hidden in man-made structures, so they blend right in, as you all well know.' He held up a finger. 'That doesn't mean we're not working to develop more effective sphere-hunting technology. We're always on the lookout for new ways to deliver these miraculous orbs into your hands.'

Holliday made a sour face, took a breath. 'You bored yet?'

There were shouts of 'No' from every corner of the room.

'Well, I'm tired of hearing my own voice. How about some questions?'

Fifty hands shot in the air, including Dom's. Heart thumping, Sully halfheartedly raised his as well. What were the odds Holliday would pick him? Sully was certain Holliday couldn't pick him out of a lineup at this point. Sully was six inches taller than he'd been the last time he and Holliday were in the same room.

Holliday pointed at the third or fourth row. 'Yeah, the woman with the beautiful smile. You. Yes.'

A black woman stood, sporting three brag badges on her sleeve. She was handed a wireless microphone from the aisle. 'Are there any pairs that you haven't burned?'

'Slate Grey,' Holliday said immediately.

Singing ability. Rarity two, under five hundred for a pair.

Sully wondered if there was anyone in the room who didn't know what ability went with every single colour.

'Why Slate Grey?' the woman asked.

He shrugged. 'I guess I believe there should be at least one thing you're bad at, so you don't get too cocky.' He waved as people laughed. 'I'm kidding. To tell you the truth, I don't know. Superstition, maybe.' Holliday turned and walked towards the wings. He said something to someone out of sight, then returned to centre stage. 'I'll tell you what. Come on up here.' He beckoned to the woman, who, after a moment's hesitation, hurried on to the stage.

A beefy guy in a black suit appeared from the wings carrying a pair of Slate Grey spheres. He handed them to Holliday, who offered them to the woman. 'A gift for you, if you'll agree to sing us a song.'

Surprised, flustered, the woman accepted the spheres. She lifted them and touched them to her temples.

There were no sparks. She didn't fall backwards or cry out in orgasmic ecstasy. When she touched the Slate Greys to her temples and then lowered them, their rich grey colour began to fade. In an hour the colour would be faded and cloudy, and the spheres would be worthless, except to people who collected used ones, which was becoming a larger part of Sully's business every year.

'Sing us something,' Holliday said.

The woman nodded shyly, looked at the ceiling, and began singing 'Like a Rainbow.' She was excellent – not pop-star excellent, but smooth and clear, and right on every note. She sang the first stanza, then gave Holliday a hug as the audience applauded, and went back to her seat.

As the crowd quieted, hands shot up again, including Dom's. Holliday's index finger drifted, pointing to the left side of the auditorium, then right. 'Someone's whispering, "Pick me, pick me," under her breath.' Holliday tapped the Turquoise (enhanced hearing) brag badge on his shirt to much laughter, then resumed pointing at the audience. Before his roaming finger reached the back where Sully was standing, he stopped and pointed at a girl halfway to the back. 'Yes – the woman in the red sweatshirt.'

The girl stood, accepted the microphone. She was Sully's age or maybe a little older, Asian, big-boned, very tall.

'Clearly your Lemon Yellow was more potent than mine,' Holliday said. The audience ate it up.

'Sorry to disappoint you, but this is the result of good nutrition and wholesome living,' the girl shot back, looking cool and relaxed. 'I was wondering if you saw the article published on *Slate* a few years back about how independently owned sphere stores burn down at a rate six times higher than stores selling other goods.'

Holliday shrugged, shook his head. The big smile had vanished. 'What's your point?'

'Have you seen the article?'

Holliday looked towards the ceiling, touched his chin. 'Let's see. Yes. June eighth, 2016, around ten a.m. I was in my office drinking tea. Earl Grey.' Laughter drifted from the audience. Sully pinched the bridge of his nose, sickened by Holliday's smarmy display. They got it – he'd burned a Canary Yellow (perfect memory, rarity level nine). 'I read the first paragraph. Everything sphere-related crosses my desk. Again, what's your point?'

The girl folded her arms. 'My aunt's store burned down a few months after one of your representatives offered to buy her out. He was really aggressive. Downright threatening. Then her store burned.'

Holliday rolled his eyes, poked the inside of his cheek with his tongue. 'Let me make sure I have this straight before I respond. You're accusing me of burning down your aunt's store?'

'That's correct.' The girl didn't hesitate. A few people in the audience gasped at her audacity. Sully couldn't believe how calm she was.

There was whispering and mutters as Holliday cleared his throat, folded his hands in front of him, and spoke softly, forcing everyone to be absolutely silent to hear him. 'I am truly sorry your aunt lost her store, but I hope you can understand if I take umbrage at your accusing me of a felony in front of two thousand people. Holliday's is not the only corporate player in the sphere industry, and it has a reputation for being the most principled. My weapon is my business model, not gasoline and a match. My integrity is worth more to me than a hundred stores.'

'*Bullshit!*' Dom shouted. 'Bull. *Shit*.'

Stunned, his heart suddenly hammering, Sully watched Holliday's face go stony as his gaze lifted towards them. A thousand people turned to look in Dom's direction.

Dom put a hand on each of Sully's shoulders. 'You recognize this guy?'

Holliday shook his head briskly. 'I'm sorry? You have a little too much Red Bull tonight, my friend?'

Dom shouted over the laughter, 'This is David Sullivan!

23

Does that name ring a bell, Mr I-have-so-much-integrity-it's-squirting-out-my-butt?'

People booed.

Sully raised both hands. 'Can I say something?' No one heard him.

'You owe this man *two point five million dollars*!' Dom shouted, stabbing a finger at Holliday.

Holliday was staring right at Sully. Sully stared right back, gave Holliday a little mock salute for good measure. Holliday shook his head, looked away.

A rough hand landed on Sully's shoulder. 'Let's go.'

Two big, solid guys in black suits had pushed their way to Sully's and Dom's seats. One was bald with a goatee, the other – the one who'd grabbed Sully – sported a bleached-blond crew cut. Two more just like them waited in the aisle. Holliday's bodyguards.

'Who are you?' Dom asked, knocking the bald guy's hand off his shoulder.

'Event security.' The bald guy curled a finger at them. 'Let's go. Outside.'

'What the hell is event security?' Dom said, nice and loud. He looked the guy up and down. 'You're not police. You're just guys in suits.'

The bald guy grabbed Dom by the front of his sweatshirt with both hands and yanked.

Dom threw a punch and nailed the bodyguard in the face, sending him stumbling into the seats.

The blond bodyguard grabbed Sully's arm. Without thinking, Sully reached with his free hand and pulled the guy's pinkie back, hard. The bodyguard shouted in pain, let go of Sully. As soon as Sully eased up, the guy spun round, lightning fast, and grabbed Sully from behind, putting him in a headlock.

'Hey, let him go.' Rob grabbed the arm around Sully's neck, tried to prise it off. The bodyguard shoved Rob, sending him tumbling over the seats.

Black spots peppered Sully's vision as he was shoved towards the fire exit.

'So much for your goddamned integrity.' The voice sounded like the Asian girl's. She shouted over the rumbling crowd and Dom's cursing, 'That's David Sullivan? The kid you cheated? Perfect. Tell us more about your pristine ethics while your goons beat on a welfare kid.' Out of the corner of his eye, Sully glimpsed another bodyguard racing up the aisle towards the girl. 'Somebody call the police. *Don't touch me.*'

The blond guy pushed the fire exit door open with his hip. Sully reached back and grabbed for his face, but only brushed his nose before the guy shoved his head through the half-open door. Sully landed on one knee on the concrete alley.

Behind him, Dom was dragged out, shouting and swinging, by two bodyguards. A third pushed the Asian girl through. As soon as the door clicked closed, the two bodyguards went to work on Dom, punching him from both sides.

Sully lunged, shouting, but the blond bodyguard shoved him back. 'Stay out of it.'

The guy was way bigger than Sully, and built like a steer. Sully got low and kicked him in the knee. It felt like he was kicking a fire hydrant. The guy let out a grunt and grabbed his knee as Sully ducked around him.

Before he could get clear the guy tackled him, driving him

to the ground. Sully's nose hit the pavement and erupted in searing pain. A second later a knee was in his back. His kidney exploded in agony as the guy landed a punch. Two more quick blows followed.

'Now stay down!' the bodyguard screamed into his ear.

The knee in his back lifted. Sully grunted, trying to take a breath. For a moment he couldn't, then his chest expanded in a spasm and a tight squeal escaped him.

He heard Dom grunting with effort, or in pain, the girl cursing, shouting, the smack of fists landing.

Applause rose inside the auditorium. Evidently the great Alex Holliday had concluded his Q-and-A session.

'Crap. We gotta get back,' one of the bodyguards said. He turned to Sully, pointed. 'Lesson over. Don't screw with Alex Holliday.' They headed off at a jog towards the front of the building.

'Should I call nine-one-one?' It was the Asian girl, her face close to Sully's.

Sully struggled to his hands and knees, touched his nose. It was bleeding, but from the feel of it, it was just a bad scrape. 'I'm OK.' He looked at Dom, who was sitting on a concrete step, head down, one hand over an eye. He pursed his lips, spat blood on the ground, pressed on one of his front teeth.

'You all right?' Sully asked.

Dom looked at him. 'Just peachy. Marvellous.' He let out a guffaw. 'Jerks.'

The girl went to Dom. 'Let me see your eye.'

Dom took his hand away, tilted his head up.

'I think you need stitches.' She turned to Sully. 'Let's get him to the emergency room.'

When they tried to help him up, Dom brushed them off. 'I can walk.'

Sully limped along between Dom and the girl.

'I'm David Sullivan, by the way. Sully.'

'Mandy Toko.'

'Dom.' Sully wasn't surprised Dom didn't give his last name. He rarely had since sixth grade, when his uncle made the name Cucuzza infamous. Dom's upper lip was swelling; blood from the cut over his eye dribbled down his temple. Dom stopped short. 'Crap.'

'What?' Sully asked.

Dom raised his eyebrows. 'You feeling a little chilly?'

'Our coats,' Sully said.

'I'll get them,' Mandy said. She was wearing hers, which was long and black. 'I'll catch up.' She turned and jogged away. They watched her for a minute, her long strides eating up ground. She looked like an athlete.

They turned and walked.

'Basketball team?' Sully asked.

'Maybe. Did you see her go after the douche who was whaling on me?'

'*No*. She punched him?'

'She punched him in the *throat*.'

'I missed that,' Sully said.

'She's kind of cute.'

'Sure.' One downside to having Dom as a friend was that he was immediately interested in – and quickly established dibs on – every girl they met.

Dom pulled out his phone. 'We forgot about Rob. He has no idea where we are.' Dom filled Rob in about their

27

injuries and said he'd call him later.

When they reached Thirty-Fourth Street, they paused. Sully had no idea where the nearest hospital was. He asked a guy wearing a fedora and a pin-striped suit, who pointed them towards a walk-in clinic.

Dom touched the cut above his eye, looked at his fingers. 'I'm gonna hurt like hell in a couple of minutes. Right now my face just feels kind of warm.'

Sully's nose didn't feel warm. It hurt. He was fairly sure it wasn't broken, though; he'd heard you knew immediately when your nose was broken.

Behind them, a voice shouted, 'Hey!'

They waited for Mandy to catch up. She held out their coats. Sully thanked her as he pulled his on.

'So where do you go to school?' Dom asked, falling back on the tried-and-true conversation starter.

'St John's.'

'A prepper,' Dom said. He looked her up and down. 'You're one of those smart people, aren't you?'

Mandy shrugged. 'I guess.' She looked at Sully. 'I didn't realize *the* David Sullivan lived around here.'

Sully rolled his eyes. 'Yeah. There was supposed to be a press release. I don't know what happened.'

A couple of years earlier, Sully had stumbled on to an article on *Slate* while Googling himself. It was about weird fame – people who were known for things that had nothing to do with talent or ability. The article mentioned Steve Bartman, who was famous for leaning out of the stands and deflecting a foul ball that cost the Cubs a chance to play in the World Series, and Monica Lewinsky, who had an affair with

Bill Clinton that almost got him impeached. And Sully, who, instead of sticking his hand in front of a foul ball, had stuck it inside a storm drain under an overpass and pulled out the rarest sphere in the world.

Warm air hit Sully as he stepped into the hallway of his apartment building. His nose was throbbing, and he was totally whipped. Starving as he was, he didn't know if he could stay awake long enough to eat dinner.

'Sul-ly.'

Sully raised his head, found Mike Lea and Laurie Heath sitting crossways on the stairs to his apartment.

Mike stood, his phone in hand. He was a year older than Sully, pitched on the school's baseball team. Sometimes Sully and Mike were friends, and sometimes Mike acted like he didn't know who Sully was. 'Sully, man. You're going viral on YouTube.' He turned his phone so Sully could see himself, caught in a headlock, struggling to break free.

Evidently word spread fast. He'd turned his phone off on the way into the auditorium and forgot to turn it back on. He pulled it out and turned it on now. He had about a hundred texts.

Mike stepped closer. 'Man, your *nose*. Those goons did that?'

Sully touched his nose. 'The sidewalk did it, but the goons helped.'

Laurie stepped closer as well, inhaling in sympathy. 'You should clean that up right away.'

Sully nodded. 'I'm guessing my mom is going to run for

the Bactine as soon as she sees me.'

Laurie nodded. It had been two years since Laurie broke Sully's heart, but there was still a slight whiff of awkwardness when they talked.

The door at the top of the stairs opened; Sully's mom burst out. 'Sully?'

'I'm fine, Mom.'

As his mom came barrelling down the stairs, Sully thought she was going to hug him, but she stopped short and held up her palm for a high five.

Confused, he slapped her hand.

'Good for you. I wish you could have got on the stage to bend that little bastard Holliday's finger back, but good for you.'

'Thanks, Mom.'

Grinning, Mike patted Sully's shoulder. 'I'm gonna get going.' He made a fist. 'Way to go, Sully.'

Laurie gave Sully a wave and followed Mike out.

'You've got seven thousand and some hits already,' Mom said as the front door clicked closed. She studied Sully's face. 'Come on, let's get your nose cleaned up. No broken bones?'

'Dom took most of the punches.'

'Bull. *Shit*,' Mom said, mimicking Dom's Italian American Yonkers delivery. 'That was priceless.' She looked back at Sully as they climbed the stairs. 'He's OK, though?'

'He's fine. Just some stitches.'

Once Sully's nose was bandaged, they ate dinner on tray tables at the couch, watching a rerun of *CSI: NY* like they always did. Pretty much all they watched were *CSI* reruns, plus *Marble Hunters* and a few of the copycat sphere-hunting shows.

Dinner was spaghetti, which was definitely *not* like always. For as long as Sully could remember, Friday had been take-out pizza night. Sully didn't say anything; his mom was hurting enough.

Sully only half watched the show. Seeing Laurie had stirred up some of the memories from that time when he'd been borderline obsessed with her. It had been the first time Sully truly understood how painful love could be. He'd been shocked by how much it hurt. Until Laurie, having a girlfriend had just been something you did, like an extension of being friends.

His first girlfriend, if you could call her that, had been Kaitlin Bie. They'd both been nine when Kaitlin's older brother dared them to kiss on the swing set in their backyard. Kaitlin's dad had seen them from the living room window, though, and their relationship ended right then and there.

Then there'd been Jen Posner, when he was thirteen. After walking around with a crush on Jen for a couple of months, Sully had mustered the nerve to send her a candy-gram – one of those Valentine's Day fund-raisers where you pay a dollar to send a flower or candy to someone during class. She'd sent one back the very next period. Unless Sully counted the peck he'd given Kaitlin on the swings, Jen was the first girl he'd ever kissed. He'd been so blown away by the sheer act of kissing a cute girl with big brown eyes and exactly the right amount of freckles that it had taken him about two months to realize he was bored out of his mind whenever she was around and they weren't kissing.

Breaking up with her, seeing the disappointment on her face, had been awful. It was nothing compared with the day

Laurie broke up with him, though. Laurie had seemed like his entire world back then. Every love song he heard had been about Laurie. Her face had floated like an overlay on Sully's vision all day long. Since Laurie, he'd hung out with a couple of girls as more than friends, but it had never got close to serious with any of them.

After dinner Sully went to his room and read through his messages, shooting texts back to friends, answering the same question over and over, about where he learned the pinkie move. He had no idea where he'd learned it; in the heat of the moment he'd seen that finger on his shoulder and wanted to snap it off the guy's hand.

It should have felt good, reading message after message about what a badass he was, but it didn't. When you cut right through it, Holliday had kicked them to the kerb. His bodyguards had taken out the rubbish while the audience cheered.

Sully sat up on his bed, then went over to his little desk, where the used Cherry Red sat on a shot glass that served as its pedestal. He picked it up, turned it in his hand.

It was hard to believe this marble and its only match had reseeded the entire planet with new spheres. The first wave of spheres had just about dried up when Holliday burned the Cherry Reds.

Sully remembered the start of the second wave like it was yesterday. At first he didn't realize he'd been cheated by Holliday, and he went out hunting along with everyone else. You could probably find a couple of spheres in your own house that first day, and by the time it was dark and Sully came home, exhausted and dehydrated from a frantic day of hunting, he was carrying six spheres in a pillowcase, including a rarity three (Mint, more outgoing).

Now the second wave was getting thin. Sully was beginning to wonder if there would be a third.

Once a month Sully had a dream about finding the Cherry Red. There were all sorts of variations: who was with him and where he found it, but the dream ended the same every time: he'd suddenly realize he was dreaming and cling to that Cherry Red as hard as he could, willing himself not to wake up. He always woke up, though.

CHAPTER 3

Sully eyed the empty space in his display case where the Forest Green had been resting front and centre until a few minutes ago, feeling a buzz of satisfaction. He'd made a hundred ninety dollars on one transaction. You couldn't beat that. The woman who bought it, as a Christmas present for her daughter, had pulled out six hundred-dollar bills like it was nothing. His customers seemed to fall into two categories: collectors/investors who stopped by regularly to see if Sully had anything new (and to talk sphere collecting), and well-off impulse buyers, who were usually just browsing, just passing an afternoon.

A kid with bright red hair and freckles, six or seven years old, picked out a bagged pair of toy Seafoam Greens and handed Sully a ten as his parents looked on.

Grinning, Sully gave the kid his change. 'Speed, eh? Be careful with those; there's a thirty-mile-per-hour speed limit in here.'

Sully watched as the kid rejoined his parents. He tore open the bag, pressed the plastic spheres to his temples as if burning them, then raised a fist in the air, made a sound like a rocket lifting off, and ran full tilt down the aisle.

'Look at that handsome face over there,' Samantha called. She was unpacking a box of scented candles. 'I need to introduce you to my niece, Paulina. Let me show you.' She rummaged in her wallet, finally pulled a picture from a plastic sleeve. She crossed over and held it in front of Sully's face.

It was a studio shot of a girl in a white lace dress, wearing a lot of make-up. She was pretty, with dark, smoky eyes and silky brown hair. She looked about fourteen.

'Isn't she beautiful?'

'She's gorgeous,' Sully said. 'How old is she?'

'Thirteen.'

Sully smiled.

'She'll be fourteen in March.'

'Yeah, that's a little young for me.'

'Three years is nothing,' Samantha said, pushing the photo closer to his nose. 'Neal is nine years older than me.'

'I'm guessing you didn't meet when he was seventeen and you were eight.'

'Oh, come on, give the girl a chance,' a girl's voice called.

Sully turned. A flutter went through him when he saw Hunter standing at his table, hand on her hip.

'Where did you come from?' Sully asked. 'I didn't even see you coming.' He was pleased, and surprised, to see her back so soon. They'd completed the Forest Green transaction just last week.

'I'm like a ninja.' Hunter slid her pack off her shoulder, squatted to pull something out.

'How old are *you*?' Samantha asked.

Hunter looked up. 'Me? Seventeen. How old are you?'

Samantha laughed. 'Twenty-nine. I've lived a hard life.'

Hunter stood. 'Me too.'

'There you go, Sully,' Samantha said, gesturing towards Hunter. 'Someone your age.'

Before Sully could turn too red, Hunter smiled and said, 'Don't look at me. I'm all business, no pleasure.' She held out a sphere: Rose (ability to hold your breath for a long time). 'Nothing like the Forest Green this time, but I take what I can find.' On the rarity chart it was a two, but scarce, as twos went. Sully could get about a hundred seventy-five for it.

Samantha slipped away, saying she'd let them get down to business.

'I'll skip the part where we haggle, if that's OK with you,' Sully said.

'That's fine with me. I'm all about minimizing the bullshit in my life.'

'One twenty?'

She pointed at him. 'You read my mind.'

Sully dropped a hundred-dollar bill on to the table, added a twenty from his wallet. 'Is this typical for you, finding two marbles in a couple of weeks?'

'I average two or three a month. Course, three years ago, I was averaging five.'

Sully nodded. 'They're really drying up.'

Hunter swept the bills off the table. It was hard to believe she was seventeen. There was an awkwardness in kids their age, as if they wanted to look and act like adults but couldn't quite pull it off. That awkwardness was completely absent in Hunter.

'They're drying up faster in the city,' Hunter said. 'More people in less space.'

'You live in the city?'

Hunter nodded. 'The Bronx. Webster Avenue.' That was a rough neighbourhood, a twenty-minute train ride from the flea market, plus a hike from the station to Webster Avenue. 'I wish I could hunt past the suburbs. Much less competition out there.'

Sully shrugged. 'Why don't you?'

She waved her hand. 'It costs thirty-five dollars to take the train there and back. I can't clear enough to make that work.'

Wheels began to turn in Sully's head. This girl clearly knew how to find spheres. 'I could give you a ride out once in a while.'

Hunter gave him a big smile. 'It's good of you to offer, but what are you going to do out in Stony Point or wherever while I'm off hunting for ten hours?'

Sully shrugged. 'I could go with you. I've always wanted to do some hunting.'

Laughing, Hunter folded her arms. 'You've always wanted to do some hunting? You mean, besides the time you found the Cherry Red?'

Sully felt that old familiar sting. He never knew if he was going to feel proud or embarrassed when the Cherry Red came up. 'That was a fluke. I was hunting carp when I found it.'

'Carp.'

'You know, big fish that taste bad?'

'Yeah, I know what carp are.' Hunter studied him, her gaze making him uncomfortable, like he was on a job interview. 'I guess we could try it, see how it goes.' She raised a finger. 'But

I get sixty per cent of whatever we find, and you pay for gas out of your end.'

Sully raised his eyebrows. 'How do you figure?'

Hunter unzipped a side pocket on her pack, pulled out a spiral-bound notebook. She turned it towards Sully, riffled through a few dozen pages. Lists, crude maps, and blocks of neat writing flew by.

'I've been doing this for five years, recording the details of every find, watching the news for details about big scores. You get the benefit of all that experience.' Hunter gave him a subtle one-shouldered shrug. 'I should be charging you instead of giving you a cut.'

Sully thought of the Forest Green, the sphere she'd brought today. If she was right about having better luck in the suburbs, it could be lucrative, and he sure needed cash. The notebook was nothing compared with the database Alex Holliday had compiled – he claimed to have information on every one of the millions of spheres his hunters had discovered over the past nine years. But no one outside his organization had access to that information, so Hunter's notebook was about as good as it got for amateurs.

Sully stuck out his hand. 'OK. Sixty-forty.' Something about this girl told him she was the type who could make a big hit, given the chance. She was . . . dynamic. That was the best way he could describe it. The direct, no-bullshit way she spoke; the fierce look in her eyes, like no one was going to stop her, and she'd tear apart anyone who tried.

'How about this Wednesday?' Sully said.

Hunter raised her eyebrows. 'Your school have a special holiday or something?'

'They won't miss me for one day.' He shrugged. 'What can I say? I want to get out there.' He needed the money way more than he needed algebra and biology.

She nodded. 'Works for me.' She didn't seem particularly concerned about school either.

CHAPTER 4

Sully took a break from wading through a book on the California gold rush and glanced around the library. He and Dom had chosen a desk by tall windows that looked out on to the car park.

Taking in the view, he tried to identify places where spheres might be hidden as practice for tomorrow. He couldn't wait to go hunting.

He was also curious about Hunter. He had considered stalking her on Facebook, but decided she wasn't the type to have a Facebook account.

He pulled out his phone, opened the Facebook app. What the hell, it didn't hurt to try.

His search returned three Hunters in the New York metro area. Hunter number one, from Queens, was a guy who'd taken a selfie with his French bulldog. The second, from Scarsdale, didn't have a picture – just a shot of a latte in a coffee shop. The third Hunter, the only one from the Bronx, was also a guy.

Sully wasn't surprised, but he was disappointed. He

wanted to know more about her — who her friends were, what music she listened to, what she thought was worth sharing with the world.

Taking a deep breath, he turned back to his book.

'How do you make yourself give a shit about everything so intensely?'

Sully looked up at Dom. 'What do you mean?'

Dom gestured towards the book. 'I mean, you're working on that history paper like it's the freaking Magna Carta. This weekend you'll bust your ass at the flea market.' He shrugged. 'My grades are just about underwater, but I can't make myself care. I just want to have a good workout and meet girls.'

'You care about things. They're just different things from me.'

'Yeah. I care deeply about losing my virginity. But who doesn't?' Dom made a face. 'Look at that douche bag.'

Sully followed Dom's gaze. A guy Sully didn't know — probably a junior or senior — was sitting at a table near the checkout desk, speed-reading a book. He'd scan the page on the left for two seconds, then the page on the right, then turn the page using his palm so it made as much noise as possible. He had a handful of brag badges on his shoulder. Besides Burnt Orange (speed-reading), he had Periwinkle (good with numbers), Indigo (enhanced eyesight), Violet (verbal acuity), and Hot Pink (adrenalin rush — handy when you had to pull an all-nighter). He didn't have the ultra-rare, million-dollar college helpers — Canary Yellow (perfect memory) and Mustard (high IQ). The guy had everything else, though. A pair of Periwinkles alone would have cost his parents over a hundred thousand. He'd probably been there cheering Alex Holliday last Saturday night.

'He can't just enjoy all those advantages his daddy bought him. He's got to show off,' Dom said. 'I can't stand people like that.'

'I know.'

Sully hated kids who could afford to burn spheres. Although hating them made him kind of a hypocrite, because if he had the money, he'd burn some too. The speed-reader must be a moron, though, if he was at Yonkers High. Most of the kids loaded up as well as him were at the Masten Academy for the Gifted.

Of course, they could all be fake. Bootlegged brag badges were a hell of a lot cheaper than spheres, and anyone could flip through pages and pretend they were speed-reading.

Dom closed his notebook, grabbed the books he was checking out for an English assignment. 'You ready? I could use a Sprite or something.'

Sully stowed his stuff in his backpack, then followed Dom to the checkout desk.

'You talk to Mandy since last Saturday?' Dom asked, keeping his voice low. Dom handed his books across the counter to the librarian. He pulled out his library card and handed it to her as well.

'Nope. We should invite her to hang out.'

'That's what I was thinking.'

'There you go, Mr Cucuzza.' Ms Yonke, the librarian, handed Dom his books.

'Cucuzza,' a voice behind them said, laughing.

Dom turned. Sully stepped out of the way as his friend, mouth tight, nostrils flared, stalked over to the speed-reader.

'You got a problem with my name?' Dom asked.

The speed-reader was a big guy with smooth red cheeks.

'I just . . .' he said, his voice a little tight. Chances were, the guy couldn't resist showing off his enhanced hearing, given the chance. Only he hadn't thought about how Dom might react.

'You just what? You just can't help being a douche bag?'

The speed-reader's red cheeks went crimson. He looked Dom up and down, sizing him up. The guy had maybe thirty pounds and four inches on Dom, but it was easy to see from Dom's bull neck, the way his shoulders filled out his brown leather jacket, that Dom wasn't someone you wanted to mess with.

The guy swallowed. 'I was just saying your name.'

Dom glared at him a heartbeat longer, then turned to Sully. 'Let's go.'

They headed back to study hall.

Sully would never forget that day in sixth grade when Haley Hinton told Dom his uncle was on CNN, then showed him on her phone. It was ironic, that Anthony Cucuzza was more infamous for walking into the Met and destroying hundreds of priceless works of art with an AK-47 than some people were for shooting living, breathing people.

The week before, Dom's aunt Terry had left Tony for a guy she'd met where she worked, the Metropolitan Museum of Art. Uncle Tony got back at her by destroying the things she loved most in the world.

'What a tool,' Sully said as they walked.

'I hope my uncle's miserable in prison. I hope the food is rancid and his cell mate is an art-loving skinhead.'

It was a weird bond they shared, being known for something. At least Sully was known for something he'd done. Dom had to live with a last name that was a verb through no fault of his own.

CHAPTER 5

'How come you always wear gloves?' Sully asked. They'd been driving up the Palisades Parkway in silence for the past ten minutes.

Hunter turned her head, gave him a badass glare.

'I'm not saying I don't like them. They look good on you. I'm just curious why you wear them, even in the car with the heat on.'

Hunter licked her upper lip, closed her eyes for a second, like she was trying to muster patience. 'I don't know, my hands are cold all the time. My blood must be thin.'

'I have a cousin who has poor circulation in her fingers and toes—'

'Take this exit.' Hunter pointed at the sign for Exit 19: Bear Mountain State Park.

'Bear Mountain?' Sully asked, trying to picture where they'd hunt there.

Hunter smiled. 'Sure looks that way, doesn't it?'

He'd been to Bear Mountain a couple of times as a kid. There was a little zoo, a big lodge and a mountain. Not many good places to hunt. Sully put on his blinker, got in the right lane.

On the ride he'd learned Hunter's parents were dead, that she 'mostly' lived in an apartment with 'a bunch' of room-mates. He wanted to ask what her life was like, but she didn't seem eager to talk about life in the Bronx. Mostly she wanted to talk about spheres. That was fine with Sully.

'You ever burn any?' Sully asked.

'Me? Nah. One day when I can afford it, there are a few I want. How about you?'

Sully pulled into the drive that led to the Bear Mountain car park. 'Same story. Can't afford it. So how'd you find your way to a flea market all the way out in Yonkers, anyway?'

'Found you on the Internet, thought I'd see if you paid fair prices. There aren't many independent dealers left in the city, and Holliday's and the other superstores rip you off, so I'm always on the lookout.'

As soon as Sully put the car in park, Hunter jumped out. Sully followed as she turned away from the lodge and zoo, and headed towards the mountain.

'We're going hunting in the woods?' If there was one thing everyone knew about finding spheres, it was that not many were hidden in nature. Once in a while someone found one wedged in a tree or stuffed in an old gopher hole on the prairie, but most were hidden in and around man-made structures.

Hunter's eyes were bright with excitement. She was walking so fast that Sully strained to keep up with her. 'Yes and no. We're going to Doodletown.'

'Doodletown?' He'd never heard of Doodletown. It sounded like a joke. A made-up place.

Hunter pulled a folded page from her back pocket and handed it to Sully. 'Once upon a time there was a little town called Doodletown, about three miles from here. Seventy houses, a school, a church. Two stores. The last residents left in 1965, and it became a ghost town. Ten years after that, the buildings were bulldozed. All that's left are a dozen foundations, a few walls, and two graveyards.'

Sully scanned the Wikipedia entry Hunter had printed out, his smile growing bigger as he read.

'When you're picking sites, you have to keep in mind, you don't know what's already been searched. You could break into an abandoned factory in the city, and it looks like the best place in the world to find marbles, but ten people have already gone through it with a fine-tooth comb. This late in the game, the key is coming up with places other pros wouldn't think to look.'

'You really thought this out.'

Hunter looked at him. 'It's all I think about.' They reached the sidewalk that ran along the base of Bear Mountain, and paused. 'One day I'm going to make a big score. Maybe not a Cherry Red like you, but big. Chocolate. Mustard. Olive . . .'

Sully nodded. Those were million-dollar marbles. He watched Hunter's face as she gazed towards the summit, her dark eyes blazing. She saw him looking. He looked away, at the mountain.

Through the trees he scanned the snow-covered boulders that filled the lower half of the climb. He used to get a kick out of climbing around on those rocks as a kid.

'Six miles, round-trip. I hope you're in shape.' Hunter

hopped on to a rock, sprang across a little gap to the next. Sully followed. He'd keep up if it killed him.

The narrow trail they'd been hiking opened on to a wider road heading uphill. Trying not to let on how out of breath he was, Sully fell into step beside Hunter.

'You in any particular camp about what they are?' he asked.

Hunter shook her head. 'I like it that no one knows. Whatever you want to believe – that they're proof God exists, that they're from another dimension, that aliens left them – no one can tell you you're wrong. You can't laugh at someone else's ideas if yours are just as crazy. And they're all crazy. How can they not be?'

Sully couldn't argue with that.

The weirdest part to him was that they were hidden. If they'd all just appeared at random one day, that would be one thing, but they'd appeared in hiding places. That was one of the arguments the God camp used. The spheres were hidden, and that meant an intelligence was behind it, and that meant God. Or Satan.

A steel sign on a tree announced that they were entering Doodletown. To their right, a concrete walk ran up a hill, leading nowhere. A few hundred yards further along they came to a three-sided stone wall surrounding nothing but snow and weeds. It looked to be a building foundation.

Hunter consulted the map she'd printed out and pushed past the foundation, towards the trees beyond. 'Let's start at the farthest point and work our way back.'

At first Sully just watched Hunter work, and she didn't

question this. He wanted to pull his weight, and before he could do that he needed to see how she approached the job.

Hunter worked methodically. Her first target was a low stone wall overgrown with vines and brambles. Squatting, crawling, sometimes snaking along on her belly, Hunter worked the crevices, especially down low. She checked for loose stones, and when she found one she pulled it out, checked the crevice, then replaced the stone. After finishing the wall she went to work on what the map identified as the second schoolhouse, starting at one corner of the stone foundation.

Sully watched a little longer, then joined her, moving in the opposite direction around the low stone foundation.

He was grateful it was the middle of winter, otherwise they'd be taking their lives into their hands jamming their fingers into crevices. Timber rattlers and copperheads would be all over these woods in the summer.

'Hey!' Hunter called. She held up an Army Green (resistance to the common cold, rarity one) for Sully to see before stashing it in her backpack. 'At least now we know this place hasn't been picked over by a pro.' Sully's cut of the sixty dollars they'd probably get for it would cover gas.

After a couple of hours of hunting, Sully's toes were numb. He and Hunter went from headstone to headstone in the cemetery, running their fingers along the base, seeking chipmunk holes. Some of the headstones were from the late 1700s. None were hiding spheres.

Hunter jotted notations on the map, plumes of condensation wafting from her mouth. 'Let's take a look at this mine.' She spun, headed into the woods to the left. She was always looking around, scanning the ground by her feet, the low branches of trees. Always hunting.

Sully had pictured the mine as a cave that ran horizontally in the side of a hill, but it was nothing but a hole going straight into the ground, roped off so no one would accidentally stumble into it.

Hunter pulled a coiled length of blue and black cord out of her pack and tied one end to a nearby tree.

'You're going down there?' Sully asked, peering into the hole.

Hunter paused, shot him a questioning look. 'Don't worry, Yonkers. Just me. You stay up here in case someone needs to run for help.'

When Sully had told her he'd grown up in Yonkers, she'd nodded, saying she knew he wasn't a city boy.

'Whatever you say, Bronx,' he shot back.

Hunter turned. 'That's *the* Bronx. It's the only place important enough that they had to put a *the* in front of it. You don't say *the* Manhattan, or *the* California, only *the* Bronx.'

Sully cleared his throat. 'Excuse me. I have to go to *the* bathroom and use *the* toilet.'

'You ought to get into stand-up comedy.' With that, Hunter lowered herself hand over hand, quickly disappearing into the mine. He'd expected her to pull out more equipment – clamps and a harness, maybe – but the cord was it.

Grasping the cord with one hand, Sully watched it rub against the stone, shifting back and forth as Hunter descended.

Ten minutes later, she reappeared, pulling herself out of the hole with ease.

'You're like Spider-Man,' Sully said.

Hunter laughed as she untied the rope from the tree. 'I do

a decent amount of climbing in the city.'

Sully knew not to ask where in the city she'd need to climb. Hunter had made it clear information related to hunting was strictly on a need-to-know basis.

Consulting the map, Hunter pointed downhill. 'The other schoolhouse is that way.' They were running out of places to look. Sully was disappointed they had only found the one common, but relieved that before too long they'd be in his heated car.

As they headed down the hill, he stifled a yawn.

'You look tired,' Hunter said.

'I haven't been sleeping much lately. Some nights it takes me a couple of hours to fall asleep, then I wake up at three or four and the thoughts start spinning and that's it, I can't get back to sleep.'

Her eyes softened, the mischievous twinkle gone. 'Yeah. I know about that.'

They cleared a rise and stepped into a space littered with old tyres, a rusting refrigerator, the front axle of a wagon and plenty of broken glass.

Hunter stopped, took a few steps back to the edge of what was obviously the Doodletown dump. She got on her knees. 'I'll start over here.' She pointed. 'Why don't you start at that end?'

Sully surveyed the dump for a moment. 'If we search this whole area it's going to be too dark to find our way back.' The truth was, he was cold and tired. He wanted to go home and watch TV.

Hunter looked at the sky. 'We'll leave ourselves time to make it back. It's downhill, so it'll be quicker. Let's search as much of this as we can. We can come back if we don't finish.'

As Sully knelt on the frozen ground and ran his hand inside the rim of a tyre, he realized something. As deadly serious as he thought he was about this, Hunter was more serious. Or more desperate. In the car she claimed she'd been hunting full-time for the past two years, and if she really meant full-time, she wasn't in school. She had no parents to fall back on. This was all she had. The worst bottom line for Sully was living in a basement in Pittsburgh, and although his mom kept warning him that they'd probably be moving there this summer, he had to admit it was nothing compared with what Hunter faced every day.

Sully watched her in the fading light as she brushed snow off the ground, her eyebrows pinched, all of her attention on the hunt.

He imitated her movements, brushing drifts of snow off rusty tin cans and broken glass. What must it be like, doing this every day? He'd always romanticized the life of hunters, but now he saw it wasn't all excitement. It was a tedious, detail-orientated job.

He exposed a corner of a glass jar, dug around it, clearing dead leaves. It was a mason jar, tinged pink. Either that, or the food someone had stored inside had turned pink over the years. . . .

'Oh,' Sully said. He leaned closer, squinting. Beneath the smoky glass was a pink curve. 'Oh,' he said again, his tone pinched with dread, as if he'd found something that might be awful. A skull, or a finger. But what he dreaded was that he might be wrong about what he suspected that delicious pink curve was.

Hunter rose. 'What is it? Did you find something?'

Sully felt around in the snow, found a stone, and brought it down on the jar. 'Oh. Please let it be —'

The top of a Hot Pink sphere peeked through the hole.

'It is. *It is*. Oh, my God.' He smashed the sharp edges of the broken jar until he could reach in. Fingers working frantically, he tugged at the hard, slick surface until the sphere came loose.

Sully stood and held it to his face as Hunter shrieked.

Hot Pink. There was no mistaking that colour. Hot Pink.

Shouting in pure primordial joy, Hunter collided with him. He shoved the sphere into her hand, wrapped his arms around her waist, and lifted her in the air. She held the Hot Pink over her head as they whooped.

It was a rarity five, worth, what? Twelve thousand dollars? More, if he found the right buyer.

Sully put Hunter down. She held the sphere out to him and he put his hand over the top of it, partially covering both of her hands.

'Oh, my God. I can't believe it,' he said.

'I've never found a five before. I've never found a *four* before.' She raised a hand to her mouth; it was shaking. 'I can get my own place. I can buy an old motorcycle to get around.'

'You'll still let me tag along once you have your own ride, won't you?'

Hunter grinned. 'Are you kidding? Mr Cherry Red. Big marbles roll right out of their hiding places when you're around.'

It wasn't a Cherry Red, not even close, but his share would be, what, close to five thousand dollars? It bought them time. It meant Sully didn't have to leave his friends, his school, or his town, at least for another year. And they'd find more.

Maybe when he showed his mom the cash she'd look the other way and let him cut school one day a week.

They found the path out of Doodletown and headed down the mountain.

A half mile on, the trail broke out on to a dazzling view of the Bear Mountain Bridge crossing the Hudson River, with mountains beyond.

'I want to sit for a minute.' Hunter settled on a waist-high rock, the Hot Pink in her hand. 'I want to drink this day in.'

Sully squatted on a smaller rock and took in the view. He was still shaking. It was ironic that they'd found a Hot Pink. Burning a pair of Hot Pinks let you summon a rush of adrenalin on demand, giving you a boost of strength and energy for a few hours at a time. Much like they'd just experienced.

His phone vibrated. It was a text from Dom.

> **Want to do something after dinner?**
> **I need to get out of here.**

Hell, ya, he sent back. **BIG NEWS. Tell u when I see u.**

'I was homeless for three years,' Hunter said.

Sully turned to look at her. 'Three years?'

Hunter nodded. 'My mom lost her nursing job when I was five. She died two years later. I was on my own for a couple of weeks before a Korean woman took me in. But she had to go back to Korea when I was twelve, and she couldn't afford to take me with her, so I was on my own. Now I rent space on the floor in an apartment that's got about twenty people living in it.' She swallowed, wet her lips with her tongue. 'I'm telling you because I want you to understand what this means to me.' She gestured at the Hot Pink with her chin. 'I hit on hunting marbles when I was ten and' – she shook her head – 'I don't know, it just *felt* right. When I found my first, a Rose, it was like beautiful music going off in my head, like the marble was telling me I was going to be OK, that their whole reason for being here was so I had enough to eat, a coat to keep me warm.' She lifted her eyes to look at Sully, and there were tears on her lashes. 'In the car you asked what I thought they were. All I know is they're the best thing there is. I know some people say they're bad, but those people are wrong. They're perfect. I wish I didn't have to sell them. I wish I could take them all inside me and keep them forever.'

Sully nodded. He agreed. They were the best things in the world.

They watched the river, the sparse traffic crossing the bridge looking like toys. Sully wasn't cold any longer. His cheeks and fingertips thrummed with warmth.

'Who was the Korean woman?'

Hunter smiled wistfully. 'I was at the public library. Libraries are heated and cooled, and they can't kick you out if you're quiet. She was a widow who worked there as a janitor. She started bringing me food. Cold noodles, pickled cabbage, pork, radishes. Then one day, out of the blue, she invited me to come home with her, and pretty much adopted me after that.' Hunter tossed the Hot Pink in the air, caught it, admired it for a moment. 'When I wasn't in school I was hunting marbles to help support us.'

'It's weird, how strangers can become like family. Remember Neal, the guy selling CDs in the stall across from mine?'

'The sixties-looking dude?'

'Right,' Sully said, laughing at her description. 'The guy's been more of a father to me than my own dad. I mean, he might be surprised to hear it, but he means a lot to me. At the flea market he and his wife, Sam, watch out for me like I was their kid.'

'It's nice to have people watching your back.' Hunter smiled as she watched a motorboat tool along the river. It was the first time Sully had seen her look so relaxed.

'So why did your Korean mom have to go back to Korea?'

'Her own mom got Alzheimer's. She had to go back to take care of her. She cried and cried when she had to get on that plane.' Hunter rubbed her hands together, then cupped them and blew into them. 'You ready?' She pushed off the rock, landed on her feet with a little hop, and headed down the trail.

As the woods enveloped the trail again, Hunter's hiking gait turned into a bobbing strut. She snapped the fingers of her free hand, and sang, 'Ten per cent luck, twenty per cent skill. Bending reality to my will.'

Sully didn't recognize the song, but Hunter just sang the refrain over and over. After a minute Sully picked it up and sang along. They danced their way down Bear Mountain with their Hot Pink.

'What should we do with it until we can sell it?' Hunter asked as they crunched through the snow, taking a shortcut off the trail.

'Right into a safe-deposit box. You want me to list it on eBay tonight?'

'No, not right away.' She blew into her hands again. 'I know you need the money bad; I do, too. But if we sell on eBay we're talking at least a thousand less. That's a lot of cash.'

'Yeah. It is.' Sully was fairly sure Mom had enough money to buy food for a few weeks. The rent was due on the tenth of January, which was almost three weeks away. They could delay two more weeks after that if they paid the late fee. 'How about this: if we can't find a buyer in a month, we sell it on eBay.'

'Sounds good,' Hunter said as she hopped from one rock to the next across a partially frozen stream.

'I can call around, spread the word that we're selling it.'

Hunter leaped on to the shore, then backstepped on the steep slope, her rear foot cracking through ice.

'Crap!' she shouted, laughing.

When the freezing water hit her foot she stopped laughing and grimaced. 'I *hate* the cold.'

Fortunately, they were close to the car. They jogged the last two minutes, and Sully cranked up the heat as soon as they were inside. As he was putting the car in reverse, he remembered the spare socks he'd tossed in the back seat in case his own feet got damp from the snow.

'Hang on.' He reached and retrieved the socks, offered them to Hunter. 'They're probably eight sizes too big, but they're dry.'

Hunter gave him a tight smile. 'Thanks, but that's OK. I'm fine.'

Laughing, he pushed the socks towards her. 'No you're not. Your foot is soaked.'

Hunter pulled out her phone, turned to face front. 'I appreciate the thought, but I'm *fine*.' There was a bite in her tone.

Sully shrugged and tossed the socks on to the back seat, not sure what her problem was.

As he pulled on to the Palisades, he glanced at Hunter's screen, expecting her to be on Instagram, posting their find like he was going to do as soon as he got home. She wasn't – she was looking at the front page of *The New York Times*.

'So what do you do when you're not hunting?' he asked. 'Do you have a group of friends you hang out with, or a boyfriend?'

'Holy shit,' Hunter hissed, holding her phone right up to her face.

'What?' Sully glanced at her phone, but couldn't read what was on the screen. 'What is it?'

Hunter dropped the phone into her lap. 'One of Holliday's hunters found a new kind of marble. It's *bigger* than the rest. It's dark blue. Midnight Blue.'

'Oh, my God.' No one had discovered a new colour since the Cherry Red. 'It's *bigger*? How much bigger?' Sully pulled on to the shoulder of the parkway.

'Half again as big as the rest, it says. The size of a cantaloupe.'

Sully leaned in to look at the phone, saw a photo of Holliday holding up the dark blue sphere, grinning like an idiot.

'Where'd he find it?'

Hunter read for a moment. 'Africa. He won't be any more specific than that.' She shook her head. 'I wish it was anybody but him. I hate that guy.'

'*You* hate him?'

'He ruins it for everyone – him and the other big marble operations. Jin Bao. ExoSphere. Hoovering up marbles with their mercenaries and computer programs. That's not the way they're meant to be found. It's the only game that's built to be fair, and they found a way to rig it.'

'A couple of weeks ago me and a couple of friends got in a brawl with four of Holliday's bodyguards.'

Hunter's head snapped up and turned towards him. 'Seriously?'

Sully nodded. 'Holliday was making an appearance to plug his new Yonkers store. My buddy Dom called him a thief. His bodyguards dragged us out of the auditorium.'

Hunter punched Sully in the arm. 'I like it.'

'Hey, come hang out with us,' Sully said.

Hunter gave him a sceptical smile. 'Sometime, maybe.' She went back to her phone. 'Holliday's offering fifty million to the person who finds the match,' she said.

'I'd love to find it, just to keep it from him.'

Hunter blew air from the corner of her mouth. 'Fifty million? Give me a break. You'd sell it to him. You'd get a good lawyer first, but you'd sell it.'

Sully chuckled. 'OK, you got me. If we find the match and you twist my arm, I'll let him have it and walk away with twenty million.'

Hunter propped her knees on the dash, watched the trees fly by past the window in the near dark. Sully was pushing the speed limit; he wanted to get home and tell Dom and his mom what they'd found. He also had an English test tomorrow that he needed to study for before going out with Dom. Another week and a half of school and he was home free. He was looking forward to Christmas vacation.

'What are you doing for Christmas?' he asked Hunter.

She turned, let her head loll, gave him a deadpan look. 'I'm hunting on Christmas. New Year's, too, in case you're wondering.'

The idea horrified Sully. 'You're going to be alone?'

She turned back towards her window. 'I'm not all that close to what's left of my family.'

Her tone said it was no big deal, but Sully tried to imagine spending Christmas alone.

'No. You're spending Christmas with me and my mom.'

Hunter guffawed, folded her arms. 'I'm not spending Christmas with you and your mom.'

'Yes you are. You just found a Hot Pink; you can afford to take Christmas off and drink some hot cider.'

'Your mom doesn't want some stranger in her house on Christmas.'

'If she knows you're spending Christmas alone, she does. She'll drive to your neighbourhood and drag you out of your apartment. She's loud, and you never know what's going to come out of her mouth, but she's got a heart of platinum.'

'I'm skipping Christmas by choice—'

'*Ah.*' Sully raised a hand to cut her off. 'I don't want to hear it. It's all settled.'

Hunter huffed a little, leaned back in her seat. 'Fine.'

Suddenly Sully couldn't wait for Christmas. Usually it was just him and Mom, and besides watching some old Christmas movie instead of *CSI* and opening a few presents it was about the same as any other day. He felt a flush of anticipation as he imagined staying up late into the night with Hunter after Mom went to bed, laughing, eating Christmas cookies, planning their next hunt.

Maybe more.

CHAPTER 6

A Copper thunked to the carpet in Sully's room. Dom retrieved it, studied the three spheres in his hand, then tossed the Rose in the air. He managed to juggle the spheres for about three seconds before two hit the floor.

'Cut it out,' Sully called from his bed. He changed the channel to ESPN. There was a golf tournament on, with sphere-burners playing off longer tees, sphere virgins off shorter ones. Golf was one of the last holdout sports still trying to level the playing field for competitors who hadn't burned spheres. It seemed unbelievable now that baseball had ever toyed with making the National League non-sphere and the American sphere. The only way you could tell a player had burned a sphere was because he suddenly got better. When Mike Trout went from hitting thirty home runs a year to fifty, or Aroldis Chapman's ninety-nine-mile-per-hour fastball suddenly leaped to a hundred four, it was pretty damned obvious they'd burned Chocolates for strength, and probably Creams for coordination. All of the records were falling. It was kind of depressing, actually. Burning spheres sure seemed like cheating to Sully, even if MLB owners and players had agreed that since there was no way to detect who was burning, it had to be accepted.

Dom dropped the Rose this time.

'Come on, cut it out.'

'It's not like I'm gonna break them. I couldn't break them with an atomic bomb.' Dom bent to pick up the dropped sphere. 'Just call her. She could be home doing nothing.'

'Why don't *you* call her?'

'Because I like her. When I like a girl, I get nervous calling. My voice shakes and my mind goes blank. I sound like a moron.' The Copper hit the floor again.

From the other room, Sully's mom called, 'Whatever you're doing in there, stop it. You promised you were going to do homework. You're not going anywhere until you finish yours, David.'

'Sorry, Mom. I will.' Sully swept his phone off the night table. 'Fine, I'll call her. But if I do, she's going to think I'm the one who likes her.'

Dom hesitated, studied Sully. 'You don't like her, do you?'

'We've gone over this already.' Sully did think Mandy was interesting, but he couldn't say he felt that spark. Since he and Laurie had broken up, Sully hadn't met anyone who lit that spark in him.

Hunter's face appeared in his mind. Maybe that wasn't completely accurate. How could he not be drawn to a girl who climbed into abandoned mine shafts? She was Catwoman. His feelings were complicated, though. He liked her, but he doubted he would like going out with her, assuming she even liked him. He believed what she said: she was all business. It wasn't that she was out of Sully's league – she was playing a whole different game.

Still, he had to admit he couldn't wait to see her on Christmas Eve. He'd always found Christmas carols cloying, but this year they filled him with warmth. The days left between Sully and Christmas felt like impositions, like annoying relatives parked on the couch yammering when it was clearly time for them to go.

'Great. Give her a call,' Dom said.

For a second Sully thought Dom meant Hunter, then he remembered they were talking about Mandy. He hit Mandy's number and put the phone to his ear. She answered on the first ring.

'It's Sully. From the brawl.'

Mandy sounded sniffly as she laughed. 'I remember you. The knee-kicker.'

'Hey, anything goes in a street fight. He was a big guy. You OK?' It was pretty obvious she'd been crying.

'I always cry before Christmas. Kind of a tradition with me.'

Dom was watching him, eyebrows raised.

'You interested in being cheered up? Dom and I are going Christmas shopping. We're taking the train into Manhattan.'

'No,' she said immediately. 'I appreciate you thinking of me, but I'm not going to be good company tonight.'

'Come out with us. You'll feel better.'

'Some other time I'd love to.'

Sully looked at Dom, shook his head. 'You sure? We're not particularly skilled fighters, but we're good at cheering people up.'

Dom surged forward, hand out. 'Let me talk to her.'

'Dom wants to talk to you.' He handed Dom the phone.

'Mandy. What's going on? You having a bad day?' Dom stuck a finger in his ear, turned towards the window. 'Come out with us.' Pause. 'Well, look at it from our side. We can't leave you alone and miserable four days before Christmas. What kind of people would we be if we did?' Dom waved his free hand. 'So bring us down. We don't care.' Another pause. Dom pumped his fist. 'Half an hour. Where do you live?'

Dom jotted down her address, said goodbye, handed the phone to Sully. 'Piece of cake.'

'I thought you got too nervous to talk.'

Dom shrugged. 'I didn't have time to get nervous.'

'She broke up with her boyfriend. That's got to be it,' Dom said as they climbed down the steps to the ground floor of Sully's building. A bitter wind hit Sully as he pushed open the door. It was below freezing, and would get even colder as the sun set.

'It could be a lot of things,' Sully said.

'Like what?'

'Maybe her mother's sick. Or her cat died.'

They crossed the car park to Dom's car, their heads down.

'If it was something like that, she would have told us right up front. "I don't feel like going out. My cat died."' Dom raised a gloved finger. 'But if you're talking to people you don't know well you wouldn't say, "I don't feel like going out, because my boyfriend dumped me." It's too personal.'

He had a point. 'We just got our fall grades,' Sully said. 'Maybe she flunked something.'

Dom burst out laughing. 'She's a brain. She probably got straight As.'

As they pulled out, Sully said, 'You're probably right, then. She just broke up with her genius boyfriend.' Dom had pulled a C-plus, two Cs and a D. To his surprise, Sully had managed all Bs except for a C in algebra. Pretty solid. No one on either side of his family had gone to college; he came from a line of mechanics, secretaries and factory workers. Further back, to his great-grandparents' generation, it was farmers and coal miners.

Mandy lived in Scarsdale, six or seven miles away, but a thousand miles removed from Yonkers. Houses there were mansions, with lawns like golf courses.

'There she is,' Dom said.

Mandy was waiting at the end of her driveway wearing a big blue parka with fake fur lining the hood, and heeled boots that made her look freakishly tall. She seemed all legs. Her nostrils were red around the rims, her eyes bloodshot.

'I don't want to talk about it,' she said, responding to their questioning looks as she climbed into the front passenger seat. 'Let's just have a good time.'

As Dom headed for the Metro-North train station, Mandy looked back at Sully. 'Who are you guys shopping for?'

'I need to get something for a friend,' Sully said. 'My sphere-hunting partner.'

'Who Sully happens to be madly in love with,' Dom said. It was so obviously intended to signal that Sully was not available that Sully almost laughed.

'Oh, really?' Mandy said. 'Maybe I can help you pick something out.'

'That'd be great. Although I don't think she's a jewellery or clothes person. Not your typical girlie girl.'

Mandy tilted her head, gave him a look. 'And I am?'

'True.' Mandy was wearing a little mascara, but no other make-up. Her parka was something Sully could see Hunter wearing. 'Yeah, you might be the perfect consultant for Hunter.'

'I'll take that as a compliment, given that you're madly in love with her.'

Sully started to say he wasn't in love with her, but decided it wasn't worth it. He was in something with her.

On the train, Dom peppered Mandy with questions about where she hung out (at home, mostly), what music she liked (obscure indie stuff Sully had never heard of; she was hardcore organic – refused to listen to any singer who'd burned Slate Greys, which ruled out pretty much all Top 40 music). Sully was happy to let Dom carry the conversation as snow flurries melted against the train's windows. He passed the time thinking about Christmas, imagining conversations he might have with Hunter while they relaxed on the couch.

'What's your last name?' Mandy asked Dom. 'You sound like you're Italian.'

The question pulled Sully out of his reverie.

'Cucuzza.' Dom said it with a well-practised lightness. Sully knew that inside, he was dying.

'Any relation to, you know?' Mandy asked.

To the infamous Tony Cucuzza, she meant. Destroyer of 276 priceless works of art at the Met.

'Nope,' Dom said, his tone still light.

'So your family is Italian?' Mandy asked.

'Yup. Third-generation American. My great-grandparents made the boat ride.'

'I'm first generation. My parents were both kids when my grandparents brought them here from Korea.'

Sully tuned out. He'd been trying to think of a gift for Hunter since he'd invited her for Christmas. He wanted something that couldn't be construed as romantic, yet wasn't impersonal. Something between a gift certificate and earrings.

There was a little extra bounce in Dom's step, his arms held further from his body than required even by his impressive muscles, as they climbed the steps leading from the subway to Fifth Avenue. When he was around women, Dom seemed to turn up his tough-guy persona a few notches.

'Tell me what she was wearing the last time you saw her,' Mandy said as they breezed into Lord and Taylor, passing women in white lab coats manning fragrance counters. The air was filled with a light, flowery scent that made Sully long for springtime.

'Jeans, combat boots, a grey sweatshirt, black gloves with the fingers cut off.'

Mandy pointed at him. 'Gloves. Perfect. Intimate, but not too intimate.' She raised her head and, gazing into the far reaches of the store, picked up her pace, so Sully and Dom had to push to keep up with her long strides.

She led them to a stretch of counters offering an elaborate array of gloves, crossed her arms, considering. 'What kind of gloves does she have?'

Sully tried to picture them. 'Just typical fabric gloves. You can see loose threads where she cut the fingers off.'

'Good, then she doesn't have leather. If you give her leather gloves, you're giving her something you know she'll use, only nicer than what she already has.'

'Anything would be nicer than the ones she has. They've pretty much had it.'

'Perfect.' Mandy chose a pair of fingerless black leather gloves, pulled one on, held out her hand.

'Nice,' Dom said.

'Yeah,' Sully agreed. They were form-fitting, simple, the leather thin and supple, the fingers ending just below Mandy's first knuckle.

'This is what I'd choose, if I was getting them for myself. If her taste leans towards androgynous, I don't think you can go wrong with these.'

They were also forty bucks. If not for the Hot Pink sitting in a safe-deposit box at the Hudson Valley Bank, they'd be out of the question. Sully took the gloves to the register, trying to suppress the idiot grin that kept forming. He couldn't wait for Hunter to see them; they were exactly right.

They made a bathroom stop after that. As Dom and Sully approached the urinals, leaving one between them, Dom said, 'I'm gonna ask her out. You think I should?'

Sully smiled. As if this was a surprising revelation. 'Never hurts to ask.'

'I feel so comfortable around her.'

'She's terrific.'

'OK.' Dom took a big, huffing breath. 'If I give you a look, back off so I have some room to work.'

'You got it.'

Mandy wanted to get a gift certificate for the Apple store for her sister, so they left Lord and Taylor and headed out into the cold.

Across Fifth Avenue from the Apple store, the black marble monolith that was the flagship Holliday's store loomed. Thick at the bottom and tapering to a slender pinnacle ten stories up, it was bathed in white spotlights. It stood out from the buildings around it like a Persian palace among hot dog stands.

'God, I hate that slimebag,' Mandy said, looking up at the store.

Dom nudged Sully. 'Let's go see what a Hot Pink is selling for.'

'I don't know.'

'Why Hot Pink?' Mandy asked.

'Sully and Hunter found one in the wild last week,' Dom said.

Mandy spun to face Sully. *Really?*

Sully nodded, unable to suppress the same huge, dumb grin he'd had while buying Hunter's gloves.

'That's a serious stone.' Mandy shook her long, straight hair out of her face. 'You want to check out the price?'

He *was* curious. Holliday's did not publish prices for the higher-end spheres online; they were way too exclusive and sophisticated for that. But even stepping inside would feel like he was acknowledging the store's right to exist.

'Come on,' Dom said. 'Let's go in.'

Sully eyed the store. The prices changed almost daily, mostly pushing ever higher. It would be useful to know what the biggest player in the business thought a Hot Pink was worth these days. Plus, Dom and Mandy both looked like they wanted to go in. He didn't want to rain on their fun.

'Sure. Why not?'

They hurried across the snow-covered street and headed into Holliday's.

The ground floor was packed with holiday shoppers, which wasn't surprising, since the common spheres – the rarity level ones – were displayed there.

Most of the space inside Holliday's was utterly wasted. The centre was hollowed out, so each floor from two and up was nothing but a catwalk with elegant railings, the spheres displayed in cases set into the walls. Sully craned his neck to peer up at the tenth floor. No one was up there except a solitary salesperson in Holliday's signature metallic silver garb, standing motionless, legs apart, arms folded behind her back.

They headed for the elevator.

'Floor, please?' a tall, thin man with a crew cut asked as they stepped in.

'Five,' Sully said.

'I'm sorry,' the elevator operator said. He remained facing the column of buttons, their glow reflecting off his glasses. 'There's a minimum credit score required for admittance to the upper floors during the holiday season. I'd be happy to take you to floors two through four, or you could sign up for a tour of the upper floors, although there's a three-month wait right now.'

Sully exchanged looks with Dom and Mandy. This place got more obnoxious every time Sully visited, although admittedly that wasn't often.

'How could you possibly know our credit scores?' Mandy asked.

'People's basic financial profiles are publicly available information.'

Sully couldn't help laughing. 'Yes, but you don't know who we *are*.'

The elevator door slid closed, but the elevator didn't move. Still facing the buttons, the operator turned just his head to look at Sully. 'Actually, Mr Sullivan, we do. All of our stores are equipped with facial recognition software that identifies you as you enter.' He smiled tightly. 'If we couldn't tell our rarity eight customers from those who can't afford a two, we'd waste a great deal of time, wouldn't we?' The operator tilted his head, touched his earlobe. Sully spotted a tiny transceiver wedged in his ear.

He turned to face Sully and his friends for the first time. 'I apologize. You've been issued a waiver.' He pressed the button for the fifth floor.

'Who issued the waiver?' Sully asked.

'Mr Holliday.' Although his expression hadn't changed, the operator's face was flushed. His Adam's apple bobbed as the door slid open. 'Mr Sullivan. Mr Cucuzza. Ms Toko. Enjoy your shopping.'

Sully stepped out of the elevator, regretting setting foot in the building. He didn't like that Alex Holliday knew Sully was visiting one of his stores. And why, exactly, would Holliday issue them, of all people, a waiver? Probably for the same reason he'd sent Sully the VIP invitation to the Yonkers store opening – to gloat.

A saleswoman was waiting, arms behind her back.

'Welcome to the fifth floor. My name is Anna, and I'll be assisting you. What can I show you today?'

'We'd like to see something in a Hot Pink,' Mandy said.

Anna bowed her head, smiling ever so slightly to acknowledge Mandy's joke. 'Right this way, Ms Toko, Mr Sullivan, Mr Cucuzza.'

It was nothing new that salespeople dealing with high-priced items treated customers with more deference than those who shopped at Walmart, but it was bizarre to see that difference so obvious inside one store. The salespeople on the ground floor were polite, but there was no bowing, no *Right this way, Mr Sullivan*.

As they walked, Anna manipulated a handheld device that looked like a slim TV remote. The glass separating them from the Hot Pink on display slid out of sight as they approached. Using both hands, the saleswoman lifted the sphere from a pedestal shaped like a silver goblet and offered it to Mandy.

'Current population estimates for Hot Pink are one per one hundred and eighty-five thousand people, actually making it closer to a rarity five point five.'

'How much is it?' Dom asked. Sully was grateful his friend had blurted out the crass question up there in the rarefied air of the fifth floor, so Sully didn't have to.

'At the moment it's . . .' Manipulating her remote, Anna looked up, as if the answer was on the floor above. Sully realized she was consulting some sort of virtual display in her glasses. '. . . sixteen thousand, six hundred.'

Sully nodded.

Dom looked at him. 'Nice.'

Ignoring the comment, Anna accepted the Hot Pink from

Mandy, restored it to its pedestal. 'What else may I show you today?'

'That's the only one we wanted to see. Thank you for your time, Anna.' Sully wanted to get out of there. That Alex Holliday knew he was there gave him the creeps.

'My pleasure, Mr Sullivan.' She winked at him, spun and led them to the elevator.

The elevator doors slid open as they approached. The operator gave them a broad smile.

As the door slid closed behind them, the operator pressed the button for the tenth floor. Sully exchanged a confused glance with Dom and Mandy. Dom shrugged. Evidently they were picking up other customers before heading back to the ground floor.

The door slid open. 'Right this way,' the operator said, gesturing towards a waiting saleswoman.

'What?' Sully said. 'No, we're done.'

'Mr Holliday instructed us to give you a private viewing of the Midnight Blue.' The elevator operator gave them an intent look, raised one eyebrow. 'You'd be stunned at some of the people who've asked to come up here and been turned down.' He gestured again. 'Please.'

Sully stepped off the elevator. The waiting saleswoman (although that title wasn't quite right, because the Midnight Blue was not for sale) extended her hand. In a delightful French accent, she said, 'Cosette Amiot. How do you do, Mr Sullivan?' Evidently the employees on the tenth floor got to keep their last names.

As they followed Cosette along the catwalk, which looked to be made of marble bordered with gold, Sully wondered what this was about. Maybe it was Alex Holliday's way of saying, *I see you. I know you're here.* He guessed they wouldn't be up here if not for Dom's outburst at Holliday's talk. That had got Holliday's attention, because it embarrassed him.

The Midnight Blue was balanced on a simple gold cylinder that resembled a candleholder. Cosette Amiot lifted it, offered it to Sully.

He couldn't help but feel awe as he held it. It was the most valuable object on the planet, and in Sully's mind, the most important. Who knew what it did when paired with its match? Maybe it was the key to understanding the spheres. By reseeding the world with new spheres, the Cherry Red had done something miraculous, and it had been normal-sized. That the Midnight Blue was twice as large must mean it did something even more miraculous.

Sully wished he could be there after its match was found, when the secret was unlocked.

'I wish I could tell you where we found it,' someone said from behind them. Sully immediately recognized Alex Holliday's voice. 'I know you'd appreciate it more than just about anyone.'

Holliday stretched out his hand as he approached, as if Sully was an old friend he was glad to see. Or an old enemy. At another time and place Sully might have refused to shake Holliday's hand, but he shook it now, stunned and a little confused.

'Ms Toko,' Holliday said, turning to Mandy. He placed his hand over his heart as they shook. 'I swear to you, I had nothing to do with the accident at your aunt's store. You know, I lived in Philly, not ten blocks from where your aunt's

74

store was, before I moved to Yonkers when I was twelve.'

'It was probably just some kids who got hold of sophisticated timers and fuel mixes,' Mandy said.

Chuckling, Holliday shook his head. 'Wanmei has a store in Philadelphia, if I'm not mistaken. Why don't you go bust his balls?'

Mandy didn't answer; she didn't even nod, just went on looking at Holliday sporting a tight half smile.

Holliday shrugged. 'I don't know what I can do to convince you. How do you prove you *didn't* do something?'

'Thanks for the tour,' Sully said, gritting his teeth but determined to be polite. 'I've enjoyed getting a chance to see the Midnight Blue up close.' He wasn't about to give Holliday the satisfaction of playing the part of the reasonable man hosting immature kids.

'When I heard you were here, I had to do something to welcome you.'

Sully offered the Midnight Blue to Mandy, but she shook her head, so he set it on the marble counter. Holliday reached over and retrieved it. 'David, let's take a walk.' He gestured down the hall, then handed the sphere to Cosette, who had reappeared with a tray of drinks in glasses made of stained glass.

Sully exchanged a glance with Dom, then turned down the hall, leaving his friends with Cosette. He was astonished by the attention Holliday was giving him and curious as to why. Holliday led him down a hallway that opened on to a vast lobby with a glass ceiling and lavish fountain, then on into a room that looked to be a combination luxury suite and control room. The walls were screens displaying data, scrolling stock prices and camera feeds that showed various parts of this store and others.

'My office.' Holliday raised his eyebrows. 'You want anything? We've got pretty much everything.'

Sully shook his head.

'Been doing a little Christmas shopping?' Holliday gestured at the bag holding Hunter's gloves.

'That's why we came down,' Sully said. 'We stopped in here on a whim.' What the hell was going on? Holliday was acting like they were old buds.

Holliday folded his arms across his chest, studied a screen of numbers that kept updating. It resembled a stock feed, but Sully quickly recognized that the letters in the columns weren't stock symbols, they were abbreviations for sphere colours.

'This is where it all happens, all the strategizing,' Holliday said. 'Three years from now I'm going to be the biggest seller in the United States. In five I'll be bigger than Bao.'

Sully wasn't sure how Holliday expected him to respond to such an egotistical pronouncement. He went on looking at the screen.

'Want to see what I really do in here?' Holliday lifted a little remote like the one Cosette had used to open the case. The data disappeared, replaced by a hyper-realistic prehistoric jungle scene. In the distance, a T. rex was prowling among the trees. 'Video games.' Holliday pointed a finger at the T. rex, pretended he was shooting.

The screen switched back to data.

'You know, I was raised by a single mother in a shitty neighbourhood, just like you.'

'Yeah, I'm familiar with your biography,' Sully said.

Holliday looked at him. 'Oh, really? Why is that?'

Because rage had been boiling inside Sully since the day Holliday cheated him, and he couldn't help but want to understand everything he could about the bastard. 'Everything sphere-related interests me.'

'I'm glad to hear that. Me too.'

Sully turned to face Holliday. He was getting tired of this game. 'Why are you glad? What difference does it make to you?'

The door opened and a woman came in carrying a bottle of water on a tray. As soon as Holliday plucked the bottle up, the woman disappeared back through the door. 'Because I'm always on the lookout for good people.' He shrugged. 'You've been on my radar. Why do you think I invited you to that opening?'

It took a moment for the words to register. When they did, Sully was sure he'd misunderstood.

'Are you offering me a job?'

Holliday took a swig from the bottle. 'You can start on the third floor. If you do well, you can advance to higher floors, or move out of sales into acquisitions, marketing, research . . .'

He wasn't talking minimum wage; he was talking real money. Benefits. A salary. Enough to take all the pressure off Sully's mom and erase all possibility that they'd have to move to Pittsburgh.

Just the thought of pulling on a silver suit each morning, standing at parade rest to help Holliday make money, made Sully's skin crawl. But he and Mom were in serious financial trouble, and he'd just been offered a way out.

What about school, though?

'I'm not sure I could work with school—'

'Drop out,' Holliday said immediately, as if he'd been anticipating the question. He gave Sully a wry smile. 'I didn't graduate from high school.'

'I know.'

Holliday pointed at him. 'Right. It's in my biography.' He took another swig of water. 'To bastardize a saying, people who can't do, learn.'

Sully couldn't work for this guy. What would Dom say? What would *Hunter* say? She'd never speak to him again. And he wouldn't blame her; he'd be a sellout. Holliday would own him.

Sully had a flash of his mom, giving Sully a high five after the fight outside the auditorium. Would she be happy if he took a job from Alex Holliday, even if it solved their problems?

No. No, she wouldn't. She especially wouldn't like it that he was dropping out of school. She would hate that.

But they were in trouble. Could he really afford to be proud?

Holliday pointed at the screen displaying sphere prices. 'Hot Pink is up another five.' When Sully didn't respond, he said, 'What can I say? I see a lot of my younger self in you.'

Sully didn't see how Holliday could know much of anything about him. Maybe he saw benefit in having the kid he'd cheated working for him. The Cherry Red was one of the few PR black eyes Holliday had taken. If Sully was working for him, it would look like there were no hard feelings.

'No, thanks,' Sully said. 'I think I'll keep on wasting my life learning for a while.'

Sully wanted to let Holliday have it. When else would he have a chance to tell him off right to his face? The problem was, Holliday was rich, and powerful. It wouldn't be hard for him to make Sully's life miserable.

'I am sorry about what happened with the Cherry Red. I didn't have a chance to apologize when it happened, because you were suing me and my lawyer advised against it. But I felt bad about how that played out.'

'Yeah. Me, too.' Sully could still picture that cheque, with all those zeros. He could still remember the elation he felt holding it, like it was a balloon rising higher and higher. He clutched that cheque with all his might as it lifted him higher and higher . . .

And then it popped, and Sully had come crashing to the ground.

'I hope you can see my side of it. I got nothing from the Cherry Reds, either. I didn't receive any benefit when I burned them.' Sully was pretty sure Holliday was reciting directly from the legal arguments his lawyer had drawn up. '*My* Cherry Red became just as worthless as yours, so you could argue I lost two point five million dollars in the transaction as well.'

'Except the Cherry Red was probably worth ten times that. I was just a thirteen-year-old kid, so I didn't know that when you told me your offer was only good for thirty minutes.'

Holliday made a sour face. 'Back then? Twenty-five? No way.'

Sully realized that for a few minutes he'd begun to think maybe Holliday wasn't the biggest scumbag on the planet.

Now he was back to his original opinion on the subject. He leaned up against a built-in desk, facing Holliday.

'To be honest, Alex, I'm surprised you'd ask me to work for you. I mean, I *know* you're a thief and a liar. I may have been thirteen, but I was still there, in that room.'

Holliday's smile flattened a little.

'I *know* some of those things you swore under oath you said to me were never said. You cheated a kid, then you lied about it.' Sully pushed off the desk, headed for the door. 'I wouldn't work for you in a million years.'

'*Hey*.' The doorknob clicked as Sully reached for it. The door was locked. 'Don't turn your back on me, Dollar Meal.' Holliday stalked over, stuck his finger in Sully's face. 'This isn't *Rocky*. This is the real world. You don't want to work for me? Fine. Graduate high school, then go flip hamburgers. But watch how you speak to me, and about me, or I will wreck you. Do you understand?'

Sully should have been scared, but all he felt was rage. He wanted to bite Holliday's finger off and spit it in his face. 'Unlock the damned door.'

'I'll unlock it when I'm finished,' Holliday said through his perfect teeth, courtesy of a pair of Ruby Reds. 'I asked you a question.'

Sully kept his gaze hard on Holliday. 'And I told you to unlock the damned door.'

Sully could almost see the wheels turning in Holliday's head. He didn't want to back down and unlock the door, but what was he going to do? Summon a bodyguard and have him beat Sully until Sully said he understood? That would just prove Sully's point, that Holliday was nothing but a criminal.

Or Holliday could take a swing at Sully himself. Sully would like that, even though Holliday was pumped up with Peach, Chocolate, and Cream spheres.

Holliday touched the remote in his hand. The lock clicked open. 'Don't ever come back here.'

'Don't worry.' Sully yanked the door open and stormed out.

Mandy and Dom were waiting with Cosette. It looked as if they'd run out of conversation topics.

'Come on,' Sully said, striding towards the elevator.

With Mandy and Dom on his heels, Sully stepped into the waiting elevator. The operator was back to staring at the buttons, the friendly smile gone.

'What did he want?' Dom asked as they descended.

'He offered me a job.'

Despite everything, Sully got a kick out of Dom's bug-eyed reaction. '*What*? What did you tell him?'

'I told him I don't work for thieves.' Sully watched the elevator operator's profile. He showed no reaction.

Mandy, on the other hand, burst out laughing.

While they were crossing the car park on the way to Dom's car, Mandy dumped a pile of snow on Sully's head, setting off a snowball fight that left all three of them panting, red-faced and laughing. As the fight was petering out, Dom raised his eyebrows at Sully when Mandy wasn't looking. Sully gave him a questioning look. Dom gestured emphatically for Sully to take a walk. He'd almost forgotten Dom's plan to ask Mandy out.

Sully got in the car. Fortunately, he could still hear them.

'That was a blast,' Dom said.

'Thanks for talking me into coming out. I feel so much better.'

'You want to do something tomorrow after school? Maybe go to Nathan's?'

'Sully, too?' Mandy asked.

'Nah. Tuesday is Sully's marble-hunting day. With the girl in the gloves.'

'Wait. Are you asking me out?' Mandy sounded perplexed. That didn't seem like a good sign.

'Yeah. I guess.' Dom sounded hesitant. He was picking up on the surprise in her voice, too. Sully turned partway round so he could see them.

'Dom, I'm sorry. I should have mentioned earlier, but it never came up.'

Dom looked at the ground. 'You have a boyfriend?'

'No. Dom, I'm gay.'

Dom's thick eyebrows pinched. He pressed a hand to his forehead. 'Damn. That's even worse. If it was a boyfriend, I could hope you'd break up with him.'

Laughing, Mandy leaned in, kissed Dom's cheek. 'That's sweet, though. *Thank you*. I was wondering why you suddenly seemed nervous.'

'I *was* nervous.'

Sully cracked the door open. 'Can I come back out now?'

Mandy peered round Dom, saw Sully sitting in the car and burst out laughing. 'Is that why you got in the car? What, did Dom give you a signal?'

'Pretty much, yeah.'

Mandy sighed. 'Very smooth.' She turned to Dom. 'We're still friends, though, right?'

'Yeah,' Dom said immediately. 'Of course. You're a blast.'

Mandy's eyes got a little misty. 'I didn't think –' She choked up. For a moment, she couldn't speak. She fanned herself with one hand, blinking back tears. 'I didn't think anything could cheer me up tonight, but I've had the best time.'

'What happened?' Dom asked. 'We didn't want to pry, but we were wondering why you were so down.'

Mandy waited as two shoppers speaking in low voices passed.

'I broke up with my girlfriend, Alexis, a couple of days ago.' She reached up and rubbed her nose, which was pink from the cold. 'As it turns out, most of our friends were her friends, or at least they're taking her side.' She shrugged. 'Suddenly I don't have many friends.'

'Well, you've got two, anyway,' Dom said.

CHAPTER 7

Sully was winded by the time he reached the fifth floor. As he approached Hunter's apartment, number 503, he could hear so many voices inside it sounded like someone was having a party.

The door swung open as soon as he knocked. A boy about ten years old looked up at him, clutching the knob.

'Is Hunter here?'

The kid turned, yelled something in Spanish. Sully couldn't see much, because the living room was divided into smaller spaces by old blankets hanging from the ceiling. Based on the voices he guessed twenty people were in there. He heard angry voices – two men having an argument – coming from a back bedroom. To his right, a blanket-free corridor ran along the edge of the room towards what he guessed was the kitchen.

One of the blankets swung back, giving him a glimpse inside as a woman stepped out. The space was packed with cardboard boxes and three rolled-up sleeping bags. There was also a little square TV and piles of clothes.

Hunter appeared in the corridor, smiling.

'Ready?' Sully asked.

Hunter nodded. She didn't turn to say goodbye to anyone, just led him out.

'Wow, that's a lot of people,' Sully said.

'That's because it's Christmas Eve, and because it's winter. On an average day in the summer there might be just eight or ten.'

Sully's little apartment didn't seem so cramped all of a sudden.

It was snowing as they pulled into the Garden Apartments. Sully thought that was perfect. Any other time of year he hated snow, but who didn't want tree branches and roofs covered with white on Christmas Eve? It even brightened the Garden Apartments, and that was a challenge. Those joyless redbrick rectangles evenly spaced on a flat parcel of land didn't have much going for them beyond being close to McDonald's and Price Chopper.

He licked his lips, suddenly nervous. 'I want to apologize in advance for anything weird or inappropriate my mother says. She means well.'

Turning to pull her pack out of the back seat, Hunter said, 'The woman's welcoming me into her house on Christmas, feeding me a turkey dinner. It'll take a hell of a lot for her to offend me.'

'We'll see if she's up to the challenge.'

The door opened before he could turn the knob. Mom burst through wearing a hat in the shape of a Christmas tree, a strip of white fur round the band.

'Merry Christmas, Mom.' Sully turned to Hunter. 'This is my friend Hunter.'

Mom opened her arms and enveloped Hunter. 'Merry Christmas, sweetheart.'

'Thank you for inviting me, Mrs Sullivan.'

Mom waved her words away. 'The more, the merrier. It's always too quiet on Christmas with just Sully and me.' She looked from Hunter to Sully and back again. 'The mighty hunters. Over dinner I want to hear you tell the story of finding the Hot Pink, Hunter.'

Sully showed Hunter his room, where she'd be sleeping while Sully took the couch in the living room. He felt a little self-conscious as she looked around, taking in the Kate Upton poster with amusement. Sully had removed all signs of baseball cards, video games, Marvel superhero comics and figures, and anything else that seemed boyish, and hidden them in his closet. He felt OK about Hunter seeing his baseball equipment, which was stashed in a corner, the framed eight-by-ten photos he'd taken on their trip to the Adirondacks two years ago. Leaving the Kate Upton poster up might have been a mistake.

He ducked out to let Hunter get situated.

His mom was in the kitchen. Sully helped himself to one of the chocolate-covered pretzels spread on a serving dish on the kitchen table. As he took a bite, Mom pointed a spatula at him and whispered, 'Don't even *think* about having sex with this girl in my house.'

Sully coughed, nearly choking on the pretzel. At least she hadn't said it with Hunter in the room. He wouldn't put that past her. 'Jeez, Mom.' He raised his hands. 'If I was going to, if she were the least bit interested, I sure wouldn't do it in my bedroom with my mother on the other side of the wall, listening.'

'I wouldn't be listening. I'd be plugging my ears and humming.'

Sully laughed, despite how uncomfortable he was feeling. 'That's good to know.' He turned towards the counter and took another pretzel; his face felt so hot he was sure it was glowing bright red.

Mom pulled open a drawer, started taking out silverware. 'So you're not having sex with her?'

Sully cringed at how loud she said it. 'You know, these walls are paper thin. I used to listen to Jay Leno through them while I was falling asleep. No, Mom, she's just a friend.'

'Awfully pretty friend.'

The toilet flushed.

A moment later Hunter joined them, still wearing her gloves with the fingertips cut off.

'So, Hunter, Sully tells me you were homeless.' Mom pressed a hand to her chest. 'That just breaks my heart. He said your mother died?'

'Mom.' Sully was trying to stay calm. 'Let her drink a glass of eggnog before you interrogate her.'

Mom pulled a Christmas cup down from the cabinet, poured a glass of eggnog, and set it in front of Hunter. 'Now, tell me your life story.'

Hunter lifted the cup, laughing.

'*Sully*,' someone called from outside. Then again, '*Sul-ly*,' this time a chorus of voices, singing his name, badly.

Sully went to the big picture window that overlooked the common area. The whole gang was looking up at him: Mike,

Laurie, Donny, Jim, Bugs, four or five others.

His phone signalled an incoming text message. Sully pulled the phone from his back pocket. It was from Donny.

Come on out! We're carolling.

He showed the message to Hunter. 'Want to go caroling?'

She shrugged. 'I don't know the words to any songs.'

'That's OK; they don't either.'

When they were in the hallway, out of earshot of his mom, Sully said, 'The carolling is just an excuse for them to get away from their folks and drink.'

'Got it. They don't look like carollers.'

Sully introduced Hunter to the gang, then they headed off along the frozen ground. Mike broke out in a loud rendition of 'Hark! The Herald Angels Sing' almost completely devoid of melody. Some of the others joined in, but after the 'God and sinners reconcile' line, everyone muttered incoherent syllables that degenerated into laughter. No one knew what came next.

'Here you go.' Mike handed Sully an open carton of eggnog. Sully took a swig, and winced. It was about eighty per cent vodka.

Mike patted his back. 'That'll put some hair on your chest.'

Sully offered it to Hunter. She took a drink and blinked as she returned the carton to Mike. 'You're supposed to leave some of the eggnog.'

'Welcome to the Yonkers alcoholics club,' Mike said.

Laurie sidled up, gave Sully a quick one-armed hug as they walked. Her pale cheeks were red, her eyes warm from shots of eggnog-flavoured vodka. It was strange to look at Laurie and feel only the faintest stirring of what had once felt like a volcano of love, a Fourth of July finale of passion. They'd gone out for only a few weeks; then she'd given him an awkward speech about 'liking him as a friend, but not . . . you know.'

Bugs caught his eye behind Hunter's back, gave him an enthusiastic thumbs-up. Sully just smiled. There was no behind-the-back hand signal for *I know, she's really something, but we're just friends*.

Donny and Jim, who were brothers, were pelting windows with snowballs. Neither was wearing gloves.

'So, Hunter, what did you ask Santa to bring you for Christmas?' Mike asked, sidling up to her.

She thought for a moment. 'I asked him for strength.'

'Strength? I think you got the wrong guy; you're supposed to ask Jesus for strength. Santa brings the swag.'

'Yeah, well, the strength I want can be wrapped in a package with a bow on top. I asked Santa for a chocolate-coloured marble.' She shrugged. 'But he never brings me what I want.'

'You must be a naughty girl, then.'

Sully felt his blood pressure rise. Mike was hitting on her. That asshat.

'Now *you're* confusing him with Jesus. Jesus is the one who cares about good and bad. Santa gives out presents based on how much your parents make; he has a way of leaving poor kids cheap crap, or skipping their houses altogether.'

Mike laughed. 'Ain't that the truth.'

When the carton of vodka was empty, the troop broke up after a round of hugs, back slaps and Merry Christmases.

On the way back to Sully's apartment they passed the complex's pathetic little playground – a couple of swings and a slide missing its ladder. Hunter made a beeline for one of the swings, swept the snow off it and sat. Sully took the other.

Across the snow-covered lawn and Germond Road, McDonald's sat in darkness.

'Your friends are OK,' Hunter said. 'You can always tell by how they treat the new kid.'

Sully chuckled. 'They're not as welcoming when the new kid isn't scorching hot.'

'Shut up, Yonkers.' She said it like she was put out, but she was grinning.

It was one of those magical moments, sitting there in the dark with the snow falling on Christmas Eve. Sully felt an undeniable urge to lean over and kiss Hunter. But, looking at her profile as she gazed off into the car park, he guessed being kissed was the last thing on Hunter's mind, that a kiss would dump a bucket of ice water on the moment.

I'm all business, no pleasure, she'd said.

'You and Laurie had a thing?' Hunter asked.

Her words startled him. 'What? How did you know?'

She grinned. 'One of my superpowers.'

Christmas music drifted from a nearby apartment. 'White Christmas'. It was muffled, the tune just recognizable.

'So show me where you found it,' Hunter said.

It. No need to get more specific than that. Over the years Sully had shown so many people where he found *it*, including dozens of journalists.

He led her to the stream that ran between the apartments and the highway, to the overpass he and Donny had waded under during their bare-handed carp-catching contest.

'There it is. I'd show you the gap in the wall I stuck my

hand through after a carp swam into it, but it's probably not a good night for wading.'

Hunter leaned out over the stream, trying to see into the dark tunnel. 'Was that the first place you looked, after Holliday burned the Cherry Reds and the second wave appeared?'

Sully laughed. 'You got me.'

She nodded. 'It made sense that the new ones might be hidden in all the same places as the last batch.'

'There wouldn't have been much challenge in that, though.'

Ice had formed along the edges of the stream, but the black water in the centre sluiced along, making a pleasant trickling sound.

Hunter's phone chimed, alerting her to an incoming text. She pulled out her phone, smiled. 'It's from my Korean mom, wishing me a merry Christmas.' She typed a reply and sent it. 'We'd better get back. Your mom's all alone on Christmas Eve.' There was a twinkle in Hunter's eye as she said it.

As they headed towards the apartments, Hunter said, 'So it's just you and your mom? No relatives nearby who'll be knocking on the door tomorrow, bringing figgy pudding for Christmas dinner?'

'Nope. Just us. If we want figgy pudding, we have to make it ourselves. Most of our relatives live around Pittsburgh. We went to Pittsburgh for Christmas a couple of times, but decided we'd rather celebrate by ourselves.'

'Bad relatives?'

Sully considered, trying to wrap his head around how to describe them. 'They're not bad people, they're just . . . strange. If you met them, they'd be friendly, all grins and handshakes and small talk. But that's as far as you'd ever get with them. You'd never get to know them. They're obsessed with mysteries and produce. That's all they want to talk about.'

'You mean, like TV show mysteries?'

Sully nodded. 'Sherlock Holmes. Those British shows on PBS where you can barely understand what anyone's saying. If they're not talking about Miss Marple, they're going on about where you can buy the freshest asparagus, how seedless watermelon isn't as good as regular.' Sully opened his mouth to ask about Hunter's relatives, then realized that might be a touchy subject. If she had any, they couldn't be worth much if they hadn't taken her in.

'You said most of your mom's family are in Puerto Rico?'

'That's right. I never met my father, so I don't really know his family, besides one aunt who isn't worth knowing.'

'Definitely no figgy pudding for you, then.'

Hunter giggled. 'No figgy pudding. No nothing. My family is one big fat lump of coal. Unless you count my Korean mom.'

In the morning, Hunter came out wearing a green sweater, along with her gloves and combat boots. They got some coffee, then sat cross-legged on the floor and opened gifts. It was the first time in his life Sully wasn't the least bit interested in his own gifts. He couldn't wait to watch Hunter open her gloves.

Hunter gave his mom a big white knitted hat.

'It's called a slouchy,' Hunter said as his mom put it on. It sank on to her head like an accordion. 'It's all the rage in my neighbourhood.'

Mom took it off, examined it carefully. 'It's gorgeous. It's handmade, isn't it?'

Hunter nodded. 'I made it.'

'Wow,' Sully said. 'Can I see it?' Mom passed it over and Sully admired it, shaking his head. 'That's beautiful. I didn't know you could crochet.'

'Yarn's a whole lot cheaper than hats and sweaters.'

Sully's mom got him a big hardcover book on spheres that he didn't have. There was a separate page on each colour.

Sully had hoped Hunter would like what he got her, but her reaction took him by surprise. She cried. She pressed the gloves to her mouth as tears rolled down her cheeks.

'I'm sorry,' she said, 'I just love these so much. They're perfect.' She scooted over to Sully, hugged him, kissed his cheek. 'Thank you for this, for all this. It's the best Christmas I've ever had.'

She scooted towards the tree, grabbed a present in cartoon snowman wrapping paper, and handed it to Sully. It was surprisingly heavy.

Smiling, Sully held the package next to his ear and shook it before setting it down. He tore open the wrapping, opened the flaps on a plain cardboard box.

Inside were two Teal spheres. Fall asleep more easily, rarity level one. Hunter must have paid at least a hundred dollars for the pair, unless she managed to find them in the wild.

'The day we found the Hot Pink, you said you were having trouble sleeping. I know you can't go burning your stock because you've got to make a living, but I figured if you got a pair of Teals as a *gift*' – Hunter shrugged – 'well then, you'd *have* to burn them, 'cause they were a gift.'

Sully couldn't believe how much thought, and money she couldn't afford, Hunter had put into this gift. 'Wow.' He lifted the spheres out, held one in each hand. He wanted to tell her it was too much, but he didn't want to spoil the pleasure she was so obviously getting from his reaction.

'Wow,' he repeated. 'This — I wasn't expecting this. Thank you.'

'Go ahead,' Mom said, leaning forward on the couch.

Sully looked from one Teal to the other, then up at Hunter. 'Should I?'

Hunter nodded. 'Go for it.'

'My first ever. I'm going to remember this for the rest of my life.' He lifted them slowly, touched them to his temples. They felt cool, smooth. As he'd heard from so many others who'd burned spheres, there was no sensation; he didn't feel any different.

The spheres' brilliant blue-green hue began to fade. He set them down on the carpet carefully, reverently.

'Your first, but not your last,' Hunter said. She leaped up. 'Now go take a nap.'

'I can't take a nap.' Sully laughed. 'I've never been so wide awake. I just burned my first marbles.'

'That's the whole point of them, though. Even when you're pumped up, or your thoughts are racing, you can fall asleep.' She held out a hand. Sully took it, and Hunter pulled him to his feet and nudged him towards his room. 'Go ahead. We'll come in ten minutes and wake you.'

So Sully went to take a nap, although he wasn't the least bit tired. It took him about two minutes to doze off.

Feeling warm, Christmassy and utterly content, Sully curled up on the recliner and flipped open his new book to the first page. The first colour it covered was Cherry Red, which made sense, given that Cherry Red was responsible for reproduction, for seeding Earth with a second wave of spheres.

His name was mentioned as the discoverer of one of the two Cherry Reds. It was kind of cool to see his name in print.

The thing about it was Sully was afraid the Cherry Red would define his entire life. When he was thirty, he didn't want someone pointing him out while he stacked soup cans at Price Chopper and saying, 'See that guy? When he was thirteen, he found the Cherry Red.'

He and his mom had had a rough year after the Cherry Red. It was amazing what it did to your head to believe you'd been handed $2.5 million, only to have it snatched back.

Sully thumbed through the pages, stopping at random: Mint (more outgoing), Magenta (night vision), Plum (erase memories).

'I don't know why someone would want to burn Plums,' Sully said to Hunter, who was sitting cross-legged on his bed, watching *A Christmas Story* on Sully's little TV. 'Who wants to erase a part of their life, whether it's good or bad? You couldn't pay me to erase even my worst memory.'

Very slowly, Hunter closed her eyes. 'That's because you've never had something bad happen to you.'

Sully laughed. 'Are you kidding me? My father's an alcoholic. He once kicked me in the ass so hard he lifted me right off the ground. My life was miserable before Mom left him.'

As Hunter turned to face him, Sully could see he'd hit a nerve. 'So tell me. Do you wake up screaming from nightmares of your drunken father kicking you in the ass really hard? Do you think about it every day? When you think about it, do you still break out in a sweat and get sick to your stomach after all these years?'

Sully regretted opening his mouth. He didn't appreciate Hunter making him feel like he'd just drowned a puppy or something. 'You know, you don't have a monopoly on hard times. My mom just lost her job. If not for the Hot Pink, we'd have no way to pay the rent next month.'

'You think that's something we have in common, don't you? That we both grew up poor. You're not *poor*. You're just growing up in the crappiest part of a tony suburb. You get three meals a day; you stop in at McDonald's for french fries on the way to your soccer league.' The way she said it, she made *soccer league* sound like a particularly pussy disease. 'You have your own *room*, for God's sake. You're not poor. You just feel poor because everyone around you is rich.'

Sully held up both hands. 'Hey, you don't have to jump down my throat. I was just saying that, to me, Plums aren't worth the price.'

Hunter's scowl softened. 'I'm sorry. It's just . . . I have friends who would trade a kidney for a set of Plums. They've been through things you wouldn't believe, that they'd do anything to forget.'

Sully could see this was something Hunter wanted him to

understand. Needed him to understand.

'Sorry. Sometimes I just think out loud without thinking through what I'm saying first.'

Hunter relaxed. 'Me too. All the time. I didn't mean to bust on you. I'm really sorry.'

CHAPTER 8

There was tightness in Sully's chest as he drove. He didn't want Hunter to go home. Seeing her away from the flea market, away from hunting, he realized he'd had her all wrong. She wasn't hard and closed down and serious by nature; she was that way because she had to be. Given the chance to kick back, she was funny and honest. Easy to be with. The apartment was going to feel empty with her gone.

When they had gone Christmas shopping, Dom had said Sully was madly in love with Hunter. Sully didn't know her well enough to go that far, but he liked her. He liked her a lot.

'Thank you for inviting me,' she said.

'You made my mom's Christmas. She wasn't just being polite when she said you're welcome back any time.'

Hunter nodded, pleased.

'You made my Christmas, too.'

She pulled her backpack into her lap, took hold of the zipper. After a long pause, she seemed to decide something, and unzipped the pocket. She pulled out her hunting notebook.

'I think I know where we might be able to find something

rare. I mean really rare. Like maybe an eight.'

Sully leaned forward in his seat. 'Where?'

'In the city.'

'I thought you said the city was picked clean?'

'I think there's a place everyone's overlooked.'

Sully's heart was thumping. Hunter had led them to a Hot Pink. If she said there was a place where they could find an eight, he believed her. 'Come on, don't keep me in suspense.'

Hunter typed on her phone, then held it where Sully could see the screen while driving.

It was a photo of a water tower on a tenement roof. The tower was round, with a roof that looked like the Tin Man's hat, and stood on crosshatched metal stilts. He'd seen towers like it all his life; they were all over the city.

'Holy –' Sully swallowed. *Inside* the water towers? Never in a million years would he have thought of that. 'But they're filled with water, aren't they?'

'Duh, yeah. We'd have to buy a wet suit, and a waterproof flashlight.'

He studied the picture of the tank. It was big, and tall. How deep was that water? Ten feet? Fifteen? 'You mean we're going to swim to the bottom of these things?'

'*I'm* gonna swim, Yonkers. I've been waiting for someone I trust who can help me get up on the roofs and help with the hatches. The hatches are heavy as hell.'

'And you know that because?' Sully said, laughing.

Hunter shrugged. 'Reconnaissance.'

It was a wild idea; he was breathless just thinking about it. 'Wait. Aren't the tanks cleaned out every so often?'

Hunter messed with her phone again, held it up. It was an

article in *The New York Times*: INSIDE CITY'S WATER TANKS, LAYERS OF NEGLECT. 'They're supposed to be, but most of them aren't.'

Sully laughed. That figured. 'How many tanks are in the city?'

Hunter covered her eyes. 'Ten to fifteen thousand.'

'Yikes. Ten to fifteen *thousand*? That would take *years*.'

'That's one of the reasons I think they've been overlooked. That, and because no one wants to swim down ten feet in dark water in those tin cans.'

It made sense. It wouldn't be easy, but she was right – it was the sort of place you might find the rarest of the rare, because the low-hanging fruit had all been picked. There were no more eights hidden in people's bushes.

'A lot of roofs have two or three towers on them. Some have six,' she went on. 'I figure we could search ten a night if we work three or four hours, say from six p.m. to nine or ten.'

There was no way his mother was going to let him do that. The only way he could pull it off was to lie, and he wasn't sure he could tell Mom such an enormous lie. He would die from the guilt.

At the same time, an *eight*. Aquamarine (quick healing), or Vermillion (need little sleep), or Olive (pain control). They were million-dollar spheres.

Maybe he wasn't giving his mom enough credit. Maybe she'd understand . . .

Understand that he was climbing on to tenement roofs at night, in the city, so Hunter could *dive into water towers*? No way. She'd probably be OK with it if they were going somewhere safe to hunt, like the suburbs.

What if he didn't lie, exactly? What if he told her they were going hunting all over, that it was the only time they both had open? He'd have to do his homework during free periods, and work in the dark (and the cold in wintertime) until bed, then do it all over again the next day. It would be gruelling.

But damn, they needed the money. An eight? That would solve their financial problems forever. And as an added bonus, it would annoy the hell out of Holliday if Sully and Hunter found a rare one right in his own backyard. Almost no one was finding rare spheres any more except for pro hunters.

'OK. I'm in.'

Hunter held up her gloved hand, and Sully slapped it. She caught his hand, squeezed it for a second before letting go.

CHAPTER 9

Perched behind his table of spheres, one foot propped on a folding chair, Sully watched Maurice Trudell clean up his painting supplies after staining a coffee table. Trudell put the lid on the can of stain, tapped it shut with the handle end of a screwdriver.

It reminded Sully of the time he'd been so eager to help his dad with some do-it-yourself project that he splashed white paint on Dad's truck trying to use a hammer to tap the lid down on a can of paint. Sully could still remember his dad's exact words: 'You stupid ass.' Then he'd smacked Sully's face and told him to get the hell out of the garage.

Hunter had said Sully's years with his dad hadn't been that bad. They'd sure seemed bad. Hunter was right, though: he wasn't haunted by them. They didn't define him. They were in the past, and he kept them there. Being homeless had likely given Hunter a different barometer of what constituted awful.

Sully stared down the aisle, remembering the moment he'd first seen Hunter. He'd noticed her as soon as she was in sight, almost as if he'd been expecting her.

For the hundredth time he thought about sitting on the swings with Hunter on Christmas Eve, the snow falling. There had been a moment when he'd wanted to lean over and kiss her. Had there been something in her expression, maybe a slight lean towards Sully, that put the idea in his head? Maybe it was wishful thinking.

Someone paused in front of Sully's table, drawing him out of his daydream. The guy studied the sign Sully had hung from his table, announcing a Hot Pink for sale. The guy was tall and skinny, with curly brown hair bursting from the top of his head like a mushroom cloud.

'A friend of mine saw this and gave me a call.' He pointed at the sign. 'You really have a Hot Pink?'

'I sure do. Not here, but I have one for sale.' The guy didn't look like someone with wads of cash to spend, but you never knew who was a highly paid tech genius or who owned the patent on a new iPhone app.

'How much you asking?'

'Fourteen five. In Holliday's they go for almost seventeen.'

The guy nodded, put a hand on his chin. 'You take thirteen five, cash?'

Sully kept his expression neutral and his voice steady even though it wanted to shake a little. 'I'll take fourteen.'

The guy took a huffing breath, looked down at the sign, as if considering. Sully waited.

The guy looked up. 'OK.'

Sully held out his hand. 'If you have the cash, you've got a deal. David Sullivan.'

'Aiden Oberon.' They shook hands. 'I can go withdraw the cash. Shouldn't take me more than twenty minutes.'

Sully nodded. 'I can get the marble here within an hour after that.'

As Aiden wandered off, head bobbing side to side, looking like he was out for a leisurely walk, Sully got on the phone to Hunter.

She sounded out of breath as he filled her in. Sully couldn't blame her; if this guy was serious, she was about to be handed $8,400.

Next he dialled Dom, who answered on the second ring. 'How would you like to make two hundred bucks?'

Dom laughed. 'As long as it doesn't involve nudity.'

After Sully filled him in, Dom insisted on starting out for the bank right away to save time.

As he hung up, Sully tugged at the front of his shirt, which was stuck to his chest. He was sweating.

'Sounds like good news,' Neal called over.

'I think I sold the Hot Pink.'

Neal held his fist in the air. 'There you go. Good for you.'

Neal's praise made Sully flush with pride. When Sully had first showed up at the flea market, a fourteen-year-old kid, Neal and Samantha had pretty much adopted him. They taught him how important it was to display your merchandise in an eye-catching way, how you could 'create' sales just by being friendly and getting to know the flea market's regular customers. He'd come a long way, thanks to them.

Fifty-six hundred dollars. Almost eight months' rent. Handing that money to his mom was going to be one of the best moments of his life. She'd told him she wouldn't accept more than half to put towards their living expenses, that he should save the rest for college, but she couldn't hide how desperate their situation was. Even when Mom finally found a job, it was going to be half of what she'd made at Exile Music.

Sully spotted his buyer heading towards the table.

'All set,' Aiden said. He pulled a bank deposit envelope out of his back pocket and opened it, displaying crisp, new thousand-dollar bills.

Sully nodded. 'Let me make a couple of calls.' He felt like Matt Damon in a big-budget thriller as he stepped away from his table and called Hunter.

'We're all set. Dom is on his way to get you.'

'We made a good call, not taking the quick sale on eBay.'

Sully had to agree, even if it had taken him right down to the wire on rent. 'Use the vendors' entrance, not the main gate. It's quicker.'

Next he called Dom and confirmed, then turned back to Aiden. 'Figure half an hour, forty-five minutes tops.'

Aiden nodded. 'I think I'll walk around. I'll stay close.'

As Aiden wandered off, Sully wondered if he was an investor, or if he planned to get a pair and burn them. In all likelihood he was an investor. The way prices kept rising, nine out of ten buyers these days were investors. You had to have serious cash to spend $28,000 on the ability to call up an adrenalin rush, cool as it would be to have that power.

Sully paced his stall, unable to sit.

He heard Dom before he saw either of them.

'Screw you!' Dom's shout cut through the murmur of flea market chatter, jolting Sully. That didn't sound like excitement; it sounded like anger. Sully scanned the flea market anxiously, looking for Dom and Hunter.

He spotted Hunter running towards him, cutting between

shoppers. She bumped into a guy in a knit cap and continued running without a word. Dom was a dozen feet behind her, shouting something Sully didn't catch.

As Hunter drew closer, Sully spotted a bloody scrape on the left side of her forehead. He left his booth and headed towards her.

'What happened?' Sully shouted as they converged. He already knew, though, and he was already feeling sick. They'd lost it. Somehow they'd lost the Hot Pink.

Hunter just kept coming. She raised both hands and drove them into Sully's chest, nearly knocking him off his feet.

'Do you think I'm stupid?' Hunter shouted.

'What happened?'

'You know what happened!'

Dom pushed between them. 'We got rolled. Two guys in the car park pulled guns on us.'

Sully had known what Dom was going to say, but the words still doubled him over. He braced his hands on his knees to stay on his feet.

It was the Cherry Red all over again.

'Don't do this,' Hunter said. 'I'm warning you.'

Sully raised his head. 'What are you talking about?'

'She thinks we're in on it,' Dom said.

'*What?*'

Hunter was shaking. She looked on the verge of tears. 'How did they know what I looked like? Hmm? A thousand people here, and they come right at me and tell me to hand it over? How stupid do you think I am?'

'You're not stupid – you're just paranoid,' Dom said.

'They knew you had it?' Sully asked, speaking over Dom.

He looked around for Aiden. If that was really his name. A friendly-looking doofus with a crooked smile to put Sully off his guard. He was nowhere in sight.

How *had* they known what Hunter looked like? He hadn't said a word to Aiden about her.

Sully turned back to Hunter. 'I don't know how they knew what you looked like, but I didn't have anything to do with this. This guy came to my table, we agreed on a price. He went off, came back and showed me fourteen thousand-dollar bills.'

Hunter glared, shaking her head. Drops of blood oozed from the scrape on her forehead.

'What happened to your head?' Sully asked.

'Hunter wouldn't give them the marble, so one of the guys pistol-whipped her,' Dom answered.

Hunter spun to face Dom. '*I* wouldn't give it to them, but *you* sure were eager to hand it over. "Just give it to them, just give it to them." I gotta say, you're not a very good actor.'

Dom threw his hands in the air. 'I didn't want to get *shot*.'

Hunter turned back towards Sully. '"Use the vendors' entrance, not the main gate." That was the last thing you said to me on the phone. So they'd know which way I was coming.'

'I said that because it's quicker to go that way. I was trying to move fast on the deal.'

She turned away, pressed her hand to her forehead. 'How could I be so stupid? I should have known better than to trust some random dude I met at a flea market.'

'Hey,' Sully said, 'I could say the same about you. Maybe *you* set this up.'

Hunter spun, gestured violently at the lump on her forehead. 'I got *hit*. With a gun.'

'And isn't that the perfect touch?' Sully said. 'Like no one's ever taken a punch to make an inside job look convincing.' He knew Hunter had had nothing to do with it. At least, he thought he knew that. But he didn't appreciate being called a thief while dealing with losing $5,600 that was going to allow him to go on living in the town he'd lived in his whole life.

Hunter went on staring him down, the anger in her eyes almost as hard to take as the loss of the Hot Pink. 'You and I both know that's not what happened. We all know what just happened here.' She glanced at Dom, then back at Sully. 'Don't ever talk to me again.'

As she stormed off, she added, 'You're just like Holliday.'

'You're wrong, Hunter!' Sully shouted after her. 'You're dead wrong about this.'

As he turned away from her retreating form, he realized people were watching. A dozen sets of eyes looked away; people who had paused went on walking.

Dom squatted on his haunches. 'Jesus, I'm so sorry. All of a sudden they were just there, one in front of us, one behind, pointing guns.'

'No, I'm sorry I put you in the middle of that. You could have been shot.'

They returned to Sully's booth. Neal and Samantha were standing in the centre of the aisle, keeping an eye on his booth as well as their own.

'We heard most of it from here,' Neal said. 'You going to call the police?'

'What are *they* going to do?' Spheres had no distinguishing marks. You couldn't leave fingerprints or DNA on them. Not that anyone would conduct a DNA test to solve a robbery.

Sully didn't even have proof he'd owned a Hot Pink, unless you counted eyewitnesses.

He steadied himself, palms on his table. All the strength had gone out of his legs. The rent was due in a week, and he and his mom had nothing left in savings. They were done. Broke.

And Hunter had the gall to accuse him of being in on it?

Howling in frustration, Sully grabbed the edge of the table and toppled it, sending crates and display cases filled with the crappy assortment of bargain-bin spheres he had left crashing to the ground.

Dom, Neal and Samantha watched in silence as Sully dropped to his knees and buried his face in his hands.

CHAPTER 10

Dom sat sideways in his chair, spinning a pen on the little desk where Sully did his homework. He meant well, but Sully wished he would take a walk or something. He wasn't sure how to tell Dom that without hurting his feelings.

'Maybe you should talk to your dad, see if he can pull some strings,' Dom said.

It made sense to consult his dad the police detective, but that would be a miserable conversation. Sully had last seen his dad three years ago. They'd gone to McDonald's and, ever since, the colour yellow made him sick to his stomach. 'It's gone. I'm not getting it back.' It took effort to speak.

How was he going to tell his mother? She'd been counting on that money as much as Sully. Head down, Sully punched his mattress. They should have put the sphere on eBay immediately, or sold the damned thing to Holliday . . .

Sully had a terrible thought: what if Holliday was behind the robbery? They'd gone to his store and asked to see a Hot Pink. A rarity five was barely worth Holliday's time, but Sully had insulted him. He could have arranged to steal it to get back at Sully, to force Sully to crawl back and accept the job offer. He also knew what Dom looked like, though probably not Hunter. If Holliday was behind it, Sully would probably never know for sure. Holliday had the power and money to hide his tracks well.

Sully checked the wall clock: 4:24. He wished it was later so he could go to sleep. Blessedly, he'd burned those Teals, so he'd be able to sleep.

Thinking about the Teals reminded him of Hunter, which set his heart racing with anger all over again. How could she think he was a thief? What sort of person jumped to a conclusion like that? He should have trusted his first impression. She wasn't his type; she was too hard.

Sully's mind kept spinning back to the same thoughts, the same feelings of betrayal and hopelessness. It was like a song in his head that just kept repeating, a bad song, a song he despised.

'I don't want to push, but I really think it'd be a mistake not to call your father.' Dom raised his hand as Sully opened his mouth to respond. 'I know he's a first-class douche bag, but he's a detective, isn't he? He might know how the men knew Hunter had the marble. You're giving up before you even try.'

The truth was, Sully didn't want his father to know he'd lost the sphere. He could hear it now: *You lost* another *one?* But if, somehow, Sully could get it back, some of the pain he was feeling would vanish. The rent could be paid.

'I'll call him in the morning.'

In the meantime, he needed to come up with some cash, or he and his mom were going to be evicted. Dragging himself off the bed, he went to his shelf, snapped a picture of the Cherry Red on its pedestal, then took it down.

'What are you doing?' Dom asked.

'Selling it.' It should bring at least a thousand dollars – a king's ransom for a burnt sphere, but still less than two months' rent. It killed him to sell it; it truly killed him.

CHAPTER 11

Old Darrel Hanks was doing a brisk business selling gloves and hats over in his corner. He had five or six customers digging through the boxes of irregulars.

'Five dollars a pair,' he shouted. 'No ups, no downs, all gloves just five dollars.' Darrel had to be pushing eighty, but it was obvious he still loved selling.

Sully wished he could say the same. Flea markets had always been his escape; now the place just reminded him of the Hot Pink, of the day Hunter came strolling down his aisle. It was hard to go back to hawking rarity ones and twos.

And, as much as he distrusted his father's judgement, the old man's words kept rattling around in his head.

When fourteen thousand is on the line, you have no friends. You got that? You trust no one. I've seen people screwed by best friends, brothers, wives, fathers. Sully could picture just how his father had folded his arms and settled back into his seat at the diner. *I'll say it again: it was Dom or the girl. My money's on the girl. She's pistol-whipped, but she's up and running a second later? That's awfully convenient.*

Whether Hunter had ripped him off or not, he was better off not having her around. He knew that, but it was still hard to get used to.

Of course, *he* wouldn't be around much longer. As soon as the school year was out, he and his mom were moving to Pittsburgh (assuming they could scrounge up and borrow enough to stay in Yonkers even that long). It was all set; Sully would be spending his senior year at a strange school, living in a basement.

Sully wondered what he and Hunter would have found in those water tanks. That had been a brilliant idea. Maybe he should pursue it without Hunter. Dom might be interested in partnering with him . . .

No. It was Hunter's idea. Even if they weren't friends any more, he wasn't going to steal her idea.

Across the aisle, Neal was whistling and bobbing his head furiously, listening to some no doubt ancient rock music on an iPod. Sully envied Neal's ability to stay full of energy. He seemed to be enjoying the hell out of his life.

Noticing Sully looking at him, Neal pulled out one of his earbuds. 'T. Rex, man. Most underrated band in the history of rock.'

Sully gave him a thumbs-up, although he'd never heard of T. Rex.

Probably noticing how unenthusiastic his thumbs-up was, Neal headed over. He had new sneakers on – bright orange Nikes. 'You've got to let it go. I know you had big plans for that cash, but if you cling too hard to what could have been it's like poison.'

Yes, big plans. Pay the rent. Spend his senior year with his friends. 'You're right. Like they say, it's all good.'

'Except it's not all good. Some things suck.' Neal pulled out the other earbud. 'What I'm trying to say is, if you can't change it, don't let it eat at you. Let it go.'

Samantha had come over as well. She put a hand on Sully's back. There was no doubt he was letting it eat at him. Going to see his old man, who'd made sure to drive home just how stupid Sully had been, had made it worse.

'Yeah, I'll try,' he said.

'That's it. It's called non-attachment. Play the game, but don't get too attached to the outcome.' Neal snapped his fingers, pointed at Sully. 'I'm going to lend you a book. Have you ever read any Zen authors? Alan Watts? D. T. Suzuki?'

'Nope.'

Neal checked his watch. 'Tell you what, I'm going to grab a snack in the motor home. I'll bring you back a book.'

Sully didn't have much time for extra reading, but maybe he'd give it a try. Neal bobbed off towards the exit, arms swinging, looking like a twelve-year-old kid, not a guy in his sixties.

'He really loves you,' Samantha said as they watched Neal's receding figure. 'He talks about you all the time.'

'Really?' It pleased Sully to hear that. Neal and Samantha were like his flea market parents, but Neal was friendly to everyone, so it was hard to know if you were special to him.

If Neal hadn't been married, Sully would have introduced him to Mom. He was perfect for his mom, because he was the exact opposite of Sully's dad. Their advice said it all. *Trust no one* versus *Let it go*. Sully was still fuming at his father's smug confidence. *There's your answer, Sully: one of your friends cheated you, because you're a sucker, you're an easy target. You need to grow up and be a man, like me.*

Sully squeezed his eyes shut, took a deep breath. *Let it go.* If only it wasn't so hard to stop thinking about something.

He checked the time: 3:48. The flea market was just about empty except for the vendors. Screw it. He picked up the display case containing his 'rare' spheres, which now amounted to a half-dozen rarity twos he hadn't listed on eBay yet. If he kept cashing out his stock on eBay at a discount until there was nothing left, he was through making money as a dealer. He couldn't stand behind an empty table at the flea market and expect people to offer to sell him spheres, and most of his stock came from walk-ups at the flea market. His inventory was pathetic; half his table was nothing but empty space.

He set the display case on top of a crate of spheres and lifted both. 'Hey, Samantha? Can you watch my stuff? I'm going to pack up early.'

'Sure.' She stepped into the aisle, where she could more easily watch all three booths at once.

Maybe he'd call Dom, see if he wanted to head over to Nathan's.

In the car park, Led Zeppelin's 'All of My Love' drifted from Neal's camper. Sully remembered the book. Shifting the crates to get a better grip, he went to the camper door and knocked.

Neal swung the door open. 'Hey, you leaving?' he shouted over the music.

'It's pretty dead in there.'

Neal held up a finger. 'Hang on a minute, I'll get you that

book.' He disappeared into the camper, ducking his head slightly. Sully couldn't imagine how two people could actually live in that camper, day in and day out. It was such a narrow space, and every nook and cranny was packed with books and boxes.

They had got a new sound/entertainment system since the last time Sully had visited. A brand-new big-screen TV was mounted on the back wall, with speakers in all four corners of the room, and a sharp-looking stereo system, currently blaring Zeppelin, set on shelves.

'Hey, that's some nice equipment,' Sully said as Neal reappeared, his orange Nikes bright against the soiled beige carpet.

'Thanks. We've been saving for a while, decided it was time.' Neal held out a beat-up paperback with a black cover.

Sully didn't take it immediately, because a terrible thought had occurred to him, and it was threatening to knock him to his knees. New TV, new stereo, new sneakers. A spending spree.

As if they'd just come into some money.

He reached up with numb fingers, took the book. 'New TV, too.'

Neal looked over his shoulder, as if he hadn't noticed. 'The old one was on its last legs. We had it fifteen years.'

Neal and Samantha knew what Hunter looked like. They would have been close enough to hear Sully's phone calls. The one to Dom, telling him to pick up Hunter; the one to Hunter, telling her to go to the bank and get the Hot Pink. It all fitted.

Dom or the girl, his dad had said. Only, Dad hadn't known about Neal and Samantha. Sully studied Neal's face, searching for signs of guilt or nervousness, but Neal looked as friendly and open as ever.

It was all an act. The warm, friendly guru gaze, the laid-back hippie attitude. Sully would never have believed you could fake an entire personality, but suddenly he felt sure. It was fake. Samantha's earth-mother routine as well. They were nothing but poor, desperate con artists.

He couldn't just come out and accuse Neal of ripping him off, because he didn't know for sure that was what had happened.

Only somehow, he did. He did know.

'All of that must have set you back a couple thousand dollars. Maybe twenty per cent?' He looked into Neal's startled eyes. 'Yeah. That seems about right.'

Sully stuffed the book in the crate, then lifted it. 'Thanks for the book.'

'Hang on,' Neal called as he walked off. 'You're not suggesting –'

Sully kept walking.

'*Sully*. What are you saying?' Neal didn't come after him. He just went on shouting from the door of his camper, as if there was an invisible force field keeping him inside. Anyone who was innocent would be out of that camper in a flash, would be blocking Sully. Only a guilty man would let him walk off.

He really loves you, Samantha had said. Enough to steal from him, to spoil things with Hunter. Sully unlocked the back of his station wagon and shoved the boxes in.

At least he knew Hunter wasn't the one who'd ripped him off. He slammed the door shut. Yes, all she'd done was leap to the conclusion that *Sully* was a thief.

As he headed back to his table, he passed an old woman digging through a green rubbish barrel at the end of one of the car park rows. A shopping cart of aluminum cans waited beside her.

Ten years ago that could have been Hunter. Only, she'd been barely a teenager.

Maybe Sully should cut her some slack for being overly suspicious, for not trusting him more.

Sully was tempted to head back to Neal's newly tricked-out camper and punch him in the face. This was all because of him. He'd stolen Sully's rent money, banished him to Pittsburgh, driven a wedge between him and Hunter.

Sully slowed. That, at least, he had some control over.

On his way out, Sully dropped Neal's Zen book into the first rubbish can he passed.

CHAPTER 12

The front door of Hunter's building was unlocked. In fact, it didn't have a lock. Sully stepped into the lobby, a dirty, nondescript hallway with mailboxes set into the wall to the right, a stairwell to the left. A single brown rubber boot lay on the bottom step.

Sully climbed to the fifth floor, knocked on number 503. The thick steel door didn't conduct sound well; he knocked harder, his knuckles stinging.

He heard footsteps inside, growing louder.

'Yeah?' A woman's voice.

'I'm looking for Hunter?'

No answer. Only footsteps, growing fainter this time. Three or four voices drifted through the door, all apparently having different conversations.

There was a sharp bang on the door. 'Get lost.' It was Hunter. Her acid tone made Sully wince.

He stepped forward until his face was six inches from the scuffed and dented door. It had been red once, but there wasn't much paint left.

'I should be the one who's pissed off. I *am* pissed off, but I didn't let it keep me from hauling my freezing ass all the way to your door.' There was a peephole in the door; Sully wondered if Hunter was watching him through it.

'I went to see my jackass father, the cop. You know what he told me? He said either you cheated me, or Dom did. But you know what? I know you didn't rip me off, because I know you. Why is it you don't know me?' He waited for an answer. 'How can you think I would cheat you?'

'Nobody knows anyone,' Hunter called from behind the door. 'You don't know if you can trust me, and I don't know if I can trust you.'

Sully thought of Neal and his new flat-screen TV. Yesterday he'd have sworn on his life he could trust Neal. 'Maybe you're right. I learned that just this morning, in fact, when I figured out who stole the Hot Pink.' He waited for Hunter to ask who had done it, but she didn't. 'I guess I'm asking you to take a leap of faith, then. Trust me. Believe me.' He pressed his palm against the cool steel of the door and waited.

Nothing. He was tempted to storm off, tell her to have a good life, if she could somehow manage that while being so paranoid.

'What the hell would I be doing at your door if I ripped you off? If that's what happened, I've got fourteen thousand dollars. I can hire a professional scuba diver and go search on my own.'

Nothing.

He was just making a fool of himself, begging forgiveness through a door for something he didn't do. He turned to leave, in black despair. It was over. He'd never see Hunter again;

they'd never find out if there were any rare spheres hidden in those water towers. Even scoring a few rarity twos and threes would be huge for him at this point.

Sully turned back. He pressed his nose to the door, closed his eyes. 'Take one leap of faith. If we find anything, you hold on to it. I'll trust *you*, even if I can't know for sure I should.'

He was halfway to the stairs when the lock clicked. The door swung open.

Hunter was wearing a ratty violet NYU sweatshirt and shorts, along with the inevitable gloves. Her old gloves – not the ones Sully had given her. She looked exhausted, like she hadn't slept in a week.

'I swear to God, I didn't do it.'

She nodded. 'I guess I believe you.'

Some of the tension in his gut, the blackness of the past week, eased. Not all of it, not by a long shot. But he'd made this one thing right.

'I'll see you tomorrow, at five.' Hunter closed the door.

CHAPTER 13

You didn't notice them, but they were everywhere. Even from street level Sully could see two, three, or four perched on every roof. Some were tall and thin, others short and squat. All were round, with funny slanted roofs.

They walked in silence. Things were still a little tense between them. It wasn't as if Sully could just forget overnight that Hunter had accused him of stealing, and Hunter didn't seem overly concerned about smoothing things over. She seemed content to walk in silence.

Head down, Hunter turned right on to a narrow street between two big, old grey-brick industrial buildings. She led Sully to a fire escape alongside three security doors that were raised so trucks could back up to them.

Sully looked at the rickety black steel staircase clinging to the outside of the ten-story building. The bottom of the ladder was ten feet above them. 'Why this one first, out of all the buildings in the city?'

Hunter shrugged in her bulky black parka. 'We start in Brooklyn because most of it is poorer than Manhattan, so it's more likely no one's cleaned the water towers in a long time. This building has four towers and it's not too tall, so I figured it's a good place to start.'

Sully unslung his pack and dropped it on the sidewalk. 'Fair enough.' He glanced left and right to make sure no one was around, then pulled out a rope ladder and extendable rod. He used the rod to hook the end of the rope ladder to the bottom of the fire escape, just like he and Hunter had practised behind Hunter's building. When they reached the fire escape, he reeled in the rope ladder and put it back in his pack.

'Do you even want to know who ripped us off?' Sully asked as they reached the third-floor landing. His voice seemed loud in the silence.

'Sure.'

'Remember Neal?'

Hunter nodded. 'Sure. The sixties-looking dude who was like a father to you.'

'Guy lives in a little broken-down motor home, and suddenly it's got a big-screen TV and a state-of-the-art stereo system. He knew what you looked like.'

Hunter passed Sully, headed up the next ladder. 'Did you call him on it?'

'Yeah. He denied it, but it was obvious he was lying. I don't know, maybe there's still a way to nail him.'

'Nail him in the face. It's gone.'

Maybe he should have punched Neal in the face. He couldn't imagine punching a sixty-year-old guy in the face, though.

Hunter took the stairs three at a time, one leather-gloved

hand brushing the top of the railing. The girl seemed to have only one gear – full throttle.

'You're like a ninja,' Sully called, half sarcastic, half admiring.

'Shut up,' Hunter shot back.

The fire escape ended at the top floor. From there, a vertical ladder led to the roof. As Sully stepped on to it, following Hunter, the ladder jerked and wobbled. The rungs were so cold, Sully could feel the metal through his gloves; the icy breeze was like hands trying to shove him loose, towards a rusting storm drain that ran down the side of the building. He had a flash of himself clinging to that storm drain, ten stories up, his legs flailing.

As he reached the roof, he flattened on to his belly and crawled to safety.

'I hadn't really thought through the climbing part of this.' Sully rolled on to his back.

Hunter was standing over him, looking rattled. She swept her braids over her shoulder. 'Man, I've never had a problem with heights, but that ladder was terrible. It felt like it was going to pull straight out of the wall.' She reached out, and when Sully took her hand she pulled him to his feet.

They looked up at the closest water tower, a dozen feet away. It was set on a six-foot-high steel frame. The tower's body was vertically slatted, like an enormous wooden barrel, and wrapped by five horizontal steel cables. A ladder curled up to a hatch in the tower's roof, maybe twenty feet above where they stood.

Hunter unzipped her coat and let it drop to the roof, exposing the black dry suit she was wearing beneath. A little research had made it clear that it was a dry suit they wanted – with a wet suit, water saturated the suit and acted as insulation, and that wasn't a good idea if the water was close to freezing. Hunter kicked off her boots, unzipped her jeans, and pulled them off. Even freezing cold on a dark roof, Sully couldn't help being a little stunned by just how incredible Hunter looked in a skintight suit, despite its covering every inch of her from the neck down.

'Whoa,' he said.

'Shut up, or I'll kick you in the nuts.'

They climbed the ladder. When Hunter reached the top, Sully had to squeeze in beside her so they could pull the hatch open together. It weighed a good eighty pounds.

Sully climbed down to the roof, his neck and shoulders tense as Hunter climbed into the tank, waterproof flashlight in hand.

Gloved hands in his pockets, and positioned so the wind was at his back, Sully daydreamed of Hunter's hand rising through the open hatch, holding a Mustard, or a Chocolate.

What about another Cherry Red? No one had found a Cherry Red since Holliday triggered the second wave. Everyone – including Sully – had assumed there'd be a set of Cherry Reds in the second wave, leading to a third wave, and so on. It was beginning to look as if there might be no more spheres once this second wave was found and burned, unless Midnight Blue was the new Cherry Red. But there was no reason to think two different colours did the same thing.

The supply kept dwindling as people burned spheres, or stashed them in safe-deposit boxes as part of their investment portfolios. And every year the big corporate operations ate more of what remained. Soon there would be none for Sully to sell. And, damn, did he need some to sell. At least he had a chance, now that he and Hunter were hunting again.

Sully heard Hunter surface inside the water tower, gasping. She took a few deep breaths, then the sound of water lapping against her arms went silent as she submerged again.

He looked out at the city, the buildings all silver lights, the streets red taillights on one side, white headlights on the other.

Hunter surfaced again. Sully heard splashing, then one of Hunter's hands appeared, grasping the lip of the open hatch. She pulled herself up, both hands empty, swung around, and found a rung of the ladder with one foot.

'One down, nine thousand nine hundred ninety-nine to go,' Sully said. 'How was it?'

Gasping, Hunter dropped to the roof and wrapped both arms around her midsection. Water dribbled from her wet braids. 'Cold. Dark. The water's deep – I really had to swim hard to reach the bottom.' She shivered. 'I hate being cold. I hate it.'

Sully handed her a towel. 'Maybe we should invest in a second dry suit and take turns.'

'No.' She shook her head fiercely. 'I do the swimming.'

Sully shrugged. 'Whatever you say, boss. If you change your mind, let me know.'

Hunter handed back the towel. Because of the dry suit, her head was the only part that got wet.

They headed to the second tank, which was identical to the

first. Sully followed Hunter up the ladder. It was starting to sink in, what Sully had committed to. Ten *thousand* of these things? Years of nights spent freezing on windy roofs? What if they found nothing?

CHAPTER 14

It was so grey outside that the lights were on in the cafeteria. Sully was tired of winter; he was ready for green leaves, birds singing. It was a bad sign, given that it was early January. February would be just as cold and grey. There was no hope for a warm day until mid-March, at least.

'Sully, wait.' Dom clapped a hand on Sully's shoulder from behind. 'We're going out for lunch. Mandy's meeting us at Nathan's.'

'I can't.' He held up his brown bag. 'I brought mine. Plus I can't afford to eat out.'

Dom snatched Sully's lunch out of his hand. 'I'm buying. You can't live off sandwiches that've been sitting in your locker for four hours every day. You need hot food. Stuff that sticks to your ribs.'

Laughing, Sully followed Dom out of the cafeteria. It was technically against the rules for juniors to leave campus for lunch, but no one stood in the freezing-cold student car park to check IDs.

'How's the water-tower project going?' Dom asked as they

headed down the main hallway, lockers lining both walls, towards the front doors.

'It's brutal.'

'How many have you done?'

Sully closed his eyes. 'Eighty-four.'

'That's a lot of freaking tanks.' Dom pushed open the front door.

'Not when you're planning to search *ten thousand*, it isn't. When Hunter told me we were going to search ten thousand, it was just a number. Now that we're actually climbing up to each tank . . .' Sully blew air through his lips.

Dom nodded, commiserating. 'You finding anything?'

Sully grimaced. 'Two commons so far. Two ones.' It was a pathetic haul for the work they'd done. Pathetic.

Dom's phone vibrated. He checked it. 'Mandy. Says she's just leaving school.'

'You guys are getting pretty tight.'

Dom grinned. 'Yeah, we are. She's pretty cool. Plus, I don't know, I like having a lesbian friend. Makes me feel all modern.'

'Whatever you say,' Sully said, laughing.

Mandy waved from a booth by the window. Dom slid in beside her and gave her a big hug as Sully set his tray down and slid in across from them.

A half-dozen kids their age passed by their table, their shoulders festooned with brag badges.

'Spare me,' Dom said after the door closed.

'It makes sense that they call it the gifted academy,' Sully said. 'Most of them are in there because of gifts their parents gave them at Christmas.'

Dom nudged him with an elbow. 'Hey, that's good. They should call it the Masten Gift Academy.'

'Be nice, now,' Mandy said. 'I almost went to Masten.'

'Have you ever burned any?' Sully asked. He'd been wondering, given that Mandy's parents had money.

Mandy set her hot dog down. 'I was hoping you wouldn't ask me that.'

'Why?' Dom took a massive bite of his super-cheeseburger, then continued talking with his mouth full. 'As long as you don't wear those damn brag badges, it's cool.'

Mandy lifted her head. 'No, what I mean is, I wouldn't burn them even if someone handed me a pair.'

Dom's eyes went wide. 'You're kidding me.'

Mandy looked apologetic as she turned to Sully. 'I didn't want to say anything, because you sell them. I'm not judging you. My aunt owned a store, and I love my aunt to death.'

Sully nodded. You came across people who were suspicious of spheres once in a while. Organic by choice. 'But?'

'But there's no such thing as a free lunch. People used to think smoking cigarettes was good for you, and look how that turned out. When Internet ads say something is absolutely free with no obligation, it never is.'

Dom leaned towards her, elbows straddling his lunch. 'You think burning spheres is gonna give everyone cancer?'

Mandy sighed heavily. 'I don't know what it's going to do. I just know there's always a price, and I don't buy anything that doesn't have the price clearly displayed.'

Sully had heard this argument before. More than once,

in fact. Everyone was entitled to their opinion, but it always struck him as a little paranoid. Why did everything have to have a cost? Warm spring days were free. Swimming in the ocean was free. Not everything good had a dark side.

'People have been burning spheres for nine years now. If there was a downside, wouldn't we know it by now?' Sully asked.

Mandy waved her hands. 'I don't want to argue about this. That's why I didn't say anything.'

Sully shrugged. 'OK. No problem.'

Looking relieved, Mandy leaned back in her seat. 'Good.'

There was an awkward silence. Finally, Mandy leaned forward. 'Did you see the rumour on BuzzFeed that the president just burned a Mint?'

CHAPTER 15

Sully and Hunter headed for the next building in silence, both of them frustrated that they had to bypass another building. Every once in a while they hit one where access to the roof just wasn't possible, because security was too tight or the roof was fenced. Whenever Sully was looking up at one of those impassable buildings, he couldn't help but wonder if it was the one. Worse yet had been the two entire streets in Flatbush where they'd found *X*s written inside all the hatches, as if someone was marking towers already searched. Maybe the *X*s were there for another reason, but Sully hated the idea someone had got to towers before them.

Hunter stopped walking, pointed at a fire escape.

'You've got to be kidding me.' Sully craned his neck to take in the tan brick tower.

'Twenty-one stories. Eight tanks.'

'Eight tanks,' Sully repeated, taking deep breaths, psyching himself for the climb. 'That'll bump us to three fifty-six.' He clapped his gloved hands, rubbed them together. 'Here we go.'

The cold burned his lungs as they climbed, the wind growing stronger. Twelve steps, about-face, four horizontal paces across the escape, then about-face again, twelve more steps. By this point Sully could climb a fire escape with his eyes closed. He wasn't about to, but he could. He climbed fire escapes in his dreams, winding up and up, sometimes down and down.

When they reached the top, Hunter dropped her coat and climbed the first water tower. Sully followed, helped her wrench the hatch open, then got out of her way.

After about half a minute, he heard Hunter surface with a gasp, catch her breath for a moment, then submerge. It usually took two lungsful of air to search a tank (three for some of the bigger ones), which meant Hunter had to make that hard swim to the bottom twice in each tank. If there was some way to reduce it to one, they would save time and energy . . .

Sully pressed his palm to his forehead. Rose spheres. Hold your breath for a long time. He had one in stock, could trade for another on SphereSwap.com.

'Hey,' he said as Hunter came down the ladder. 'It just hit me. I'm going to get you Roses.'

Hunter frowned. 'What?'

He cleared his throat, realizing what he'd just said. 'Rose *marbles,* I mean.'

'Oh,' Hunter said. Her eyes opened wide. '*Oh*. Jeez. Why didn't I think of that? I knew there was a reason I was cutting you in on my million-dollar idea. You're the brains of the operation.'

She hopped down, accepted the towel Sully offered. He

was still flushing with embarrassment. *I'm going to get you Roses*. What an idiot.

He followed Hunter to the next tank.

Three hundred fifty-six down when they left this roof. Only 9,644 to go. Beautiful.

'This one's going to be a piece of cake,' Hunter said, taking in a nine-story concrete building, hands on her hips.

'Why is that?'

Hunter trotted up the front steps, gave the steel door a shove. It creaked open. She turned back towards Sully. 'It's abandoned. We can take the stairs.'

The ground floor was stripped to the beams; bricks were stacked relatively neatly in a corner, while concrete and other junk was piled in the centre of the space.

The stairwell was heavily tagged with graffiti, and, not for the first time, Sully wondered what the hell they would do if they encountered three or four men who wished them harm. The building seemed deserted, though. Huffing, Sully tried to keep up with Hunter.

'Really, there's no hurry,' he said between breaths. 'The tower's not going anywhere.'

Hunter picked up her pace.

Groaning, Sully followed.

After pushing open the door to the roof and stepping out, Hunter paused. Sully joined her, and was met with the bass thump of dance music.

'What *is* that?' Sully asked, looking around. There was no one in sight. He took a few steps, paused. The music was coming from their left. He turned, headed towards the far end of the roof, where two water towers were perched side by side on a square steel frame. An orange extension ladder was propped against the underside of one of the towers.

Sully stopped at the base of the extension ladder. There was no doubt about it: music was coming from inside the tower.

'Look at that.' Hunter pointed.

There was a hatch cut into the tower's underside, just above the end of the extension ladder. Light bled through the seams.

A sharp note of laughter rose over the thump of the music.

Sully gripped the base of the ladder. 'I have to know.'

'You and me both.'

As they climbed, the music grew louder; conversation and laughter drifted down. When Sully reached the hatch he raised his fist and knocked.

The hatch swung open; from his vantage point, Sully could see shelves filled with liquor bottles set into the slatted wooden walls. A woman's face appeared – round, pudgy cheeks and a head scarf – blocking out the shelves and the bottles.

'Hi. Do you have an invitation?' the woman asked.

Sully laughed. 'An invitation? To go inside a water tower in an abandoned building? Do you have a *permit*?'

The woman frowned. 'How did you find this place, if you didn't get an invitation?'

'We followed the music,' Hunter called up from just below Sully. 'Come on, it's cold out here.'

The woman stood. 'OK, fine. We'll make an exception.'

Sully climbed another rung.

'There's a handhold to your right,' the woman said. 'Here.'

She took his hand, placed it on a steel pipe set in the floor. Sully pulled himself up.

Inside, the water tower was packed. There was a little bar at one end, a few small tables along the walls. People were holding wineglasses and bottles of Heineken; some were dressed up in jackets and fancy hats, others wore jeans.

Sully squatted, gave Hunter a hand up. They stood in the midst of the most unlikely bar Sully could ever have imagined.

The woman studied Sully's face for a moment, then shouted over to the bartender, who was shaking a metal tumbler, 'Andy? Soft drinks only for these two.'

Andy gave her a thumbs-up.

The drinks, as it turned out, were free. Evidently you paid in advance when you received your invitation. Sully got a Coke, Hunter a Mountain Dew.

Sully took in the high ceiling, the pipe running up the centre of the room. So this was what Hunter had been diving into for the past month.

'Excuse me.' A man in a grey fedora, smoking something from what looked like an ornate fountain pen, tapped Hunter on the shoulder. 'I couldn't help noticing that you're wearing a wet suit. I have to ask why.'

Hunter looked down at herself. 'I'm not wearing a wet suit; I'm wearing a dry suit.'

Amused, the man raised an eyebrow. 'Well then, why are you wearing a *dry suit*?'

'Why are you in a bar in a water tower?' Hunter shot back.

Chuckling, Mr Fedora pointed at Hunter. 'Touché.'

'What *is* this place?' Sully asked.

The guy shrugged. 'Trespass theatre, according to the

designer. It's only open for two more weeks.'

When they finished their drinks, Sully got them a second round. They overheard that one of the other guests was some relatively famous actress who'd been in a Lord of the Rings film, but if she was there Sully didn't recognize her.

'I can't get over this. What a great idea,' Sully said.

Hunter nodded. She was moving ever so slightly to the beat of the music, half smiling.

'So tell me something about you,' Sully said. 'You're like this mystery who shows up in your superhero suit at night, dives into freezing-cold water for four hours, then vanishes.'

She smiled up at him. 'I don't *vanish*. You drop me off at the crappy apartment I share with fifty other people.'

A Daft Punk song came on. Four or five couples started dancing, heads back, arms raised towards the ceiling. Sully bobbed his head to the music; Hunter moved her hips, still smiling at him. She was beautiful in the bar's soft light.

'You know, even after two hours of swimming around in those tanks, you're stunning.'

Hunter's smile widened; she slid just a little closer to him. Sully leaned in and kissed her. Her lips slid against his.

She turned her head, took a half step backwards. 'Bad idea. Bad, bad idea.'

A spasm of disappointment squeezed Sully. For one moment, for one magical moment, he'd thought it was really going to happen. 'Why is it a bad idea?'

Hunter heaved a sigh. 'I'm just not girlfriend material. Trust me on that.'

Someone once told Sully that if a girl tells you she's bad news, take her word for it. In this case, Sully would have ignored that advice, given a choice. Since starting the water tower project, he'd got more and more hung up on Hunter, until now he went to sleep thinking about her, and she was the first thing he thought about when he woke.

Hunter dropped her head, sighed again. 'Let's stay focused on the prize. OK?'

'Absolutely. I'm sorry.'

'No, it's my fault as much as yours.' Hunter checked the time on her phone. 'It's after eight. We can finish the end of this block at least.'

They climbed down and headed towards the stairwell door without speaking. Sully needed to call his mom, tell her he was going to be late again. She wasn't happy that he was out every night. If she knew what he was doing, he'd be toast. Right now she thought he was in a quaint little burb called Tarrytown, twenty miles north of Yonkers.

'Hang on,' Hunter said. She was studying the far end of the roof.

Sully followed her. She squatted at the edge and studied the narrow gap between the building they were on and the one next to it.

'How wide would you say that is?' Hunter pointed to the gap.

'Maybe five feet?' Sully leaned close enough to the edge to glimpse the alley eight stories below. The sight made him queasy. 'Why?'

Hunter looked up at him. 'If we jump it, we save sixteen flights of climbing.'

Sully burst out laughing. 'And if we trip, we die.' He held out his hands, palms up, raised and lowered them like he was comparing weights. 'Let's see: avoid sixteen flights of stairs versus die a horrible death. Hmm. Tough one.'

'How tall are you?' Hunter asked, rising to her feet.

'Five ten.'

'Lie down.' She pointed at the roof.

'Why?'

She folded her arms. 'Just do it, OK?'

Grumbling, Sully lay down, wondering just how much filth the darkness was hiding. He'd barely got settled when Hunter's sneakers flew over his face. She landed with a thud.

'I cleared you by four feet.'

Sully sat up. 'That's without a pack. Plus, the roofs have that low ledge you have to clear, and if you don't clear it, you trip and fall eighty feet.'

Hunter lifted her pack, slung it across her shoulders, and turned towards the gap.

'Wait, what are you doing?' Sully asked.

'I'm jumping,' she said. 'If you want to climb all those stairs, go on ahead.' Fingers splayed, Hunter backed up a few steps, studied the roofline.

'Hunter, no. It's a terrible idea.'

Hunter took off, sprinting towards the edge. She planted one foot on the ledge and launched herself over the void.

She landed on the far roof, still on her feet. Her arms shot into the air. She let out an earsplitting howl of triumph.

'Did you see that?' She danced in a circle, laughing. 'Did you see that? I *am* a ninja.'

Sully went to the edge of his roof. Hunter stood across from him, hands on her hips, grinning.

'Now you're going to have to wait in the freezing cold while I climb the stairs.'

'Maybe I'll build a little fire. Cook some wienies. While I wait for a wienie.' She slapped her thigh, cackling madly.

'Nobody calls me a weenie.' Sully grabbed his pack, flung it across the gap. It landed at Hunter's feet. He backed up, eyeing the gap.

This was stupid. He knew it was stupid, and he knew if it was anyone else standing on that other roof taunting him he would take the stairs.

It was a tiny gap, though. If the drop was two feet instead of eighty, he could jump it a hundred times without missing. The only way he could screw up was to psych himself out by thinking about that eighty-foot drop.

His heart raced as he rocked forward and back, his body sideways to the gap, left foot in the lead.

'You can do it!' Hunter shouted, clearing out of his way. 'Don't think, just jump!' Suddenly she was an expert, because she'd done it exactly once without dying.

'You got this,' he said under his breath. What was the Olympic long jump record, something like thirty feet? Heart tripping like mad, Sully sprinted for the edge. As he drew close, he realized his stride was off. He took a few stutter steps, then leaped.

Out of the corner of his eye he glimpsed the long, long drop underfoot as he sailed over the gap.

He landed six or seven feet beyond the edge, stumbled, hit the ground with an *'Oof'* as he broke his fall with his outstretched hands.

Hunter whooped, clapped her gloved hands. 'You get a

nine for distance. Your landing needs work.'

Sully climbed to his feet. He felt remarkably wide awake, like he'd just chugged three Red Bulls. He clapped his hands together. 'Piece of cake. Let's go find a Vermillion.'

CHAPTER 16

Sully stopped talking as they drove over the culvert on Germond Road, wondering if Dom was reminded of the Cherry Red each time he went over the culvert the way Sully was. Probably not. He hadn't even been there when Sully found it.

With the culvert in the rear-view mirror, Sully continued. 'I just wonder sometimes if we'd be better off going back to the suburbs, where we've had more luck. I mean, we're climbing those fire escapes in the freezing cold, at *night,* and I doubt we're making a dollar an hour.'

Dom shrugged. 'So tell her you want to bag the towers and focus on the suburbs.'

'I guess. She's going to be disappointed, though. She's convinced there's a big score in one of those tanks.' They pulled into the Garden Apartments car park, bounced over a series of deep potholes. 'I'm afraid she'll stick with the water towers and just replace me.'

'Got it. And she's your edge. She has all the hunting expertise.'

'Plus, I'd miss her.'

Dom pointed at him. 'Ah, now the truth comes out. So how's it going on that front? Any sharing of bodily warmth on those cold roofs?' He waggled his dark eyebrows.

'It's not going to happen – I keep telling you.'

Dom pulled into a spot in front of Sully's building. 'Would you like it to? If she was interested?'

A month ago, Sully would have said no. 'As miserable as this project has been, I don't know what I'm going to do when I don't get to see her every day.'

'Sounds like you really like her.'

Sully put off answering until they climbed out of Dom's Toyota.

'Remember when I was hooked on Laurie?'

Dom laughed. 'Like I could forget. All you talked about for months was Laurie, Laurie, Laurie. When you guys broke up, I just about had to force-feed you, because you wouldn't eat.'

'Yeah, well, I'm pretty sure I like Hunter more than I liked Laurie.' It felt good to admit it out loud.

Dom shook his head. 'Man. In that case I sure hope she comes around to the Sullivan charm.'

It was pointless unless Hunter liked him, too, but Sully had trouble believing she was capable of harbouring a secret crush, direct as she was. More likely she saw him as a clueless white boy who thought getting kicked in the ass by his father was the worst thing that could happen to someone.

Mom wasn't home from filling out applications for part-time jobs, so Sully let himself and Dom in. When they got to Sully's room, Dom eyed the two crates on the desk, which were filled with Sully's remaining inventory. 'Whoa. That's all that's left?'

'That's it.' Eleven rarity ones, one rarity two. It hurt to look at them.

While Dom dropped on to Sully's bed, Sully pulled a chair to his computer desk. He might as well get this over with.

'Like I said, I've got nine hundred bucks in the bank,' Dom said. 'I'm happy to lend it to you so you don't have to do this.'

'Thanks. I may take you up on the offer, but I'll leave it as a last resort.' Sully listed two Baby Blues (tolerance to heat) as a set for ninety-five dollars. There was a bitter, tinny taste in his mouth. He actually felt a little queasy. A pair of Baby Blues sold for one twenty-five at the flea market.

There would be no more flea market after this. He hated to think he'd never set up his table again. A chapter of his life was over.

But it had got embarrassing to stand behind that mostly bare table, empty boxes set on it in a pathetic attempt to make it look like he had more merchandise than he did. Sully had been going mostly to buy, but there hadn't been many sellers in the past few weeks. January was a slow month.

At least he wouldn't have to see Neal's and Samantha's faces ever again. They'd kept their distance, mostly looking right through Sully like he wasn't even there. No more offers of sandwiches from Samantha, no more sage wisdom from Neal.

Sully listed every sphere except one Army Green, the commonest of the commons. He'd keep that one as a souvenir of his flea market days, unless things got really bad.

CHAPTER 17

A taxi driver leaned on his horn, then pulled round an elderly couple creeping along Twenty-Second Street in a shiny Hyundai Sonata, the old man's nose almost touching the steering wheel.

Sully returned to watching his feet, chin tucked against the cold. His right Reebok swung into view, wrapped with black masking tape. His left one was beginning to split at the toe and would require taping soon.

Hunter led him into a narrow alley squeezed between two tenements, a green fire escape linking the two buildings.

'Hey, look at that. We won't have to jump across,' Sully said.

Hunter reached up, pulled down the ladder. 'You want to go first?'

'Sure.' Sully gripped the rungs, looked up. It was a short one, probably seven stories. If they finished searching every water tower in New York, Sully was confident he would be able to glance at a building and know exactly how many floors it was. But they weren't going to finish. He took a deep breath and, as he climbed, began the little speech he'd prepared.

'Have you thought about whether we'd be better off hunting in the suburbs? Now that I'm not going to the flea market any more, we could switch to weekends.'

He glanced back. Hunter had stopped climbing. She was staring up at him, open-mouthed.

'You quitting on me, Yonkers?' Sully'd been afraid she'd be disappointed, but she sounded worse than disappointed. She sounded defeated.

'*No*. I'm just wondering if we should change our game plan.'

Hunter set her pack on the stairs, pulled out her notebook. 'I've been working this out for five years. No one's searched these towers. If they had, we wouldn't be pulling commons out of them. This is our best chance of making a big hit, and that's what we want, isn't it? A seven. An eight.'

Sully stared at his taped sneakers. Yes, he wanted to find an eight, but right now he'd settle for a steady supply of ones and twos, maybe the occasional three. He didn't want to quit on Hunter, and hated the thought of not seeing her any more, but he had to start making some money. At the rate they were going, he'd be better off working at Price Chopper. Dom could put in a word for him with the manager.

'Come on, Yonkers. Don't give up.'

A blast of freezing wind cut Sully right to the bone. He wanted to say yes. He *always* wanted to say yes to Hunter, but he couldn't afford to dream about the big score any more.

'If we don't find something decent soon, one way or another I'm going to have to give up. I have to bring in some money.' He'd stick it out till the end of the week, he decided.

He couldn't bring himself to say it out loud, though.

Hunter gave him a sad smile. 'I hear you.' She slipped past him, continued up the stairs.

There was only one water tower. They swung the hatch open with well-practised movements, then Sully climbed back down while Hunter took a swim. She didn't have to come up for air, thanks to the Roses he'd bought her.

Five minutes later they moved on, to water tower number 459.

Sully squeezed his hands in his armpits, trying to infuse extra warmth into them as he heard Hunter surface inside tank number 463. Her dripping-wet head poked out through the hatch. She gripped the edge awkwardly, because she was holding something. Something round.

Sully rushed to the base of the tower, the cold forgotten. 'What is it?'

Hunter flipped the object to the roof. It landed at Sully's feet.

A doll's head, black with mould.

'I almost had a heart attack when I saw it.' Hunter jumped the last three feet. 'It just had to be something round, and the right size.' She swept her dripping braids back, her jaw quivering from the icy water.

Sully nudged the head with his foot; it rolled half a turn, stopped face up. 'What do you think our odds are, really?'

Hunter closed her eyes and smiled. 'I'm not much of an odds person. I just follow my gut.' She headed for the fire escape. The next roof over was blessedly too far to jump.

When they reached the roof that was home to water tower number 465, Sully pulled his phone out and checked the time. It was after ten. By silent assent they were pulling a marathon session. Sully needed to call his mom again and tell her he was getting home later than he'd thought.

They didn't talk as he helped Hunter open the hatch. She was all business now, and maybe that was for the best. He wondered if he'd still see her if he quit the project. *When* he quit the project. A sting of sadness hit him at the thought of not seeing her.

He was still a little angry about the Hot Pink debacle. She hadn't apologized, unless she thought *I guess I believe you* was an apology. She could be a real pain in the ass, stubborn beyond belief. Yet he'd never felt so energized, had never laughed as hard as he did with her.

I'm not girlfriend material, she had said in that strange and magical water-tower bar. She wasn't, really; yet Sully felt like he was floating when he was around her. He was fascinated by her, by the layers of her – the hard shell, the dreamer beneath who wanted to take on the world and show it she was someone to be reckoned with.

Inside the tank, Hunter screamed.

'Hunter?' He leaped for the ladder, climbed so fast his foot missed a rung and he clipped his chin hard on a higher rung.

Hunter screamed again – a full-throated cry, as if something in the tank had its jaws round her leg and was pulling her down. Sully looked up, saw her pulling herself through the hatch, her eyes wide with shock, her jaw working soundlessly.

She was clutching something. Something round, bright, and golden. It was like a sphere, but too big, and not the right colour, because there were no Golds. There were no Golds.

Hunter perched at the top of the ladder and stared at the thing in her hand, her chest rising and falling, her breath coming in gasps. She looked down at Sully.

'It's real?' he asked, pleading. 'Please say it's real.'

Hunter nodded. 'Is this really happening? I'm so afraid I'm dreaming. If this is a dream and I wake up . . .'

'Can I see it?' Sully asked. 'I need to touch it so I know it's real.' A new colour. Oversized, like the Midnight Blue.

Hunter climbed down the ladder with one hand, releasing one rung and quickly snatching the next. When she reached the roof, she held out the Gold with both hands, clutching it tightly so Sully could touch it but not take it from her.

Sully pulled off his glove and ran his fingers over the Gold's surface. It was smooth and hard. Ice cold. It was a sphere. No doubt about it.

This time they weren't going to screw up.

'We have to take it right to a safe-deposit box.' Sully's lips felt numb. 'We don't take it out again until we've been paid.'

Hunter pulled it away. 'You said *I* could keep it. You said you'd trust me.'

'You can keep the key – the only key. But it needs to be locked away where no one can get it.'

She took a step away from him. 'That's not what you said.'

This was nuts. All that mattered was that they keep the sphere safe. 'What do you want to do with it, if we don't put it in a safe-deposit box?'

Her voice was low, almost threatening. 'That's for me to decide.'

'Do you know how much this is *worth*? We're not talking

about fourteen grand, we're talking *millions*. Fifty million. *More*. It's one of a kind. We might get—'

'*I know what it's worth.*' She closed her eyes, calmed herself. 'I'll take good care of it. You'll get your share when the time comes.' She looked at him, her eyes big, imploring. 'You said you'd trust me.'

His father's voice boomed in the back of his head. *When fourteen grand is on the line, you have no friends. You trust no one*. Only, it wasn't fourteen grand any more. It was millions. Sully couldn't believe it; he reached up and touched his face to make sure *he* wasn't dreaming. If they could keep from screwing this up, they would be rich.

He felt like the roof was tilting and he would be thrown right off. He bent his knees, drew closer to the ground, took deep breaths.

When the roof settled, he stood tall again. 'All right. That's what I agreed to, so that's the deal.'

The lines on Hunter's forehead smoothed, her shoulders relaxed.

'If we fight, we're going to screw this up,' Sully said. 'We're in this together. We're a team. I trust you.'

He offered Hunter his hand, and she grasped it, hard. She broke into a huge grin.

'We did it, Sully. We did it.'

Sully laughed. 'We were hoping for an eight, and we pulled in a ten. An eleven.'

Hunter raised the Gold sphere to him, this time cupping it in her hand rather than clutching it, offering it to him. He took it, held it close to his face.

'I wonder what it does,' Hunter whispered.

It was twice as heavy as a normal sphere, the colour bright and rich. 'Maybe it does what most people think the Midnight Blue does. Protect you from disease, guarantee you a long life.'

Softly, Hunter said, 'Maybe you can fly.'

Sully nodded, although he doubted it. The spheres worked within the bounds of what humans could already do or be. Humans could pump adrenalin. They could solve problems. They couldn't fly.

He handed the Gold back to Hunter.

She took it, then threw her arms around Sully and squeezed. Sully hugged her back, drinking in the feel of her, her wet braids against his palms, the heat of her face against his neck.

As Hunter's arms relaxed and fell away, Sully wanted to hang on.

'I should have believed you when you said you didn't take the Hot Pink.' She covered her eyes with one hand. 'God, I'm so sorry.'

She lifted the Gold. 'Thank you for trusting me, even though I didn't trust you.'

She knelt, slipped the Gold into her backpack.

'I'll be at your place by ten tomorrow,' Hunter said, speaking low so none of her dozens of room-mates would overhear through the door. 'Then we'll plan our next move.'

Sully was so excited and nervous he could barely stand still. 'Are you sure you don't want to stay at my place? My mom wouldn't mind. I can text her.'

'I'll see you at ten.'

'But what if—'

'I'll see you at ten.'

Reluctantly, Sully nodded. 'OK.'

Hunter fished a key out of her pocket, unlocked the dead bolt. Her hand on the knob, she paused. 'Do you want to sell it to Holliday?'

'No,' Sully said immediately. 'Hell no. Anyone but him.' When this moment had been nothing but a dream, Sully had thought the dollar signs would outweigh his hatred of Holliday. To his surprise, they didn't.

'Good,' Hunter said. 'I was hoping you'd say that.'

'Take care of it,' Sully whispered as Hunter's apartment door clicked shut. He felt incredibly uneasy. She was living in an apartment full of desperate strangers who couldn't afford even a one-room apartment of their own.

As soon as he was in his car, he texted Mom.

I know it's late, but you'll forgive me when you hear what we found. Home soon.

He'd texted her around nine, before they found the Gold, and she'd been pissed off that he was still out.

An answer came in about ten seconds.

It better be worth a million dollars! I am not happy.

That made Sully smile. **It is, Mom, it is.**

He was tempted to call Dom, but it was almost midnight. Dom's dad would have a stroke. He'd call tomorrow.

In fact, he wanted Dom's help on this. Mandy's, too. He and Hunter needed people they could trust to help them figure out the best way to proceed.

He turned on the radio, jumped from station to station looking for something good. His victory drive required music.

He found an old Mumford and Sons tune, cranked it and started dreaming about being rich.

If they sold the Gold for the fifty million Holliday had offered for a matching Midnight Blue (Sully figured fifty million was the minimum the Gold would bring), his cut was twenty million dollars.

Unbelievable.

The hell with rent – he and Mom could move out of their crappy apartment and buy a house. He could buy a new car. He could lay thousand-dollar bills on the counter at the Corvette dealership. He'd give a few million to Mom, a few hundred thousand to Dom.

CHAPTER 18

Sully heard footsteps on the stairs at exactly ten a.m. He opened the door before Hunter could knock.

'Everything OK?' he asked.

'Relax, Yonkers. I got it right here.' She unslung her backpack and followed him into the apartment.

'Where's your mom?' she asked, looking around.

'CVS. She got a part-time job.' Doing her part to keep them in Yonkers until the school year ended. But she wouldn't have to work for long. Sully was going to see to that.

Hunter dropped her pack on the coffee table, produced a key, unlocked and unzipped a side pouch, and took out the Gold.

'Where did you keep it while you slept?' Sully asked. Just the sight of it set his heart thumping.

Hunter laughed. 'Sleep? I didn't sleep. But while I was trying I had the pack tied to my wrist, plus I was curled around it like it was my baby.'

Sully would have been happier if it was in a safe-deposit box, but what Hunter had described wasn't as bad as what he'd imagined.

'Hey, you remember Dom, right?' Before they got talking, he wanted to call Dom and get him to come over.

Hunter nodded.

'I think we could use his help. And we've got a friend, Mandy, who—'

Hunter leaped from the couch. 'You *told* them?' She made it sound like something obscene.

'Not yet, but of course I'm going to tell them. They're my friends. Plus, we could use some help.'

'We agreed we wouldn't tell anyone until we figured this out.'

'No we didn't!' Sully would have remembered agreeing to that.

Hunter sat. 'Well, it goes without saying. That's one of the things we need to plan this morning: who we tell, if *anyone*.' She squeezed her temples. 'As soon as we tell people, they're going to tell other people, and pretty soon someone's going to be pointing a gun at us. Only, this time it won't be street thugs, it'll be paramilitary with automatic rifles.'

Sully tried to stay calm. 'My friends won't tell anyone. We can trust them. Plus, I want to hear what they—'

'*No*. We don't need any help.'

Sully stood, went to the window. He didn't like the way Hunter seemed to think she had the final word on this. Yes, she owned sixty per cent of the Gold. That didn't mean her vote on everything counted for sixty per cent.

'After all this, you still don't trust me.'

'I don't trust your friends. There's a difference.'

'No there isn't. *I* trust them. If you don't trust them, you don't trust me.' He turned to face her. 'When we lost the

156

Hot Pink, you *immediately* assumed I had cheated you. You didn't take *one second* to consider maybe I'd been cheated, too, maybe I was just as devastated as you. Even after you find out you were wrong, even after I trust you with the Gold, it all means nothing.'

Hunter seemed surprised by the ferocity of Sully's anger. Good. Maybe it was time she saw he could bite back when he wanted to. 'I apologized to you about the Hot Pink,' she said. 'More than once.'

'You said the words, but nothing's changed. You're still acting like I'm trying to cheat you.'

Hunter jumped up again. 'I'm treating you like you're a rube, like you're someone who handed over the Cherry Red for a piece of paper, who figured some guy at a flea market carrying fourteen grand in cash must be someone you can trust. I'm not going to let you blow this for me.'

'So now I'm a rube.' At another time that would have hurt, but now it just made him angrier. 'First I'm smart enough to cheat you out of the Hot Pink, now I'm too stupid to be trusted? Or, hold on, you also said the problem was my friends can't be trusted. Which is it? Who can't be trusted? Oh, wait, that's right: *no one* can be trusted.'

Hunter dropped heavily on to the couch, her eyes narrowed, jaw clenched.

'You know, I'm not the one with all the secrets here,' Sully said. 'I've been nothing but up-front with you from the start. You met my mom, for God's sake. I'm not the one who shuts down any time someone asks anything personal.'

Hunter reacted like Sully had slapped her. She put a hand over her mouth, shook her head slowly. He'd hit a nerve.

Maybe that was a good thing; maybe it was time to get things out in the open.

'You want to know my secrets?' She said it softly, almost whispering, her voice trembling. 'Here. Here are my secrets.' Not taking her eyes off him, she propped one foot on the coffee table, leaned forward, and tore at the laces of her boot until they came undone. She grabbed the toe and heel of the boot and tugged it off, then flung it at Sully, hitting him in the knee. She yanked off her sock.

Half her foot was gone. She had no big or second toe; the ones that remained formed a crooked triangle.

Sully looked at her, his eyes questioning.

'It was a freezing-cold night.' She swallowed. 'We had nowhere to go. My mother took me under the High Bridge to sleep.' A tear formed in the corner of her eye and rolled down her cheek. 'She covered us with cardboard, then gave me her coat.' Hunter raised a quivering hand to her mouth. 'When I woke up she was dead. She froze to death. I had to prise her hand from mine. I was *seven*.'

Sully's anger evaporated. He didn't know what to say. *I'm sorry* seemed so small and empty in the face of what she'd just told him. That was why she'd refused to put on Sully's socks when she stepped in the stream at Bear Mountain.

'Are you happy now? Now you know my secrets.' She wiped the tear from her face with a savage swipe, as if it had no business being there.

Not knowing what to say, Sully went and sat beside her. He wrapped an arm round her. She started to move away, then relaxed. Her whole body was trembling, as if she was freezing cold.

He thought back to their conversation about the Plums. Now he understood why she'd got so angry. She'd been talking about herself. *She* would give a kidney for a set of Plums so she could forget the day her mother died. And there he was, talking about how worthless they were.

Hunter was right: he didn't know real suffering. Not the kind she'd gone through.

Still trembling, Hunter curled up on the couch and closed her eyes. Sully stood to give her more room, but she grabbed the sleeve of his sweatshirt and pulled him back down.

The room was warm, but Hunter was shivering, her jaw trembling. Sully wrapped his hands over hers to warm her fingers. That was why she always wore gloves, why she'd got angry when he asked about it.

'Better,' she said, the words barely audible.

Sully tried to imagine waking up next to his mother's body, dealing with the guilt of knowing she had died protecting him. Hunter had been standing under that bridge, her mother's body at her frozen feet, no one to tell, no place to go. Seven years old. Had she left her mother? Had she cried out for help until someone came? He wasn't about to ask. No wonder she didn't want to talk about her childhood.

He studied her face, her cheeks even sharper than usual because of the tension in her jaw. Soon she'd be a millionaire. Sully took solace in that thought. These were such strange days; he felt both sad and elated, sitting there holding Hunter's hands.

'Go ahead and call your friends,' Hunter said. 'Tell them to come on over.'

'Are you sure?'

She nodded. 'If you trust them, I guess I can trust them too.'

Sully took out his phone. 'Thank you.'

He texted Dom.

Pick up Mandy. Come over IMMEDIATELY.
Big news. Huge.

Hunter opened her eyes. 'I'm sorry I brought you down with that. We're going to be millionaires, and I'm telling sad stories and throwing boots. We should be dancing.'

'No, I'm glad you told me. Now I understand. I couldn't fit all the pieces of you together. You didn't make sense to me. Now you do. And I like you even more, although I didn't think that was possible.'

Hunter gave him a heavy-lidded look. 'Don't feed me that line.'

'It's not a line.' Sully paused, wondering if it would be a mistake to tell her how he really felt. Maybe he owed it to her, after what she'd just shared with him. Time to get everything out in the open. 'Half the reason I was out there freezing my butt off every night was so I could be with you.'

Hunter didn't say anything. She gave him an unreadable look that might have been surprise, or worry, or confusion. He shrugged, wanting to break the tension. 'Not to mention I got to see you in that skintight suit.'

Hunter threw back her head and laughed. She reached up and punched his shoulder. 'Shut *up*.'

Sully fanned himself with his hand. 'Just thinking about it.'

She shook her head, her eyebrows pinched. It was her

What am I going to do with you? face.

Barely realizing what he was doing, Sully leaned down to kiss her.

Hunter pulled back, gave him another unreadable look, then leaned in and kissed him.

She didn't turn her head like in the water-tower bar. She let her lips linger on his before finally pulling back, clearing her throat, smiling ever so slightly.

'OK, then. We've got a fifty-million-dollar marble to think about. Let's try to stay focused.'

'Oh. Right. The fifty-million-dollar marble. It totally slipped my mind.'

Hunter lifted her hand as if she was going to slap him. 'Going to school on the Cherry Red sale, I think the first thing we do is hire legal representation.'

Sully pointed at her. 'Definitely.'

Hunter reached for her sock, pulled it on. 'My foot's pretty disgusting.'

Sully shrugged. 'It's a foot. You walk on it. I don't think anyone's feet are all that attractive.'

Hunter laughed. 'I guess that's one way to look at it.'

They strategized about how to sell the Gold until there was a rap on the door. 'It's Dom. And Stretch.'

'Don't call me that,' they heard Mandy say.

Hunter looked at Sully. 'So that's your dream team out there, come to save the day?'

Sully went to let them in.

When he turned back towards the room, the Gold was gone. Back into Hunter's pack, he assumed.

'So what's the huge news?' Dom looked from Sully to

Hunter and back. 'You said to get here immediately.'

Sully put his hands on Dom's shoulders, leaned in close. 'You can't tell anyone. Not anyone. If word got out, we could be killed. Seriously.'

Dom nodded. 'I swear to God.'

Sully turned to Mandy. 'You, too. No one. Not your parents, not anyone.'

She looked confused. 'You're serious? Why would someone want to kill you? Did you do something illegal?'

Sully huffed, trying to catch his breath, excited all over again. 'We found a sphere in one of the towers.'

Dom grabbed his shoulder. 'Holy crap. Is it an eight? Tell me you found an eight.'

Sully's belly did a flip. 'Better.'

Dom started to say something, but it caught in his throat. It was sinking in: if it was better than an eight, Sully was talking millions.

'It's a new one. It's gold, and it's bigger, like the Midnight Blue.'

'Oh, my God,' Mandy whispered. She put a hand on her head. 'Oh, my God.'

'I know.'

Dom was squatting, hands on his knees, like he'd just been punched. 'Where is it?'

'It's safe,' Hunter said.

Sully caught Hunter's eye, nodded. 'We can trust them.'

Hunter gave him a look. 'How long have you known this girl? A couple of months?'

For a second there, Sully'd thought some of Hunter's hard edges had been smoothed by the moment they shared.

Evidently not; she was back to being all business.

Dom straightened, folded his arms. 'That's about as long as Sully's known you, isn't it?'

Hunter pinched her lower lip. '*No one* can know about this until we've got things figured out.'

Dom and Mandy both nodded.

'Cross my heart and hope to die,' Dom said.

Hunter lifted her pack from the couch, set it on the coffee table, pulled the Gold from a side pouch.

Mandy whispered something under her breath and approached like she was afraid she might startle the sphere if she moved too quickly. She knelt, brought her face close. 'Can I touch it?' Tapping her forehead, she added, 'I'm Mandy, by the way.' She offered her hand to Hunter. 'I probably should have started with that, *then* asked if I could handle your priceless sphere.'

Clearly still not happy about the situation, Hunter nodded. 'Go on.'

Mandy lifted it as Dom leaned in at her elbow. He reached out, ran a finger over the top of it.

'Either of you know how to find a good lawyer?' Sully asked. Were there lawyers who specialized in spheres? He had no idea.

Evidently his friends didn't, either. 'I could ask my parents, but it would be hard to do that without telling them what it's about.' Mandy set the Gold back on the table.

Tilting her head, she studied the sphere. 'Weird.' She picked it up, set it down again.

Her hand froze, hovering above it. 'Did you see that?'

'See what?' Sully asked.

Mandy lifted the Gold and set it on the table yet again.

It shifted ever so slightly towards the table's edge.

'Did you see?' Mandy picked it up, set it down closer to the centre of the table.

It shifted again, in the same direction.

'The table's not level,' Hunter said.

'That's probably it.' Mandy picked up the Gold, took it into the kitchen. The rest of them watched from the living room as Mandy set it on the kitchen table.

Even from there, Sully could see it shift slightly.

'It did it again. Same direction.' She looked at Sully. 'Do you have a sphere I can see for a minute? Doesn't matter what colour.'

Sully went to his room, grabbed the Army Green from his desk, where it sat alongside three commons that hadn't sold on eBay. He brought it out to Mandy. She set it on the kitchen table.

It sat there, not budging a millimeter.

Mandy picked up the Army Green. 'Here, catch.' She tossed it across the room to Dom. 'Set it down on the coffee table.'

Dom did. No shift.

'Now why would that be?' Mandy asked, her voice low. She knelt, set the Gold on the linoleum floor.

It shifted.

'It's always in the same direction,' Sully said.

'Maybe it's lopsided,' Hunter suggested.

'That's possible,' Mandy said. She lifted it straight up, set it right back down.

Again, it rolled ever so slightly.

'That's just freaky,' Dom said.

He went and knelt beside Mandy, lifted the Gold, then set it down.

They all watched it tilt.

Sully's skin was prickling. It was as if the sphere was alive, or something was moving inside it.

Mandy stood, put her hands on her hips. Brushing her hair behind her ears, she pointed in the direction the Gold was leaning, which was towards Sully's bedroom. 'Which way is that?' She looked at Sully. 'Do you have a compass?'

'What do I look like, a Boy Scout?' Sully closed his eyes, visualized the apartment building. McDonald's and Price Chopper were in that direction. The sun set over the roof of Price Chopper.

'West.'

Mandy slumped a little. 'I was hoping it was north. That might mean the Gold acts like a compass for some reason.'

'What would make it pull west?' Dom asked. 'What's west?'

Nothing was west. If it was drawn towards water, the Atlantic Ocean was closer. It was morning, so the sun was in the east, which meant it wasn't pulled towards sunlight. But that was exactly what it looked like – like something was pulling it.

What if it was something closer, maybe something in his room? What was in his room, though?

Spheres.

'Hold on. I think I've got it.' Sully sprang up, carried the Gold into his room with everyone following. His hands were shaking. If it *was* attracted to spheres, they could use it to find more. He pulled the three spheres from his desk and placed them on the floor in the centre of his room, then set the Gold on the floor. He let it go.

It shifted west, away from the spheres.

'Damn,' Sully hissed.

'That was a brilliant thought, though,' Mandy said. 'If something is attracting it, other spheres make the most sense –' She inhaled sharply. '*Wait*. Oh, my God.'

'What?' Dom asked.

Mandy's eyes were wide. They shifted back and forth, as if she was tracking something invisible to the rest of them. 'What if it *is* attracted to a sphere? But only one.'

'The other Gold,' Hunter said.

Mandy nodded. 'Assuming there's only one.'

Sully froze. The other Gold?

'Oh, my freaking God,' Dom whispered. 'That makes so much sense.'

It was just a guess. Maybe the Gold was drawn towards redwood trees, or movie stars, or Japan. Maybe it wasn't drawn towards anything; maybe it moved for a reason they didn't understand, just like they didn't understand the spheres themselves.

Only, in some ways the spheres made more sense than anything. Magenta spheres always gave you night vision and Lemon Yellows always made you taller. You always needed exactly two to burn in order to gain what they offered.

'They could be like polar opposites, drawn towards each other,' Mandy said.

Sully looked at Hunter. She was staring at the Gold, but her eyes had a faraway look.

They snapped back into focus as she looked at Sully.

'What would the *pair* be worth?'

Sully picked up the Gold. There was no telling. If someone bought both, he or she could burn them and find out what they did. That made them way more valuable. 'Even if Mandy's right, though, it could be anywhere. It could be in Russia.' He didn't need a second Gold; he was already set for life. Even if Sully's mom would let him hop in a car or on a plane and chase the Gold's match, which she definitely wouldn't, it wasn't worth the risk. They should sell the Gold and be done with it.

Hunter was back to staring into space, the wheels turning.

'My parents would never let me go,' Mandy said.

Dom stuck out his tongue, made a raspberry sound. 'Mine either. No way.'

'I could go,' Hunter said. 'If I had a thousand dollars.' She looked from Mandy to Dom. 'What do you say? You bankroll me, you get a cut of the second Gold if I find it.'

'Hang on,' Sully said. 'Let's not get greedy. We don't need the other one.'

Hunter gave him a calm, easy smile. 'You really want to stop now, Cherry Red? Honestly?' She took the Gold out of Sully's hand, held it for a heartbeat, then set it on his dresser.

It leaned towards the west, then went still.

'If all it takes to find the other Gold is following whichever way this one points, do you really want to sell it and let the new owner fetch the other?' Her eyes were bright, her dimples prominent. 'I know you better than that.'

'That's easy for you to say,' Sully said. 'You don't have a mom to stop you at the door.'

Her smile wavered. 'Lucky me.'

Sully kicked himself, realizing what a dumb thing he'd just said. 'Sorry.'

Hunter shrugged, shook her head. *No big thing.*

All they had to do was go whichever direction the Gold pointed. It sounded simple enough. 'What if this other Gold really is in Russia? What are we going to do, hop on a plane?'

'What if it's in Jersey?' Hunter asked. 'We won't know unless we try.'

Would his mother let him go? She was unhappy when he came in late from hunting, let alone a trip that could last for days. But that was before he found the Gold, which was going to change her life as much as his. Hadn't he earned a little slack? Plus in less than a year he'd be eighteen; he'd be a legal adult, able to book a flight to Timbuktu if he wanted, and stay as long as he liked.

He looked at Dom. 'If we did this, could you bankroll us?'

'I've got nine hundred in the bank. If I kick that in, and I come, what do I get?'

Sully stifled a laugh. 'No way your old man's going to let you come.'

'Who says I'm going to ask him?' Dom tilted his head. 'What would my cut be?'

'If you come and we find it, you get an even cut,' Sully said.

Hunter clapped her hands to her temples. 'Are you out of your mind? For nine hundred dollars? More like five per cent.'

Dom nodded. 'She's right. You guys dived in all those tanks and found the Gold; I'd be ripping you off if I got the same as you.' He looked at Hunter. 'Ten per cent?'

She nodded. 'That's fine. I ain't greedy.'

Sully stepped close to Hunter, so their faces were only a few inches apart. 'Come on. We're already set for life with the first.'

Hunter squinted, shook her head slowly. 'You're a soft touch, Yonkers. You know that?' She turned to Dom. 'Fifteen per cent.'

'I want in, too,' Mandy said. 'I'll match Dom's nine hundred.'

Sully nodded. The polar-opposites idea had been Mandy's, so it seemed only fair.

Hunter looked like she'd just swallowed a bug. 'Fine. But just to be clear: if we find nothing, you get nothing. This Gold belongs to me and Sully, sixty-forty. Period.'

'Yeah, of course,' Dom said.

Mandy nodded. 'Agreed.'

'I feel like we should be forming a circle and stacking our hands like the Fantastic Four,' Sully said.

'Yeah, let's skip that,' Hunter said. 'When do we leave?'

They looked at each other.

'Tomorrow?' Mandy suggested. 'Tomorrow's Sunday. That's one less day of school we'll miss.'

'How are you going to get your parents to sign off on this?' Sully asked. 'The way you talk about them, they barely let you go to the bathroom alone.'

Mandy gave him a sly smile. 'I'm going to bribe my brother at Virginia Tech to say I'm coming for a visit. There's going to be some *huge* educational enrichment thing going on at Virginia Tech this week. I haven't made it up yet, but it's going be an opportunity my folks wouldn't dream of letting me miss.'

Dom shook his head. 'My folks would never buy that. They know I have no interest in educational enrichment.' He frowned, looked at Mandy. 'I thought you didn't trust marbles.'

Mandy shrugged. 'I don't. This isn't about burning them – it's about selling them. I don't think Sully or my aunt are wrong for selling them, or that people are wrong to collect them, I just think it's a big mistake for people to actually *burn* them.'

'Why shouldn't people burn them?' Hunter asked.

Mandy gave Hunter an *Isn't it obvious?* look. 'No one knows where they came from, what they're made of, who hid them, or how they do what they do. It's like a stranger walking up to you on the street, handing you a pill and saying, "Here, swallow this." And you swallow it.'

'Or it's like watching someone pluck a berry you don't recognize off a tree and eat it,' Hunter countered. 'Then when it doesn't poison them, you know it's safe to eat.'

Sully didn't want to have this debate. He'd heard both sides a thousand times, in class, on the news, everywhere. No one ever changed anyone's mind.

He clapped his hands. 'OK. Tomorrow, nine a.m., here.'

'Load up on snacks and drinks, because we ain't stopping till we find that Gold,' Hunter said.

CHAPTER 19

Sully snagged the edge of the M&M's bag sitting behind the gearshift and dragged the bag into the back seat. He poured a generous pile into his palm.

Hunter's open palm appeared under his nose. Sully filled it with M&M's, tossed the bag back up front.

Disclosure blasted from the speakers. Dom bobbed his head to the beat, driving with one hand, the other holding a bottle of Rage.

They passed a green sign: DAYTON 86 MILES.

'Ooh, the new Emma Watson movie comes out Friday,' Mandy said from the front. She was messing with her phone. 'A paranoid thriller. I love paranoid thrillers.'

'Really? I would have pegged you as a Lord of the Rings girl,' Dom said.

Mandy looked up from her phone. 'I am not a geek. I hate fantasy. Except Harry Potter, because Emma Watson was in that. Don't stereotype me because I'm Asian and studious.'

'What do your parents do for a living, again?' Dom asked.

Mandy heaved a big sigh. 'Yes, my father's a neurologist,

my mother's a dermatologist. I know — the high-achieving Asian family. It fits the stereotype. I'm also six foot one and gay.'

'You tell him,' Hunter said.

'Hey, stop ganging up on me,' Dom said. He nudged Mandy's shoulder. 'So you think Emma Watson's hot?'

'Hell yes.'

'She's kind of skinny, though. Not much boobage.'

'Boobs are nice,' Mandy agreed.

'Do your parents know you're gay?' Dom asked.

It took Mandy a moment to answer. 'They know, but we never talk about it. They've always been cool with the *idea* of gay people, but somehow *me* being gay makes them turn red and stammer.'

Dom pulled his phone from his pocket, checked it, cursed. 'My father.'

He put the phone to his ear. 'Hey, Dad.' In the rear-view mirror, Sully saw Dom roll his eyes. 'I told you, I'm running away from home to seek my fortune.'

Dom's father was shouting so loudly Sully could hear him from the back seat.

'I already told you: I can't say.'

More shouting.

'Fine. You do that. Yeah, I'm grounded till I'm eighteen. Got it. If this pans out, you won't have to wait till I'm eighteen to get rid of me.'

Louder shouting.

'Well, thanks, Dad. I appreciate your support.'

He disconnected. 'If we don't find that other Gold, I'm dead when we get back.'

This entire trip felt dreamlike to Sully. Not only what they were after, but being on his own with his friends, with Hunter, driving across states he'd never set foot in before.

He took the Gold out of Hunter's pack and set it in his lap. Whenever it was out of sight, Sully started doubting its existence. He knew it was real, but there was a part of him that just couldn't grasp it.

'Hey, Dom,' he said. 'What are you going to do with your share if we find it?'

Dom turned the music down. 'First I'm going to move out, get my own place. Then I'm going to drop out of school and open my own business. Screw school – I want to get started with my life.'

'What sort of business?' Mandy asked.

'I have no idea,' Dom said, laughing. 'No clue. I'll tell you when I figure it out. Maybe a gym.'

'How about you, Mandy?' Sully asked.

She thought for a moment. 'I'll probably put most of the money in the bank. There's nothing I'm dying to spend it on right now.' She propped a foot on the dash. 'Mostly I came because I didn't want to miss out, you know?' She looked at Dom, who nodded. 'Don't get me wrong – the money would be awesome. I didn't want to miss the adventure, to have you guys come back and hear stories about everything you did.'

She put a hand on Dom's shoulder, pointed at a sign for a rest area. 'Why don't we see if we're still heading in the right direction?'

As Dom turned on the signal, Mandy went on. 'Ever since I was little, my parents worried about me getting hurt. I swear, if they could, they'd make me wear a helmet and kneepads to school in case I trip. I miss out on a lot of things because they're so worried about me. I didn't want to miss out on this. Whether or not we find the matching Gold, we're going to remember this for the rest of our lives.'

'Yeah,' Hunter said. 'That's right.'

Dom pulled into the rest area. 'It's not just about the money for me, either. The Gold is gonna be big news. If we find the match, it'll be even bigger. I want to be part of that news. Then when people hear the name Cucuzza, they'll think about the Golds, not my uncle shooting up a museum.'

Mandy didn't react, so Sully assumed Dom must have come clean at some point about his relationship to the infamous Tony Cucuzza.

'What about you, Hunter?' Sully asked as they pulled to a stop.

'First thing I'm going to do is fly to Korea and give my Korean mom half.'

'*Half*?' Dom said.

'Half. She was the only one who helped me. I was a kid, filthy, hungry. Everyone else just looked right through me like I wasn't there, or handed me a couple of dollars and walked away. After that, I'll take my half and live like a queen. Like two queens.'

Exhausted from sixteen hours of driving, they checked into a Fairfield Inn with an indoor pool outside Springfield, Missouri.

As soon as they got to their room, Hunter took out the Gold and tested it on the dresser. It rolled about an eighth of a revolution before coming to a stop.

Mandy set a carpenter's level on the dresser. 'It's level. The pull is definitely getting stronger.'

Sully checked the compass they'd bought at a truck stop in Pennsylvania. The roll was pointing them west-south-west. He checked the big foldout map of the United States they'd also picked up. They weren't heading towards California; more like New Mexico, and beyond that, Mexico.

Beyond that was the Pacific Ocean.

Sully nudged Hunter's sneaker. 'Come on. Come swim.'

Hunter looked up. 'I don't ever want to swim again. I got my fill in the towers.' She reached beside her lounge chair and picked up a bottle of water.

He held out a hand to her. 'Please? We'll stay in the shallow end.'

'I don't have a bathing suit. Plus I'm not leaving my backpack.'

'You can swim in that.' She was wearing shorts and a T-shirt.

Hunter's smile faded. 'Sully, no. I'm not taking my shoes off.'

Sully wanted to tell her it was no big deal, that no one would be looking at her feet and, even if they did, no one would care.

There were a lot of things he wanted to tell her, once there was time. He wanted to tell her he thought about her more than he thought about the Gold.

They hadn't talked about that moment on his couch. Sully

had no idea where they stood, whether they were together in Hunter's mind, or if that kiss was just a momentary thing that had sprung out of the emotions she'd been feeling.

'OK.' He leaned in to kiss her cheek. To Sully's surprise, Hunter turned her head so their lips met. She kissed him softly, tenderly, her lips sliding along his.

As they parted she looked away, smiling. 'Don't let that go to your head, Yonkers.'

He leaned back in his lounge chair and closed his eyes, smiling. 'Your foot doesn't seem to slow you down much. You don't limp at all. Your balance is great.'

'It took some getting used to, but I barely notice it now. If you think about it, some people lose their whole leg below the knee and can still run. What's a couple of toes compared to that?'

Sully's phone vibrated. He retrieved it from beside him and checked the message.

A little birdie told me you found something.
Let's talk.

It was from Holliday.

Sully jumped out of the chair. 'No. Oh, no.'

He turned his phone so Hunter could see the message.

She leaped to her feet, stuck two fingers in her mouth, and whistled sharply. Dom and Mandy, who were bobbing around in the deep end, looked her way.

'We gotta go. *Now.*'

Sully collected their stuff. Dom and Mandy dripped on the carpet in the motel's hallway as they rushed back to their room to dress and check out. On the way, Sully filled them in. He didn't see how Holliday could track them to the hotel, since they'd paid cash, but he wasn't taking any chances.

Mandy and Hunter were both bent over their phones as Dom pulled out of the Fairfield Inn car park.

'There's an entire discussion thread on MarbleMadness about the Gold,' Mandy said. 'No one knows who started the rumours. A lot of people think it's a hoax.'

'I don't see anything in the news yet,' Hunter said.

Even if it got into the news, Sully couldn't see how that was a problem unless someone reported who actually *had* it. What they didn't need was for their names and photos to be published before they found the other Gold, assuming their Gold really was leading them to its match.

Sully checked his phone, found another text from Holliday.

How much do you want?

He read it out loud.

'How did he *hear* about it?' Dom asked. 'Who knows, besides us?'

'My mom,' Sully said. He dialled her number.

'Sully? Is everything all right?'

Sully moved the phone away from his ear. 'Everything's fine, Mom. We're still on the road. We think we're closing in.' More or less.

'Where *are* you?'

Sully debated admitting they were almost halfway across the country, decided it would be a mistake.

'Maryland.' That seemed a good compromise.

'*Maryland?* Oh, my God. Sully, I'm not sure this was a good idea. Mr Cucuzza is out of his mind. When I said you could go, I didn't know Dom didn't have his parents' permission.'

Sully squeezed his eyes closed. 'Mr Cucuzza called you.' Of course he did.

'I just told you, yes. He's ready to string Dom up.'

'Did you tell him about the Gold?'

There was a pause, because his mother had promised not to tell a soul. 'What was I supposed to tell him? That I let you take off on your own and miss school for no reason?'

'No, I understand.' There was no point in making her feel bad about it. 'Look, Mom, can I call you later? We're about to stop for breakfast.'

'Sully, this was a bad idea. Come home.'

'Mom, *no*. We're close. We'll probably find it today. You know how much money we're talking about.'

'We have more than we'll ever need from the one.'

'What about Dom, though? If we find the second one, Dom gets a share. If we turn round now, he gets nothing.' Sully neglected to mention the quarter of a million dollars he intended to give Dom, since that wouldn't help his case.

'Nice deflection,' Dom muttered from up front. Sully's mom loved Dom.

Mom sighed. '*One more day*. I want you back here by tomorrow night at the latest. And *be careful*. All of you.'

Sully assured his mom they would.

'Now we know where the leak came from,' he said as he disconnected.

'Is there any way Holliday can find us?' Dom asked.

Sully had watched a lot of thrillers where people used high-tech means to track people, but those were movies, and usually it was the police or the CIA that were doing the tracking.

Mandy tapped away on her phone in the front seat. Sully leaned forward and looked over her shoulder.

'Theoretically, he could track us through our phones. We need to take the batteries out and stop using them.' Mandy looked at the ceiling. 'The GPS. The car's location could be tracked from it.'

Hunter unbuckled her seat belt. 'Here, I can fix that.' She crawled halfway into the front, between Dom's and Hunter's seats, her phone in her left hand.

Dom glanced at her. 'What are you doing?'

Hunter brought her phone down on the GPS unit, shattering the screen. She hit it again, and again, caving the whole thing in as Dom made pained sounds.

Finally, she crawled back into her seat. 'There. I owe you a GPS. As soon as I'm a millionaire I'll buy you a new one. Connected to a really nice car.'

'Works for me,' Dom said.

'Are we being too paranoid?' Sully asked.

'Maybe,' Mandy said. 'But, given the circumstances, I think that's appropriate.'

No one argued with her.

Sully took a jam doughnut from the Dunkin' Donuts bag and bit into it carefully to avoid a replay of the previous doughnut, which had squirted jam on to the crotch of his trousers.

'Dead Throne' by The Devil Wears Prada was playing for the eleventh time as the sun sank into the trees outside Sully's window. Dom and Mandy were talking in low tones, Mandy now driving. It would be Sully's turn in a couple of hours.

Beside him, Hunter's head drooped, then jerked upright.

Sully grabbed his coat from the floor, put it in his lap. 'Here.' He tugged her sleeve, drew her down until her head was in his lap.

'Thanks,' she said, curling her hands under her chin.

Sully rested his hand on Hunter's hip.

Mandy pulled into a rest stop just beyond Las Cruces, New Mexico, twenty miles from the Mexican border. There was no one else there at two a.m., so, leaving Hunter asleep, they set the Gold on the sidewalk right in front of Dom's idling Camry.

The Gold rolled a full half-turn before stopping. They'd travelled so far west that the Gold was now moving almost due south.

'We've got to be close.' Mandy looked up at Sully and Dom. 'Keep going?'

Sully's stomach did a somersault at the idea of driving into Mexico. They'd come this far, though.

'Don't we need passports?' he asked.

Mandy shook her head. 'I read up on it while we were at the hotel. We can get tourist cards at the border inspection station. Twenty dollars each.'

Sully nodded. 'I guess we keep going.'

A nervous laugh escaped Dom. 'We're going to Mexico. Cool.'

CHAPTER 20

'Sully. Wake up.'

Sully opened his eyes. It took him a moment to remember why he was sleeping in Dom's car.

He sat up, looked around. They were parked on a street crowded with vehicles, the sidewalks teeming with people. Across the street, people were lined up at the window of a mobile food stand with a red-and-white awning. Its sign read TACOS LOS GUICHOS. He spotted Dom standing in line.

Sully ran his tongue over slimy teeth. 'Where are we?'

'Mexico City.' Hunter raised her eyebrows. 'The Gold is rolling *north*. It's *rolling*. Keeps on going until you pick it up.'

A laugh escaped Sully. They were past the spot the Gold was pulling towards. It wasn't on the other side of the Pacific, and it wasn't just some quirk of the sphere. It was moving towards something. Something close.

Dom appeared with a handful of tacos. Climbing out of the car, Sully eyed them suspiciously. 'What time is it? Isn't it breakfast time?'

'*Huevos*.' Grinning, Dom offered a taco to Sully. 'That

means "eggs". They're filled with scrambled eggs.'

They were good. Really good. Eggs, tomato sauce and chilli peppers inside a big, crunchy corn chip.

'What's the plan?' Sully asked as he ate.

'The traffic is bad, so we're going to leave the car and walk,' Mandy said.

Sully nodded. 'Good plan. Let's go. I need to find a bathroom, though.'

'Don't we all,' Mandy said as they headed down the busy street.

The buildings were colourful – lots of red, yellow and green – with striped awnings. The colours were faded, though, the buildings old. A lot of the store signs were homemade, painted right on the facade or strung up on banners.

'You think we can just go into one and ask to use the bathroom?' Dom asked.

Up ahead, a row of old bicycles stood outside one of the stores. The painted sign over the door read BICIMANIACOS. Sully didn't need to know Spanish to figure that one out.

He led the way into the store, trying to think of a way to ask if they had a bathroom, and to say they wanted to buy four cheap bikes, without knowing Spanish. There was also the small detail of having only US dollars on them.

The shop was tiny, with more bikes lining the walls. A thin, small woman was behind the counter.

'Do you speak English?' Sully asked.

She shook her head.

'Bathroom? Restroom?' He mimicked flushing a toilet.

Hunter stood watching, arms folded, trying not to laugh.

'If you think you can do better, you're welcome to try.'

Sully swept a hand towards the counter.

'Yeah, why don't I give it a try?' Hunter turned to the woman behind the counter and said, '¿*Por favor, dónde está el baño?*'

'Ah,' the woman said, then answered in Spanish while swinging open a half door.

Hunter turned to Sully, grinning. 'It's in the back. You know, the –' She mimed flushing a toilet. 'Why don't you go while I buy us some bikes?'

Dom and Mandy were laughing so hard there were tears in their eyes.

'Your mom was Puerto Rican,' Sully said.

'My mom was Puerto Rican, *sí,*' Hunter said. She pointed to the bikes in front of the store, began speaking rapid-fire Spanish to the shopkeeper as Sully slid into the back to find *el baño*.

Hunter counted *ocho* twenty-dollar bills on to the counter as a kid who looked about twelve unlocked bikes and set them by the door. After setting up three, he walked away, hands in his pockets.

'There are only three bikes,' Sully said to Hunter as she was accepting change in pesos.

'Funny story,' Hunter said. 'No one ever taught me to ride a bike.' She shrugged, breezed past him, slid on to the seat of one of the bikes as Mandy and Dom claimed the other two.

'Can't ride a bike, fluent in Spanish.' Sully squeezed in front of Hunter, placed his foot on the pedal. 'Got it.'

They rode slowly, single file, with Mandy in the lead. With

their phones disabled, Sully assumed Mandy had no idea where she was heading. She was heading north; at the moment that was probably all that mattered.

'Did you and your mom speak Spanish to each other?' Sully asked as they rolled along, hugging the kerb. A bus roared past, spewing a cloud of exhaust that burned Sully's eyes.

'She spoke Spanish. I usually answered in English,' Hunter said.

Sully tried to imagine that.

An image came into his mind unbidden: Hunter's mom, saying in Spanish, *Take my coat. Here. Let's wrap you tight.* And Hunter, a little girl, answering in English, *Thanks, Mommy.*

Mandy and Dom were a dozen feet ahead, talking.

'Can I ask you something?' Sully said.

'Yeah.'

'I feel like there's no way to ask this without it coming out wrong . . .'

'If it comes out wrong, the worst that'll happen is I punch you in the kidney.'

'I know you were just a kid, and maybe you don't know the answer, but why didn't your mother take you to a shelter that night?'

'Because she was crazy,' Hunter said matter-of-factly. 'She was a good mother, but she was crazy. She thought Michael Jackson was trying to kill us.' Glancing back, Sully could see Hunter studying him, seeking a reaction.

'Was she always that way?'

'It started when I was about four. That's why she lost her job. She was a nurse. We were doing fine until then.' She put a hand on the back of his shoulder. 'Can we talk about something else?'

'I'm sorry. Sure. The other thing I keep wondering is, now that there's no reason to dive in water towers, when will I get to see you in that dry suit again?'

She slapped his back. 'Try another topic.'

'Can you speak Korean?'

'Not really. My Korean mom taught me a few sentences, names for some Korean foods. Mostly we spoke English.'

Mandy turned right, on to a relatively quiet one-way street of colourful two-story attached houses.

She slowed to a stop. 'Let's see how we're doing.'

Hunter had emptied her backpack of everything but the Gold. Acting as if she needed to find something in the pack, she set it down flat on the sidewalk.

An instant later, she snatched the pack off the ground, zipped it, and pointed towards what looked to be the heart of the city. Tall, modern glass skyscrapers loomed in the thick smog.

No one paid Sully, Dom or Mandy any notice as they stood admiring a towering monument that rose in the centre of a busy traffic circle on the Paseo de la Reforma, the long, straight road that cut through the centre of the city. Hunter squatted behind them, one hand in her pack as she checked which way the Gold was pulling.

The monument had to be a hundred feet high; on top was a stunning gold statue of a winged woman holding what looked like a hat.

'I want to come back here sometime,' Dom said.

'To this spot?' Sully asked.

'To Mexico City, I mean. It seems like a cool place. I'd like to look around when I'm not in a hurry.'

It wasn't Sully's idea of the perfect vacation spot, but he could see what Dom was saying. It was so different from New York, kind of wild and exciting.

Hunter zipped her pack, straightened. 'Straight across.'

'We've got to be close,' Hunter said as they waited for the light. 'It rolls like crazy as soon as I put it down.'

The light changed and they crossed to the centre of the roundabout, then climbed two dozen steps leading to the base of the monument, which was ringed with statues of lions and women on thrones. They circled the monument, continued down the steps on the opposite side, and waited for the light again before crossing to the far side of the massive traffic circle.

Once there, they took up the same positions: Sully, Dom and Mandy acting like tourists admiring the monument, Hunter squatting behind them, looking in her pack.

'What if it's hidden in someone's apartment?' Dom asked.

'I guess we offer them a cut,' Sully said. 'In which case we're going to be mighty glad Hunter speaks Spanish.'

Hunter stood, slung the pack across her shoulders. She was staring at the monument, frowning.

'Which way?' Sully asked.

Hunter pointed at the monument. 'That way.'

Sully's heart went from zero to sixty. Back the way they'd just come, which meant it was between the two points. Just to be sure, they went a quarter of the way around the traffic circle and tried again, working in silence.

Once again, the Gold pulled right towards the monument.

'What *is* it?' Dom asked, staring up at the tower.

Hunter looked around, approached a woman carrying a shopping bag. '*Perdóneme. ¿Qué es eso?*'

The woman answered at length. When she finished, Hunter thanked her and turned back to them. 'It's called *The Angel of Independence*. There's a spiral staircase in the column that takes you to the observation deck. The angel on top is Nike, a Greek goddess, and she's holding a wreath directly over the spot where a dude named Hidalgo is buried. He's the father of Mexican independence.'

Sully had no idea whom Mexico had fought to gain independence. He couldn't remember being taught much of anything about Mexico in school. He shaded his eyes with his hand and looked up. A man and a woman were on the observation deck, which was a small, fenced area. *The Angel of Independence* was perched on one foot atop the spire, her arms and other leg outstretched. Now that there were people on the observation deck for comparison Sully could see the statue was huge – four or five times as tall as the people. Unlike much of the city, she was bright and clean. She looked like she was made of gold.

'How are we gonna search a public monument?' Dom asked. 'I doubt they're going to let us stop every couple of steps to feel around in the cracks.'

'Maybe it's hidden around the base, in a hollow part of one of those statues, or a drainpipe,' Hunter said.

There were six statues ringing the base: four women sitting on what looked like thrones, each clutching a sword and a book, and two lions being led by boys. The statues were black, maybe two-thirds the size of the angel at the top, and set about ten feet off the ground. Sully and his friends would have to scale the monument to get to those statues. There was no way they could do that in the middle of the day; they'd have to wait until dark.

'We're gonna look like terrorists, poking around that thing,' Dom said, shaking his head. He was right. It was a national monument; four teenagers weren't going to spend hours combing it without drawing attention from the police, day or night.

They'd come all this way, and now it was beginning to look like they'd be stopped a hundred feet from their goal.

Sully's gaze rose and fell as he scanned the monument from top to bottom, trying to imagine where the sphere might be. Maybe one of the stone steps leading up to the monument was loose, and the Gold was wedged beneath it?

The Gold. It was interesting that the statue at the top was gold-coloured. From this distance Sully couldn't make out many details, but there didn't appear to be any nooks or crannies on the angel where a sphere could hide. It looked to be all one piece.

Mandy had pulled a camera from her bag, was snapping photos of the monument, fiddling with the focus. It was a nice camera, and she seemed to know how to use it.

'Can I see that?' Sully asked her.

She handed him the camera.

At full zoom, the statue just about filled the viewfinder. The angel was gorgeous. Sully could see the individual feathers on her wings; each had a wispy texture. Her skirt was creased a thousand times, making it look like she was walking into a stiff wind. She was holding the crown high, her arm fully extended. The crown was slightly lopsided.

Sully lowered the camera. 'Wait, didn't you say she was holding a wreath? Did you mean a crown?'

Hunter shook her head. 'The woman said a wreath.'

Sully moved a few steps to the right, squinted and strained to make out the thing in the angel's hand. It did look like a wreath; he could see leafy edges, which gave it a jagged look. He could just make out something smooth and round partially blocking the hole in the centre . . .

Sully nearly dropped the camera. 'Holy crap. Oh, my God.' It was right there, in plain sight. Thousands of people saw it every day.

Hunter's face was suddenly two inches from his. 'You found it. Tell me you found it.'

He held out the camera, his hand trembling. 'Look at the wreath.'

Dom took a few steps back, stopped at the kerb, squinting up. 'The wreath? You mean way up there?'

Hunter lowered the camera, her gaze still raised towards the angel. 'We found it.'

'How are we going to get it, though?' Mandy asked as she took the camera from Hunter.

'I'll get it,' Hunter said. 'Or die trying.'

CHAPTER 21

Sully studied the photo of Nike, Greek goddess of victory, aka *The Angel of Independence,* in the glossy souvenir booklet. Among the many other things Sully had learned in the past hour, he now knew where a shoe company had got its name. Outside the hotel room window vehicles honked and engines rumbled.

When anyone stepped out on to the tower's observation deck, *The Angel* was directly above, reaching out, perched on one foot atop the domed roof of the tower. The observation deck was maybe a dozen feet below that domed roof.

'How far do you think it is from the observation deck to the wreath?' Sully asked. 'Can we buy an extension pole, like the kind painters use, and poke the Gold right out of it?'

Mandy studied the photo over his shoulder. 'The statue is twenty-two feet tall. Plus you have the top section of the tower she's standing on. That's at least another ten feet. I doubt they make extension poles that long.'

No, probably not.

'There's no other way,' Hunter said. 'I have to climb up.'

'But everyone will see you,' Sully said. They kept circling around the same problem. 'You'll get arrested and they'll take away the sphere.'

In the United States there were laws that said if you found a sphere it was your property, unless you did something illegal to get it. They were assuming the laws were the same in Mexico, and by climbing the statue – which was illegal – they'd risk having the Gold confiscated. They didn't dare activate their phones to make sure. If Holliday located them, he could jump in his private jet and be in Mexico City in a few hours.

'As soon as I get the sphere, I toss it down,' Hunter said. 'Somebody catches it and runs like hell before anyone knows what's happening.'

'You drop it a hundred and eighteen feet –' Dom began.

'A hundred and *forty*,' Mandy corrected. 'The *tower* is a hundred and eighteen feet. The statue is another twenty-two.'

'A hundred and *forty* feet,' Dom went on, 'and one of us *catches* it? That's going to be quite a trick. And if we miss, it's going to hit the steps' – Dom ran a finger down the twenty-five or thirty steps that ringed the base of the monument – 'and bounce out into traffic.'

Hunter took a breath, locked her hands behind her neck. 'Then I stash the marble in my pack. I let them arrest me, and hand off the pack to one of you as they're taking me away.'

'Will they let you do that?' Mandy asked.

No one answered. They knew a great deal about *El Ángel de la Independencia* now, but not much about Mexico City police procedures.

'There's no other way,' Hunter said. 'The tower's locked at

night. We have to do it during the day.'

'You can't climb up there. You'll kill yourself,' Sully said, still eyeing the photo of the statue.

'I'm a ninja, remember? I'll tie off on the statue's planted foot, so if I fall I won't fall far.'

Assuming the knot held.

'I'll do it,' Mandy said. 'I mess around on the climbing walls at the gym all the time.'

'No, I'll go,' Sully said.

'No!' Hunter's shout startled them. She looked from face to face, her nostrils flared. 'This is what I do. You all go to school, you have jobs, you play sports. I hunt marbles. I've been in tunnels six stories under New York City. I've climbed the rafters over factory floors. I dived into six hundred water towers in the middle of winter.' She chopped her palm with the edge of her other hand. 'This is what I do.'

Sully hated the idea, absolutely hated it, but he knew Hunter was going to do it whether or not he supported her. Plus, she was right. He'd watched her go down into that mine in Doodletown like it was nothing, and jump from one eight-story-building roof to the next. She had the best chance of pulling this off. He tried to convince himself that if she was tied off the worst that could happen was the police confiscated the Gold, and he and the others would have to bail her out of jail. But he'd learned things rarely went the way you planned.

CHAPTER 22

The metal stairs inside the spire were narrow, pie-shaped wedges, the space dim and claustrophobic. Their guide was a skinny man in his sixties with thick grey eyebrows. Two middle-aged women, both Mexican, were the only other people taking the first run of the day up to the balcony that stood in the shadow of *El Ángel de la Independencia*.

Sully felt light-headed with worry. He and Hunter had made some harrowing climbs up to the water towers of Manhattan, but they were always on ladders. Climbing *El Ángel* would be different.

As if reading his thoughts, Hunter reached back and took his hand.

They were still holding hands when they reached the top and stepped out the door to the balcony that circled the pillar. *El Ángel* loomed above them.

The view was dizzying; the vehicles zooming around the roundabout looked like toys. Buildings and trees and glimpses of wide avenues stretched out below, the horizon framed by mountains.

Sully spotted Mandy looking up at him from the steps of the monument. He hoped if it came down to it she'd stick with the plan: if he and Hunter were arrested, she was supposed to run back to the hotel, where Dom was waiting with the Gold.

Hunter squeezed his hand. 'OK. Here we go.'

Sully kissed her impulsively, hitting the side of her mouth. 'Be careful.'

Since the balcony circled the top of the spire, wherever the guide was, if Hunter was on the opposite side, he couldn't see her.

When Hunter entered the guide's blind spot she reached up without hesitation, gripped the ornamental grillwork set into the spire, and pulled herself three or four feet off the balcony. Sully had worried about how Hunter would navigate the lip on the spire's roof, which jutted out three or four inches, but it barely slowed her. With the toes of her shoes wedged into the grillwork, she reached up and round, gripped *El Ángel*'s ankle and hoisted herself on to the tower roof.

Sully's heart was galloping as Hunter pulled the cord out of her pack, tied one end round the statue's ankle and cinched Sully's belt around her waist. The other end of the cord was already tied securely to the belt.

She reached into a fold in the statue's billowing skirt and began to climb.

There were no good footholds low on the statue; Hunter's foot slipped twice before she gave up and pulled herself up with her arms, like she was doing a chin-up. She managed to hoist her head even with her hands, but there was still nowhere to wedge her feet. Her legs flailed around until she finally swung her left one up so it was level with her hands, and hooked the same crevice.

Hunter lunged for a billowing curve in the skirt three feet higher. She got her fingertips round it. A growl of fear and effort escaped her as she pulled herself up, finally managing to get her right foot into a crevice.

There was a cry of surprise. One of their fellow tourists, a small Mexican woman, was staring at Hunter, one hand covering her mouth.

'¡Baja¡' the woman shrieked at Hunter. '*Senorita, baja.*'

Hunter was clinging to the side of *El Ángel*'s skirt from narrow pleats, fifteen feet above Sully's head. She ignored the woman's shouts as she shimmied up *El Ángel*'s bare waist, her body pressed tightly against the slick gold.

'No!' This time the shout came from their guide. 'No! ¡Baja ya!'

Hunter reached out and grabbed *El Ángel*'s bare breast. At another time it might have been a comical sight, but under the circumstances Sully was just grateful the breast was there. The guide went on shouting as Hunter found footholds on the statue's waistline, then reached and caught its outstretched arm with her left hand. She let go of the breast and gripped the arm with her right hand as well, then pushed off with both feet and swung her legs up so she was sitting on *El Ángel*'s arm.

Her breath coming in a tight squeal that Sully could hear from thirty feet below, Hunter shimmied out on to the arm, wobbling as it grew ever thinner, until she couldn't go any further. The sphere was three feet away. Hunter leaned forward until she was hugging the statue's forearm with one hand, then reached with the other.

Her fingertips brushed the sphere.

She stretched, stretched, leaning forward.

She lunged. As one hand closed around the Gold, she lost her balance and flipped, swinging underneath the arm. She was hanging upside down, her legs still wrapped around the arm, one hand scrabbling for purchase while she clutched the Gold sphere in the other.

'*Hunter!*' Sully screamed. 'Just drop it! Hang on!'

Hunter lost her grip and fell. She plummeted past Sully, past the edge of the balcony.

The rope went taut. He heard her slam into the side of the tower.

Sully sprinted to the rope, grabbed it with both hands, strained to pull her up.

Hands gripped the rope behind him. The guide and the other tourists helped Sully pull until Hunter's outstretched hand rose into view. Gasping, she grabbed the balcony's steel railing. They kept pulling until Hunter came over the top of the railing and dropped to the floor.

Sully knelt beside her. 'Are you hurt?'

'I think my arm is broken.' She was cradling her left arm against her body.

The guide said something in Spanish. He was furious.

Hunter answered, then said to Sully, 'He wants to know why I was vandalizing their statue.'

Sully nodded. The sphere matched the gold of the statue so perfectly the guide still didn't realize what Hunter had been after. The sphere was nowhere in sight. Either she'd dropped it or stashed it in her pack. 'Let's get you to the hospital.' He looked up at the guide. 'Hospital? Ambulance?'

Two police officers appeared in the doorway to the stairs, breathless from the climb. The guide went to them, speaking quickly, gesturing at Hunter.

'Can you stand?'

'Yeah,' Hunter said. 'Help me up, and immediately take my pack from me, like you're doing it because of my arm.'

Sully did as she said, gently sliding the pack off her shoulders and draping it over his own as the officers came over. One of them, a stout woman, asked Hunter something.

'Come on,' Hunter said. 'She wants us to go down.'

'Are they letting us go?'

'I'm being arrested, but first they're taking me to the hospital.'

There was only room for one person at a time on the stairs, so a police officer went first, then Sully, in case Hunter fell. Hunter walked gingerly, and seemed woozy, but she made it down on her own.

A crowd had gathered at the bottom. Sully wrapped a hand round Hunter's waist and helped her towards a police car. He'd been expecting an ambulance, but maybe she didn't seem hurt enough for an ambulance.

'*Perdóname, Señora Agente.*'

The police officer who was walking beside Hunter turned towards the voice. Sully glanced over his shoulder.

His knees almost buckled.

Alex Holliday was approaching the officer, accompanied by two men in dark suits.

'Damn it,' Hunter hissed. 'How the hell did he find us?'

Hunter listened carefully as Holliday spoke to the officer in rapid Spanish.

'*No,*' Hunter nearly shouted. She stepped towards Holliday and the officer, shaking her head and protesting.

'What is it?' Sully asked, staying close.

Hunter turned to Sully. 'He's telling them I'm wanted in the United States on felony drug charges. That I'm probably high on meth right now.' She turned and shouted something at the police officer.

Holliday reached out to shake the officer's hand, and slipped something into it as he did. The gesture was subtle, but Sully caught it. The police officer smiled as if she and Holliday were old friends. She nodded, said something.

Sully could see this wasn't going their way. 'Run,' he said to Hunter under his breath.

He'd barely got the words out when Hunter took off, right into traffic. Brakes squealed and horns blared as Sully followed. A van coming right at him veered, sideswiping a tiny car.

Shouts rose from behind Sully as he reached the kerb on the far side of the roundabout. He was gaining on Hunter, who was cradling her arm against her stomach. They had to get out of sight in a hurry – Holliday had burned Seafoam Green spheres, so he was fast.

Hunter had evidently reached the same conclusion. She headed right for their hotel, bolted through the automatic doors. She and Sully didn't slow down until they were on the second floor, pounding on the door to their room.

When Mandy flung the door open, Sully headed straight to the window.

One of Holliday's bodyguards was standing a dozen feet from the hotel entrance, his hands clasped in front of him.

'What happened? Did you get it?' Dom asked.

'Yes,' Hunter said. 'But Holliday found us.' Her breathing was ragged, her eyes closed.

Sully still wasn't sure exactly what it meant that Holliday had located them, only that it was bad. Did he plan to kill them and take the spheres for himself, or just hold them hostage until they agreed to sell the spheres to him? Sully knew Holliday was a criminal who'd cheat kids and burn down competitors' stores, but was he a killer?

'Is he out there?' Dom joined Sully at the window.

Sully pointed. 'That's one of his bodyguards.' The man was tall and wiry, not one of the human bowling balls who had beaten them outside the Hammerstein. Sully would bet this guy was a lot more dangerous, maybe ex-Special Forces, pumped up with Seafoam Green and Chocolate spheres.

'Call the police,' Dom said.

Hunter sat on the edge of a bed. 'And tell them what? That Holliday is trying to steal our spheres? If we do, they'll arrest me and confiscate *both* Golds.'

Sully nodded. That seemed likely. He got his phone and battery off the nightstand and inserted the battery. 'We can use our phones now.' He was tempted to call his mom, but didn't want to scare her. Maybe he should call his father and ask for advice?

What did his father know about the situation they were in? Nothing. He'd just lay out all the things Sully had done wrong.

Sully's phone rang. It was a number he didn't recognize, with a New York area code. He answered it.

'David, *buddy*,' Holliday said. 'Come on, what are you

doing, making me fly all the way down here? Let me give you a free tip: don't bother disabling your GPS once someone IDs your vehicle. They can still track you visually via satellite.' He sounded jubilant.

He'd been following them the whole time.

'Good to know,' Sully said. 'Now why don't you go find your own marbles with your army of hunters and your computerized database?'

'Put him on speaker,' Mandy said.

Sully activated the speaker function so the others could hear.

'I will, I will. Just as soon as we take care of business. I'll give you fifty thousand – cash – for the pair.'

'Unbelievable,' Sully said. 'You are just a criminal, aren't you? All that crap about your integrity, your business model.'

Holliday spoke slowly and carefully. 'See? This is exactly your problem. You don't understand the rules of the game. You think Jin Bao wouldn't be outside your hotel if he knew what you'd found?'

Sully didn't answer.

'Let me tell you a little story. I'll be quick, I promise. Back during the Great Depression, unemployed men would gather outside factories looking for work. If a crew boss needed, say, ten workers that day, he'd throw ten apples into the crowd. The ten men who brought him those apples got the work. Not the ten men who *caught* the apples – the ten who brought them up. The crew boss figured the men who were both quick and smart enough to catch the apples, and tough enough to keep them, would make the best workers.'

Dom cursed under his breath. Hunter stood, still

cradling her arm, and went to the window.

'I have to hand it to you, Sully,' Holliday went on. 'You're a talented hunter. You have a gift. I saw that in you – that's why I offered you a job. The thing is, you're smart enough to catch the apples, but you're not tough enough to hold on to them.'

He sounded like Sully's dad, who beat on kids, then justified it by saying you needed to toughen up.

'We want a hundred million,' Hunter said. 'Each.'

'Yeah, that's not going to happen,' Holliday said. 'Again, Hunter, you don't have a good grasp of the rules of this game. You have no leverage in this negotiation.'

'You're not getting them,' Sully said. 'We'll call the police and let the Mexican government have them before we give them to you.'

'How can I say this nicely?' Holliday said. 'I can't, so I'll just say it: if you call the police, three highly trained operatives will kick down your door, take the spheres from you and hurt you in the process.'

'You don't even know what room we're in, dipstick,' Dom said, nice and loud.

'Hi there, Dom. Give me three minutes. One of my guys is bribing a maid as we speak.'

Hunter spun from the window, looked at Sully. 'Hang up.' She grabbed her pack and Dom's with her uninjured hand and headed into the bathroom.

Sully and the others followed. Once they were inside, Hunter turned on the shower. She took out both Golds, leaned against the sink.

'We're not leaving here with these. We all know that,

right? They have guns, and money, and power.' She raised the Gold in her right hand. 'All we have are these.'

'So we negotiate the best deal we can get,' Dom said, crossing his arms. 'We tell him ten million, cash, and we don't budge.'

Hunter shook her head. 'Even if Holliday gave us that kind of money, he wouldn't let us leave Mexico with it. As soon as we were on the road, his men would take it back.'

'We don't stick the cash in our trunk. We take it straight to a bank,' Dom said.

Sully doubted Holliday was going to hand them ten million dollars to begin with. It wasn't that ten million meant that much to him, but if he gave it to them he couldn't claim total victory.

This was payback for Sully's lawsuit after the Cherry Red fiasco, for turning down Holliday's job offer and insulting him in the process. Holliday wanted the Golds, but he also wanted to rub Sully's nose in it.

'We can still beat him,' Hunter said.

'How do we do that, exactly?' Mandy asked.

Hunter looked right at Sully. 'By burning them.'

It took a moment for Sully to grasp what Hunter had just said. *Burn* them? Whatever ability the Golds gave, you couldn't divvy it up four ways.

'No!' Dom shouted.

'Keep your voice down,' Hunter said.

'If we burn them, one of us gets all the benefit,' Sully said. 'That wouldn't be fair.'

'We draw straws or something,' Hunter said. 'What's unfair about that?'

'I don't *want* to burn them,' Mandy said. 'Was I not clear on that point? What if they do make you immortal, and you can never, ever die, no matter what? Or what if they make you grow six extra limbs?'

'It's not something bad,' Hunter said. 'It's never something bad.'

Mandy threw her hands in the air. 'Well, excuse me if I'm not willing to bet my life on that.'

'Fine. If you win, you can choose who burns them.' Still holding the Gold, Hunter rested her left arm against her side.

'I don't want to do it, either,' Dom said. 'I want the money. That's the deal we made.' He looked at Sully. 'Right? That was the deal.'

'I know,' Sully said. 'It was. I'm just not sure how we do that now.'

Dom pointed at Sully. 'What if we call Jin Bao, or one of the other big dealers? We make a deal on the phone, and *he* can fly down and handle Holliday.'

'How long do you think Holliday is going to wait out there?' Hunter asked.

Dom turned on her. 'If you burn them, you're stealing from us, and you're no better than he is.'

'Hang on,' Sully said, raising his hands. 'Everyone slow down. We're just talking. Everything should be on the table; that doesn't mean we've decided anything.'

He turned to Hunter.

Searching his eyes, she held out the Golds. 'You do it. Whatever gift they give, I'm giving it to you.'

'Hey,' Mandy said, 'who put you in charge? You own exactly thirty-five per cent of one of those.'

'Sully' — Dom pointed at the Golds — 'I own a piece of one of those too, and I'm saying right now I'm not OK with anyone burning my share.'

'What's your better idea, again?' Hunter asked.

Lips pressed tight, Dom glared at Hunter.

'Right.' She turned back to Sully. 'Do you want them or not?'

Sully's phone rang.

'Go ahead.' She pressed them into his hands, ignoring the phone.

Sully nudged the Golds away. 'We have to find another way.'

'*There is no other way.*' Hunter narrowed her eyes. 'Let's show him. Let's hold on to that apple harder than Holliday ever would have guessed.'

Sully's phone went on ringing. His head was spinning; he needed time to think. Was this really their only option? Could they overpower Holliday and run for it, assuming there were no armed bodyguards out there with him? Could they cut a deal with the Mexican government, negotiate a finder's fee and turn the Golds over?

'Wait,' Mandy said. 'What if we just threaten to burn them? One of us holds them close to our temples, and we use that leverage to walk out, or demand a million dollars each.'

'What stops Holliday's bodyguard from shooting whoever's holding the Golds? It's hard to burn marbles after you've been shot,' Hunter said.

There was a crash outside the bathroom. The door to their room had been kicked in.

'Take them,' Hunter said to Sully.

'*Sully,*' Dom said, his tone a warning.

Sully looked at Hunter, then down at the Golds. Burn them? Him? Whatever they did, he knew it would be monumental; it would change him and his life forever. Was that what he wanted?

The truth was, Sully had never dreamed of being extraordinary by burning spheres. It seemed like a cheat, just like stepping on someone else's throat to get where you wanted to go was a cheat.

'I don't want them.'

Hunter lifted the spheres towards her head, then paused, looking at Sully, waiting for his OK.

'Hunter, I'm warning you.' Dom stepped towards her.

Dom and Mandy were right – it wasn't Hunter's decision to make. But there was no time for democracy. There was no time for another plan. Sully nodded. 'Do it.'

Grunting from the pain of keeping her injured arm raised, Hunter touched the Golds to her temples.

'*No.*' Dom dived at Hunter. Sully reached out to block him, but Dom barrelled past and knocked the spheres out of Hunter's hands. Hunter screamed in pain, clutched her left arm as the spheres hit the floor. Sully grabbed Dom's arm and yanked him away from Hunter just as the bathroom door crashed open, knocking Sully against the sink.

The tall, lean bodyguard stood in the doorway, aiming a handgun at them. Everyone froze.

Raising his hands over his head, Sully knelt. Very slowly, he picked up the fallen Golds.

The colour was dimming.

Sully gaped at Hunter, who had sunk to the floor, and tried

to wrap his mind around what she'd just done.

Still holding her arm, Hunter looked up at Dom. 'I'm sorry. I'll find a way to make it up to you. I promise.'

Holliday appeared behind the man with the gun. He stared at the spheres in Sully's hands.

Sully underhanded them through the doorway; they thumped to the carpet, rolled past the two men. 'They're all yours.'

Holliday watched the Golds roll to a stop. He looked up at Sully. 'You're dead. All of you.'

A jangle of terror ran through Sully. 'A hundred witnesses saw you chase us here.'

Holliday pointed at him. 'Shut up. Don't say another word. Not another word.'

Hunter inhaled sharply. Her eyes went wide. 'Oh, God. What —' She glanced around, her head snapping left, right, up, in quick succession.

'Hunter?' Sully knelt beside her.

'What's happening?' she breathed. She covered her face with both hands.

Holliday was standing over them, one shiny black shoe inches from Sully's knee. He grunted. 'Maybe she did me a favour.'

Hunter screamed from deep in her throat. It was the sound of someone in hell.

Sully touched her face. 'I'm here.' There was something wrong with her skin. It had a strange pallor.

Mandy leaned in close. 'Jesus. What's wrong with her?'

It wasn't just her skin: her hair was also lighter. Her eyes were almost glowing.

'We have to get her to a hospital,' Mandy said.

'No,' Hunter said. 'Take me home. I want to go home.'

'Jesus. That's one messed-up girl.' Holliday bent, studied Hunter up close. Sully wanted to shove him away, but the bodyguard with the gun was watching from the doorway.

He flinched as Holliday patted his back. 'Like they say, you broke it, you bought it. Good luck. I'll be in touch.'

As Holliday stalked off, Hunter clutched Sully's wrist. 'I want to go home.' She clenched her eyes. 'Oh, God, make it stop.'

As gingerly as possible, Sully reached under Hunter's arms. 'Dom, get her legs.'

Dom slid one arm under her legs, then slipped his other arm around her back. 'Just let me have her. We'll move faster if I take her.'

Sully handed Hunter off.

As he did, he saw her skin was worse. It was bad enough now that he could see what was happening.

Hunter's skin was turning gold.

CHAPTER 23

Dom drove like a bat out of hell. The sound of the engine filled the car as they flew past vehicles on Route 10, the burnt Gold spheres rolling around on the floor at Sully's feet whenever Dom changed lanes.

'No. *Get away from me*,' Hunter said, pushing at the air with her right hand.

Sully kept holding her. He didn't know what else to do. She wasn't sick, didn't have a fever. It was like she was lost in another world and couldn't get out.

'What is that? *What is that?* No.' She pressed her hands over her ears. If her left arm still hurt, she wasn't showing it.

Mandy held a water bottle out to Sully. 'See if you can get her to drink.'

Sully took the bottle, put it to Hunter's lips. She knocked it out of his hands, sending the water spraying.

Her skin glistened. It wasn't as bright and lustrous as the Gold spheres had been, but the rich hue seemed to grow sharper by the minute.

The spheres were supposed to do something. They were

supposed to give Hunter some wonderful ability or shower gifts upon the world. All the Golds had done was drive Hunter crazy.

'Assuming the car isn't impounded for us speeding, it's going to take about thirty-two hours to get home,' Mandy said. 'Maybe we should stop halfway.'

'If we take four-hour shifts, how many shifts is that each?' Sully asked.

Mandy looked up, calculating. 'Three, more or less.'

Sully shook his head. 'We can do that. Let's drive straight through.'

Mandy nodded. She studied Hunter. 'What if it gave her the ability to read minds? What if she's in a thousand people's heads at once, and it's too much?'

That was a possibility. Hunter seemed completely over-whelmed.

'I can't see this,' Hunter muttered. 'It's impossible. Impossible.'

Hunter was going to have to stay with Sully and his mom when they got back. He'd better let Mom know. He pulled out his phone.

'Did you find it?' Mom asked as soon as Sully said hello.

'We did, Mom. But there's a problem.' He told her about Holliday showing up, had to talk fast to convince her not to call the police immediately when he told her about the guy with the gun.

'Mom, listen. Listen to me. Holliday didn't get the Golds. Hunter burned them.'

The line went stone-cold silent. Then Mom whispered, 'Oh, my God. What do they do?'

Sully looked at Hunter. Her head lolled to the left, then flopped to the right as she stared, terrified, at nothing. 'She's turning gold, Mom. Her skin, her hair, it's all gold.'

'I don't understand. How do you turn gold? What does that mean?'

Sully took a deep breath. 'You'll understand when you see her.'

When Dom pulled into the Garden Apartments car park, Sully felt such relief his chest hitched like he was about to cry. It was three a.m., but Mom came bursting out of the building door before Dom could turn off the ignition.

Mom opened Sully's door. 'Let me see her.' She reached in, pulled back the hood of Hunter's coat, and gasped. 'Oh, my God.' She lifted Hunter's chin so she could see her face.

Hunter's skin shone as brightly as the Gold spheres had. Sully was sure if he could hold a pre-burnt Gold to her face, the colours would match perfectly.

Hunter let out a scream that sank into Sully's bones. Her golden eyes flew open, but she was seeing something entirely different from the rest of them. Something terrible. Something unspeakable.

'She needs to go to a hospital,' Mom said.

Sully eased out of his seat while keeping Hunter upright. 'One look at her and they'll call the police, and the police are going to call the FBI or the CIA.'

Dom came around the car and lifted Hunter.

'She's not sick,' Sully said. 'The Golds are doing something to her. A doctor isn't going to be able to stop it.'

He and his mom followed Dom towards the door. Mandy ran ahead to open it.

'Then we should call the FBI,' Mom said. 'They'll be able to get her to someone who can help her.'

'No one even understands what these things *are*.' Sully gave his mom a pointed look. 'If they take Hunter away, she's never coming back. You understand that, right? They won't ever let her go.'

Mom shook her head. 'I shouldn't have let you go. I'm a terrible mother. I'm the worst mother in the world.'

'No you're not, Mom. This is Holliday's fault. Everything would have worked out fine if it wasn't for him.'

CHAPTER 24

When Sully woke, Hunter was standing pressed against his bedroom wall, perfectly still, her head against the Kate Upton poster. His mom's white penguin pyjamas hung from her, way too big.

'Get it away from me.' Her eyes were wide, her dark-gold lips trembling.

Sully slipped out of bed.

'No. Stay away. It'll get you.' She looked to her left, then back at him. 'Don't you *see it*?'

'Hunter, there's nothing there. We're alone.'

'Oh, no, we're not.' She laughed, panicked, her throat tight. 'Oh, no, we're not alone.'

She'd gone crazy. Maybe the Gold was supposed to do something else, but it had been too much. It had driven her crazy.

'What do you see?' Sully asked.

'It's like . . .' She looked to her left again. 'I can't describe it. Can't you see it?'

Mom appeared in the doorway. 'How is she? How are you, Hunter?'

'Wait a minute,' Hunter said. 'I know why you can't see it. It's not out there. It's *inside* me.' She clutched her chest. 'Oh, God, get it out of me.'

Mom stepped close to Hunter, brushed her cheek with the backs of her fingers. 'What's inside you, sweetheart?'

'I don't know. Get it out. Please get it out.'

Mom took Hunter's hand and tried to lead her to the bed, but Hunter pulled free. 'I can feel it moving around. Oh, God, it's trying to talk to me, but it has no mouth.'

CHAPTER 25

Sully held the spoonful of chicken noodle soup to Hunter's lips. 'Hunter, you have to help me. If you don't eat, we'll have to take you to a hospital. We won't have a choice.'

Her eyes a thousand miles away, Hunter opened her mouth ever so slightly. Relieved, Sully slipped the spoon into her mouth, which closed around it. 'There you go. Good girl.'

Sully couldn't take his eyes off Hunter's skin. It shone, reflecting the kitchen's overhead light. She was terrifying and breathtaking. *El Ángel* come to life.

Her arm seemed better. Either she'd only bruised it or the Golds had healed it.

'I think I want to die,' Hunter whispered. 'If I decide for sure, will you help me?'

Sully slipped another spoonful of soup into her mouth, fighting against the despair threatening to swallow him.

'We'll get through this,' he said. 'I love you, you know?' His own words startled him. He'd never said that to anyone besides his mom.

Hunter's eyes focused on him. 'You do?' She nodded.

'That's nice. No one's loved me in a long time.' She sounded like a little girl, the way she said it.

Sully kissed the side of her head. 'Whatever this is, fight it, OK? Don't let it beat you. You're a ninja.'

'Yeah,' Hunter whispered, as if that was the best idea she'd ever heard. 'I am a ninja.'

She was the only one who'd had the courage to burn the Golds. Maybe living on a razor's edge her whole life, she was the only one desperate enough for the sort of salvation you could only find in spheres. Sully suspected it had never been about money for her. It had always been about the spheres themselves.

CHAPTER 26

When Hunter let out a tight shriek, Sully realized he'd dozed off on the couch. He checked the clock: 3:22 a.m. Hunter was sitting on the floor, rocking, one hand over her eyes.

'I don't want to see any more colours. Anything else. Show me anything else.'

Looking bleary-eyed, Mom came out of her room in a bathrobe. 'Why don't you sleep for a couple of hours?'

Sully desperately wanted to take his mom up on the offer, but she'd been up with Hunter most of the night before.

They could really use some help, but that would mean Dom or Mandy, and it was possible Dom's dad would never let him leave the house again, except to go to school. Sully had missed the entire week; he refused to leave Hunter for a minute, and Mom hadn't once suggested he should.

Mandy's parents had no idea about any of what had happened. They still thought she'd spent those three days at Virginia Tech. Now she was back at school.

Hunter inhaled sharply. She stood, looked around for a moment, then disappeared into Sully's room. Sully and Mom watched the doorway until she reappeared, carrying two Army Green spheres, a couple of commons that were just about the end of Sully's stock. She returned to her spot on the couch, drew up her bare legs, and rested the spheres on her knees.

'How are you doing, sweetie?' Mom asked.

Hunter stared at the spheres.

'She doesn't need a doctor,' Mom said. 'She needs a psychologist. She reminds me of a soldier coming home from combat.'

'They're like sperm and egg,' Hunter said.

'What?' Sully asked.

Hunter gestured at the spheres. 'They come together inside you.'

Just the thought gave Sully a crawling feeling. 'You're saying they give birth to something inside the person who burns them? I've never heard that idea before.'

Hunter turned her luminous gaze on Sully. 'It just popped into my head.' She looked at the ceiling. 'You know what?'

'What?' Sully asked.

Still staring at the ceiling, Hunter stood. Sully and Mom followed as she dragged a chair from the kitchen and set it in the little hall that connected Sully's room and the bathroom. She climbed on to the chair and pushed away the panel that covered the crawl space in the ceiling. Hoisting herself up, she disappeared.

There was nothing up there. Sully had checked it out once, but the space was just a latticework of two-by-fours over dusty insulation.

'Hunter,' he called, 'what are you doing?'

She didn't answer.

'If we took her to a psychologist, do you think we could get him or her to promise to keep quiet?' Sully asked.

Hunter reappeared before Mom could answer. She dropped on to the chair and hopped down, holding a Ruby Red. White, even teeth. Rarity level two.

'Where did you get that?' Sully asked.

Hunter pointed up. 'Under the insulation. In the corner.'

Sully peered into the dark. 'How did you know it was there?'

Hunter followed his gaze. 'I don't know.'

Sully's heart began to beat slow and hard. She'd found the sphere as if she knew right where it was, like she had built-in sphere-detecting radar.

'Oh, my God,' Mom whispered.

'Do you think you could find another like that?' Sully asked.

Hunter frowned in concentration. 'There's a Lemon Yellow not far away.' She pointed. 'That way.'

'Oh, my God,' Mom repeated, pressing a palm to her forehead.

Sully fetched Hunter's coat, pulled the hood up to hide her face. 'Let's see if we can find it.'

He had no doubt they would. The mystery was solved. Gold: the ability to locate other spheres. In a million years he wouldn't have guessed.

Hunter gasped.

'What is it?' Mom asked.

'I know where there's another. No – two more.'

Sully grabbed his coat.

They should have brought a bag. Sully's arms were so full of spheres he couldn't open the building door. Giggling, he set them on the stoop as gently as he could. A Lavender rolled into the bushes. He would get it later.

Inside, they piled the spheres on the couch. Mom was shaking. 'My God, this is better than if you'd sold the Golds. Except for what it's done to Hunter.'

Hunter looked like she was about to throw up.

Sully touched her back. 'How are you feeling?'

'I'm here and I'm not,' she said. She pulled off her parka, swept her brilliant hair away from her face. 'I don't know how to describe it. I get these flashes. Shafts of colour that make the strangest sounds. Then I'm moving very fast, going on and on. Sometimes I think something and it makes no sense. It's not even words.'

Mom was listening intently.

'You seem to be a little better, though,' Sully said.

Hunter shook her head. 'I don't think I'm getting better. I'm getting used to it.' She pressed a palm to her chest, tilted her head, as if straining to hear something. 'I can feel it inside me. I can hear it.'

'What?' Sully asked.

'*It*. The Gold. It's inside me, and it's never coming out, because it can't.' She pressed both hands to her face. 'It can't live on its own. That's why they always give us something: they're paying rent.'

Mom sat next to Hunter. She'd gone very pale.

'You're saying *everyone* who's burned spheres has

something living inside them?' Mom asked.

'It's beautiful, in a way. If you think about it just right, at just the right angle, it's beautiful.'

Sully wasn't sure he could find that angle. He wasn't even sure he believed Hunter. Then again, there was no denying the dazzling hue of her skin. It was as if she'd become half Hunter, half sphere. Or half alien.

The idea made his skin prickle.

Hunter drew her legs up and hugged them. 'It wants me to see this as a beautiful thing, but I'm not sure I can.'

Sully looked at his mom, trying to sense what she was making of this. Was Hunter delusional? Or was she communicating with whatever had been born inside her when she burned the Golds?

'Is that how you know where spheres are hiding?' Mom asked. 'Because it's telling you?'

Hunter considered. 'More like it's *showing* me.' She picked up one of the spheres they'd found – an Auburn. 'Can we get Dom and Mandy over here? I want them to see I didn't cheat them.'

CHAPTER 27

Sully parked Mom's station wagon in the Yonkers High car park and ducked down so no one passing by would see he wasn't getting out of the car. He watched for Dom's Camry.

This would be his fifth consecutive day of missing school. He wasn't exactly a stellar student; it was going to be hard to catch up when he went back on Monday. *If* he went back on Monday.

Drop out. Holliday's words echoed in his head. *Those who can't do, learn*. Maybe it wasn't the worst advice in the world, given the situation. He and Hunter could spend all day harvesting spheres.

It was still hard to grasp that there was no need to hunt, that they could just drive around and pluck the spheres from their hiding places.

Mom would not be happy if he dropped out, though. Maybe if he had Dom's parents it would be easier to ignore what they wanted, but Sully had a wonderful mom, and he hated to repay her by dropping out when trying hard in school was one of the few things she asked of him.

Dom's Camry pulled into the lot, a plume of black smoke in its wake. It was amazing the thing had taken them to Mexico and back.

Watching in his side mirror, Sully waited for Dom to draw close, then rolled down the window. '*Dom.*'

Dom looked his way. Sully motioned at the passenger door. 'Get in.'

As Dom slid in, he gave Sully a dark look. 'We've been friends our whole lives. You meet a girl, and suddenly you're on her side.' He squeezed his eyes closed, lifted his hand and made a fist. 'Millions of dollars, Sully. Millions. And it's all gone. I can't just forget that and move on like it never happened.'

Sully pulled out and headed towards Rockland Avenue. 'I didn't take her side because I like her. I took it because she was *right*. Holliday and his goon were coming through the door. Holliday would have taken them, and we would have had nothing. I wasn't going to let that happen again.'

Dom sprang forward in his seat. '*We ended up with nothing anyway*. Unless you count Hunter having gold skin and going crazy as something. Besides, you took her side *before* they broke down the door.'

'No I didn't. I said we needed to keep our options open. You were the one who was saying Hunter's idea was off the table.'

'That's because it was a bad idea.'

Sully pulled up to a stop sign. He looked at Dom and smiled.

'What?' Dom said. 'You think there's something funny about this?'

'Yes. But I know something you don't.'

Dom studied his face. 'What's that?'

Sully drove on. 'You'll see. I promised not to tell. Call Mandy. See if she can sneak out of school.'

Sully turned the knob, motioned for Dom to go first, then pushed the door open.

There were spheres all over. Almost a hundred of them. Mom hoisted a milk crate of Lemon Yellows and Lavenders. She was sorting them by colour.

'Holy –' Dom said, taking it in. 'Where did you get these?'

Hunter appeared from the kitchen carrying a glass of Coke. 'I told you I'd make it up to you.'

'I don't understand. Where did they come from?'

'Hunter knows exactly where spheres are hidden. That's the power the Golds gave her,' Sully said.

Dom clutched his heart. 'You're serious? Oh, my God.' He ran to Hunter and hugged her, then ran to Sully and hugged him.

'Where's mine?' Mom asked, opening her arms. Dom ran over and hugged her as well.

'Except that's not exactly the power they gave me,' Hunter said. 'At least, that's not what it's meant to be. It's a side effect.'

'A side effect?' Dom looked around and spotted their best finds lined up on the couch: Sky Blue (sense of humour, rarity four); Indigo (enhanced eyesight, rarity five); Periwinkle (good with numbers, rarity six); and good old Plum (erase memories, rarity six). 'That's some side effect. What's the main effect?'

'Mine is talking to me,' Hunter said.

'Your *what* is talking to you?'

223

Hunter shrugged. 'Whatever they are. My alien, I guess.'

Dom looked sceptical. 'What's it saying?'

She took a sip of Coke. Her hands were shaking. 'I'm still trying to figure that out, but I'm pretty sure it's telling me I need to find the other Midnight Blue.'

'There are only two?' Sully asked.

Hunter nodded. 'Two Midnight Blues. Two Golds.'

That's what Sully had figured. Now he knew for sure.

'You know where it is?' Mom asked.

Hunter nodded. 'It wants me to burn the Midnight Blues. I don't know how I can do that, since Holliday has the other one. And, anyway, I don't think I want to.' She closed her eyes, swallowed. 'But it says if I do, something wonderful will happen. And not just for us.'

It felt like something was crawling down Sully's back. He was beginning to think they were in way over their heads.

'Hunter, I'm scared,' Mom said, echoing his unease. 'I think it's time we tell the authorities what happened.'

'That would be a mistake,' Hunter said.

'Why? Why would it be a mistake?' Mom asked.

Hunter shrugged. 'I'm just telling you what it said.'

Mom froze. 'It can hear me?'

'I guess so. Or maybe it's hearing me think about what you said.'

There was a knock on the door, which Sully had left open. Mandy was standing in the doorway, her hand still raised, gaping at the spheres all over the living room.

Sully motioned her in, turned back to Hunter. 'Do you know what the wonderful thing is? Is it a third wave?'

She looked towards the ceiling, her lips moving

silently. 'Yes. But these will be bigger.'

Mandy was looking from Hunter to Sully. 'What's going on?'

'Well, let's see,' Dom said, finger to his lips. 'How do I summarize this? Hunter says she's talking to the alien inside her. It told her where the other Midnight Blue is, and says if she burns the Midnight Blues something wonderful will happen.'

Mandy absorbed this. 'The *alien* inside her?'

'That's what she said.'

'Do you believe her?'

Dom looked slightly stunned. 'Do I believe something is talking to her?' He shrugged. 'She turned gold. She can find marbles. I figure that earns her the benefit of the doubt.'

'No, I mean, after what happened to her when she burned the Golds, do you believe something wonderful will happen if she burns the Midnight Blues?'

'It doesn't matter,' Sully said. 'Holliday would never give us the Midnight Blue, so we'll never know unless we find the other and sell it to him so he can burn them.'

'Holliday can't burn them,' Hunter said. 'I'm the only one who can burn them.'

Mom headed towards the kitchen. 'That's it. I'm calling the authorities.'

'Whoa, hang on, Mrs Sullivan,' Dom said.

Sully beat her to her phone, which was sitting on the counter.

Mom looked like she was going to cry. She held out her hand for the phone. 'It's too big, Sully. It's too serious.'

'We're not getting both Midnight Blues, so nothing is going

to happen,' Sully said. 'Except we're going to find a buttload of spheres, and we're all going to be rich. Think about it: if they take Hunter away, no more spheres.'

'Do I get a say in this?' Hunter padded into the kitchen in her socks.

'Of course.' Sully slid an arm round her waist.

Hunter fixed Sully's mom with her luminous gaze. 'Please don't call anyone. We're the ones who found the Golds, so we're the ones who get to use them. Not Holliday. Not the government. That's how it's supposed to be. That's the rule.'

'It sounds to me like the rules are changing.' Mandy was still in the living room, hands on her hips. 'Since when can only one person burn a pair of spheres? I don't like this.'

Looking pained, Mom turned to Hunter. 'Just don't do anything without asking me first, OK?'

'Sure,' Hunter said. 'You got it.'

Dom held up a canvas shopping bag he'd found in the living room. 'Come on, I'm dying here. Let's go find more marbles.'

CHAPTER 28

'Turn right up here,' Hunter called to Dom from the back seat. They turned down a stretch of road lined with cyclone fences and dotted with businesses: a concrete supplier, a cabinet factory, a transmission repair shop.

'Here we go,' she said, pointing at a dirt driveway. The beat-up sign out front read DELL'S AUTO WRECKING AND SCRAP METAL.

'I'll go ask them for something so they don't get suspicious,' Mandy said, heading for the office. It had taken some cajoling from Dom to get her to come. That she would miss out on retrieving a fortune in spheres if she didn't tag along probably helped as well.

'What are you going to ask them for?' Dom asked.

'I don't know. A carburetor for a 1994 Chrysler LeBaron.'

Dom pointed at her. 'Nice car. Convertible or hardtop?'

'What do you think?' she called over her shoulder.

Hunter led them through rows of junk vehicles at a jog, to the back of the football-field-sized space. She stopped by the back fence, in front of a school bus that was more rust brown than yellow, with no back wheels.

'What are you seeing?' Sully asked. 'What do they look like to you?'

'It's like an overlay. I see everything just the way I used to, but I also see what the Gold is seeing: the spheres are colours floating in space; the rest is just wedges of coloured light that twist and angle. It doesn't see the bus at all.'

Trying to imagine what that would be like, Sully followed Hunter through the bus's open door and gripped the bar at the top of the steps.

The seats were piled with engine parts. Hunter went straight for the back, knelt beside the second-to-last seat, and dug around in the springs and padding under the seat.

When she stood, she was holding a Mustard.

High IQ. Rarity nine.

Dom let out a whoop that came straight from his belly. He raced to the back of the bus. 'Can I see it?'

Hunter handed it to him.

'Oh, my God.' Dom lifted the Mustard and kissed it. 'We're so rich. We're so freaking rich.' He threw his arms around Hunter. 'I'm so sorry I doubted you. You were so right, and I was totally wrong.'

Hunter patted Dom's back. 'There's more where that came from.'

Dom spun, tossed the Mustard to Sully. 'Think fast.'

Sully snatched the sphere out of the air. He held it up, admiring it. A Mustard. He never thought he'd hold a Mustard. He stashed it in his pack.

They followed Dom back to the car.

'I don't think we should sell them all,' Hunter said to Sully as Dom headed into the office to fetch Mandy. 'We should burn some.'

Sully was startled by the thought. He'd been thinking purely in terms of making money. 'You said burning spheres meant taking living things inside you. I don't know if I like that idea.' He'd already burned the Teals, though, so it was kind of a moot point. Still, after what had happened to Hunter, the things Mandy had said about there being no free lunch were making more sense.

'I told you – they can survive in our world only if they're inside us, hitching a ride in our brains. They've got a personal stake in us staying healthy and happy.'

'Then why did the Golds make you flip out?'

Bundled in her parka, Hunter raised one golden-bronze eyebrow. 'Because it's in my head, and I can feel it there, and it's really weird. They're using our brains, you know; they're locked right into us. But they mean well, and it's getting easier for me. I'm understanding it more and more.'

How many people had burned spheres without anything bad happening? Something like two billion? Sully had always envied the kids who could speed-read, the track stars who'd burned Seafoam Greens.

'There's another Mustard maybe an hour from here,' Hunter said. 'We can head in that direction, pick up others along the way.'

Burn a pair of Mustards? The idea made Sully's head spin. What were a pair of Mustards worth? But they already had an apartment full of spheres, and more on the way. As many as they wanted.

'You can sense a Mustard from an hour away?' Sully asked,

finally registering what Hunter had said.

'It's getting easier.'

Dom and Mandy were laughing as they exited the office, Mandy carrying what looked to be a carburetor.

'Hey, guys,' Hunter said. 'We're gonna burn some. In a few days me and Sully are gonna take a long trip, and we can use every edge we can get.'

'Are you still talking about finding the Midnight Blue?' Mandy asked.

Hunter nodded.

Mandy put a hand on the Camry's hood. 'Look, if you're going to find it so we can sell it, I'm all for that. But I don't think we should screw around with burning these big ones any more after we almost lost you.' She gestured at Sully's backpack, where the Mustard was. 'We can get all the marbles we want. Why risk screwing it up?'

'I have to agree with Mandy on this one,' Dom said. 'We've got a good thing going here. A *great* thing.'

Hunter held up a finger. 'You're forgetting something. It's not just the four of us in this.' She poked her chest. 'The thing living inside me wants this. Bad. And *it's* showing us where to find these marbles, not me.'

Dom considered this.

'Is it saying it'll stop telling you where to find marbles if you don't go after the Midnight Blue?' Mandy asked.

Hunter shook her head. 'Not exactly. It's begging more than threatening.'

On that note, they climbed into the Camry and headed towards the parkway.

Sully had always known the explanation for the spheres'

appearance had to be something unbelievable, something that would change the world, but not knowing what it was had kept the strangeness from getting too overwhelming.

When the spheres first appeared, it sent shock waves around the world. On TV, experts and pundits had debated where they came from all day. As the years went by, though, and no solid answers to the mystery materialized, everyone started taking the spheres' existence for granted.

Beside him, Hunter reached into the basket of commons they'd picked up along the way, plucked out two Tangerines, and pressed them to her forehead.

Sully was about to ask why she'd just burned a couple of commons that did nothing but let you mimic sounds, when Hunter said, in a near-perfect impression of Dom, 'Hey, there's a Burger King. I could use a burger and fries.'

Everyone laughed except Dom, who said, 'Come on, that doesn't sound anything like me,' as he pulled into the Burger King.

Sully reached over to Hunter's hand resting on the seat and laced his fingers with hers. The contrast of his white fingers and her gold ones was mesmerizing.

'Will you come with me to get the Midnight Blue?' Hunter asked, her voice low. Dom and Mandy were joking around up front.

'Where is it?'

She closed her eyes. 'India, I think.'

'India?' Sully couldn't even find India on a map. 'Are you sure we have to do this? Can we at least put if off for a year or two?'

Hunter shook her head. 'I can't put this off.'

The truth was, the Midnight Blue made Sully uneasy. There was almost no way Holliday was going to let them have the matching Midnight Blue, but what if he did? Mandy was right: burning the Gold had nearly driven Hunter crazy, and now she was going to try to burn the other oversized spheres? It was Russian roulette.

'I'm not sure this is such a good idea,' he said.

Hunter lifted their hands to her chin. 'Please, Yonkers. I'm scared, but I know going after the Midnight Blue is the right thing to do. You said you loved me. Well, I love you, too. I don't want to do this without you. I'm not sure I *can* do it without you.'

Part of him wanted to put the brakes on, but another part wanted to keep going. There was no getting around it: his life was deeply intertwined with the spheres. He'd made a living off them, he'd discovered two of the rarest in existence and now they were about to make him and his friends rich.

He was worried about Hunter, but if she was sure she had to do this, and the spheres wanted it, Sully would stand by her. And them.

'OK. We've gone this far; let's see it through to the end. Or at least as far as we can.'

Hunter grinned, looking relieved. 'Thank you.'

She kissed him. Her words echoed in Sully's ears as he kissed her back.

Well, I love you, too.

Hunter loved him. They were rich. Sully realized he'd never had a moment in his life that was so perfect.

CHAPTER 29

As the limo pulled up to the terminal, Sully was terrified that as soon as Hunter stepped into the line at the security checkpoint, she'd be whisked off by TSA officers. Maybe it wouldn't take that long – maybe the first police officer who saw her would come running, gun in hand.

'Ready?' Sully asked as the driver opened Hunter's door.

She took a deep breath, wiped her sweaty palms on her knees, and nodded. 'Cool and badass, like it ain't no big thing.' She definitely looked the part of a model, in heeled boots, black trousers, and a black leather jacket that reached her knees. Her gold skin was brilliantly offset by the black outfit.

A valet hurried over to take their bags as they climbed out of the limo and headed for first-class check-in. His heart in his throat, Sully forced a big smile and tried to act like there was nothing strange about his gold-skinned companion, like they flew all the time. The truth was, Sully had been on a plane exactly twice, both times to visit his grandma in Florida, and Hunter had never been in an airport in her life. Sully had walked her through the process from check-in to baggage claim, and they'd watched a YouTube video for newbie fliers, so she could pass for someone who flew all the time.

People stared. People whispered. Thanks to the Turquoises he'd burned, Sully could hear what they were whispering:

'Is she someone?'

'Is that, like, a new look? Is it make-up, or spray paint?'

'What's wrong with her?'

Airport security did not come running with guns drawn.

As the moments ticked by, Sully relaxed a little. He took a deep breath, revelled in how wonderful he felt – strong, quick, smart. He could read the departure screen at the far end of the terminal, probably a thousand feet away. He could smell the onions and green peppers from the Western omelette a passing businessman had eaten for breakfast. He felt like a superhero, and had the biceps for the part.

The employee at the check-in counter, a black Caribbean woman, asked what Hunter's colouring was for.

Hunter tsked, as if the whole thing was such a bother. 'I'm doing a commercial. The make-up artist is in New York, the shoot in Calcutta. What are you going to do?'

'Have a good flight,' the woman said, smiling, as she handed over their tickets.

As they turned away, Sully took Hunter's hand. It was clammy with sweat, but you'd never know she was nervous from the way she was speaking and moving. She was a good actress.

And so it went, at the security checkpoint, at the gate, on the flight.

What else were people going to think – that Hunter's skin, hair and eyes were really gold? Who would possibly believe that?

CHAPTER 30

Having spent his life on the outskirts of New York City, Sully thought he knew bad traffic, but Calcutta traffic was like nothing he'd ever imagined. He watched as a periwinkle-and-yellow city bus – with passengers hanging off the sides and sitting on the roof – nudged its way past their hired car. There didn't seem to be any *lanes,* just an endless tangle of vehicles.

Hunter was looking out of the back window. She was dressed in an orange-and-gold sari and veil, her hands covered with gold silk gloves. 'I think we're being followed.'

The words jolted Sully. He scanned the crush of vehicles. 'Where?'

'See the white Volvo?' She pointed.

It was ten or so vehicles behind them. 'How can you tell it's following us in this mess?'

'I'm pretty sure I saw the same car parked outside our hotel last night. I noticed it because white Westerners got out.' One of those little details that you mostly forgot, unless you'd burned a Canary Yellow. Sully peered through the hazy, exhaust-filled air, trying to see the Volvo's occupants. It was a man and a woman, and they did look like white Westerners. Could Holliday's people have possibly tracked them all the way to Calcutta?

Why not? He'd tracked them to Mexico City with no problem.

Sully leaned towards their driver. 'Naman? Can you take us on some side roads, even if it takes a little longer?'

The driver nodded. 'No problem.' Naman had offered his services as a driver/tour guide inside the airport, and to their surprise had been waiting when they stepped out of the hotel the next morning. Sully was grateful to have help from someone who knew the city and spoke the language.

They turned right at the next intersection, on to a slightly less congested street. The sidewalk was lined with tiny plywood stalls covered with tarps, where people seemed to be selling anything and everything. There was rubbish everywhere. A boy sat on the kerb washing in the water from a partially opened hydrant.

'There they go. They're not following.' Hunter was still watching out the back window.

'Maybe they just don't want to be too obvious,' Sully said. 'They could be tracking us by satellite, like in Mexico.'

They parked a block from the temple. As they walked, everyone seemed to be staring. A young boy reached out and grasped at Hunter's sleeve. She yanked her arm away as Naman said something to the boy in rapid Tamil. Or maybe it was Hindi. Sully couldn't believe how many languages were spoken here.

It was a strange place. He doubted he would like it if they were doing it on the cheap, with no guide, having to flag down auto-rickshaws to get from place to place. But with fifty grand on a debit card, the place was awesome. The room they'd stayed in the night before had a freaking waterfall. It had bugged Sully to take the thirty per cent hit required to sell a cache of spheres so quickly (to a private local collector he had contacted through Craigslist), but they'd needed the transaction to be fast and simple, and $850,000 was still a nice payday, even after Dom's and Mandy's cuts.

A woman stepped in front of Hunter, said something to her. Before Naman could get between them, the woman lifted Hunter's veil and let out a sharp cry of surprise. After the airport arrival and sari shopping, Sully wasn't exactly getting *used* to intrusions from strangers, but they didn't surprise him any more.

Naman backed the woman up, repeating the same word, which Sully guessed was 'make-up', but others surged in to fill the void, speaking excitedly and clutching at Hunter's veil.

'Get *off*.' Hunter slapped at their hands, turning her face away.

Naman grasped Hunter's arm. 'Hurry. This way.'

They ran, weaving through the crowd, leaving the excited, high-pitched shouts behind.

There were monkeys swinging in the trees around the temple. The branches of the trees laced together to form a canopy over the temple.

'Quick, I need five hundred rupees.' Naman held out his hand. 'Foreigners aren't allowed inside the temple. We will have to make a contribution to convince them to bend the rules.'

At the current exchange rate of forty-six rupees to the

dollar, five hundred rupees was ten dollars and eighty-seven cents. It gave Sully such pleasure to calculate that in his head. He pulled a crumpled wad of rupees out of his pocket and found a five-hundred-rupee note.

Naman approached the guard at the temple's entrance as Sully and Hunter hung back. Naman couldn't have been more than two years older than them, but he seemed a lot older, probably because he knew the city so well, while they were like lost kids in this foreign place.

Sully dabbed at the sweat already gathering along the back of his neck and glanced at Hunter. 'Are you hot in that?'

'What do you think?'

The rupee exchanged hands. The guard waved them in.

'This way,' Naman said, putting an arm around each of them and corralling them through the gate.

Leaving behind the crowds, they passed under a colourful arch into a courtyard with a fountain in the centre and statues of various gods along stone paths. Monkeys chattered in the trees.

'What kind of trees are those?' Sully asked.

'Banyan,' Naman replied without looking up.

Hunter led them right to the fountain, which was more pond than fountain, with ornamental grasses around the edges and lily pads floating in the water. She gestured to Naman to hang back; he nodded, gave them some space. On the way from the airport he'd asked about Hunter's colouring, but hadn't asked anything about what they were doing in Calcutta.

Hunter unzipped Sully's pack. 'If anyone asks what you're doing, tell them I dropped my earring in the pond. You're trying to find it. Dig where I drop the earring.'

'How deep?' Sully asked.

'Not deep.' She held her hands about six inches apart.

Hunter leaned over the edge of the pond as if admiring a lily, touched the side of her face, and dropped one of the gold elephant-god earrings she'd bought at the hotel gift shop. It plopped into the pond and kicked up a tiny cloud of mud when it reached the bottom.

'My earring,' Hunter said, loudly but not too loudly.

'I got it.' Sully knelt, setting his pack down, and sank his fingers into the mud. It was loamy and gave easily. He scooped up a handful, set it aside without taking his hand out of the water, then dug deeper and set that mud aside.

He was beginning to suspect Hunter had made a mistake, when his fingers brushed that unmistakable smoothness. Scrabbling, he got his hand around the sphere and pulled it free.

'I got it. The earring.' He pulled the mud-covered Midnight Blue from the fountain, stuffed it in the pack, and zipped the pack, his movements lightning fast thanks to the Peaches he'd burned.

Slinging the pack on to his back, he stood and stuffed his hands in his pockets so no one would see the mud on his right hand.

'Shall we go?' he asked, smiling.

'Yes. Let's have lunch. I'm getting hungry,' Hunter said.

They strolled down the temple's concrete steps, back into the chaos of the street.

'Give me the pack,' Hunter said, holding out her hand.

Confused, Sully handed it to her. It blended with his jeans and New York Mets T-shirt much better than her sari.

Holding it by the strap, she headed down the sidewalk.

'Miss Hunter,' Naman said, pointing. 'The car is this way.'

Hunter kept walking.

Sully hurried after her. 'Where are you going?'

'I'm going to get the matching Midnight Blue.' She sounded perfectly confident.

'What are you talking about? It's in New York. And anyway, Holliday's not going to give it to you.'

'I think he might, if we handle this right.'

Then Sully spotted the white Volvo, parked at the kerb. Hunter was heading right towards it.

'*Wait*. What are you doing?'

She turned to face him, walking backwards for a second. 'You'll see.' She stopped beside the Volvo.

The car's tinted window lowered, revealing a woman with black-rimmed hipster glasses in the passenger seat and a bald man in the driver's seat. Both white Westerners.

Hunter dropped the backpack into the woman's lap. 'Once Holliday figures out this is useless to him, tell him to get in touch with us and we'll show him how they work.'

Looking startled, the woman raised the window. The Volvo roared off.

Sully stood watching, dumbfounded.

'That was kind of cool,' Hunter said.

'What did you just do?'

Hunter headed towards Naman, who was waiting outside the temple. 'After Holliday tries everything he can think of to burn them and it all fails, what is he going to do?'

Sully didn't answer. He was still trying to absorb what Hunter had just done. It had happened so quickly.

'He'll come to us. And once I convince him that he'll never be able to burn them, I'll offer to trade him a buttload of marbles for his Midnight Blue.'

Sully stopped walking. Hunter stopped as well.

'You think maybe you could have consulted me first? I mean, we travelled halfway around the world to retrieve that sphere, and you just dumped it in a stranger's lap without even asking my opinion.'

She seemed surprised by his anger. 'The whole plan came to me as we were leaving the temple, when I saw the Volvo parked there. There wasn't time.'

'Yes there was. Chances are they would have been parked outside our hotel when we got there.'

Hunter drew her veil back from her face, serious now. '"Chances are." I didn't want to take that chance.'

People began to stop and stare at Hunter, so she and Sully started walking again. Sully still couldn't believe Hunter had just dropped the Midnight Blue into that woman's lap. Since she'd burned the Golds, Sully had occasionally wondered if Hunter was still completely Hunter, or if he was talking to the alien as well as the girl he knew. Her most recent move convinced him that she was still herself. This was classic Hunter. Head down, charging like a bull, not letting anyone tell her what to do. Not even her friends.

Still, he was shaking. They'd travelled thousands of miles, spent thousands of dollars, and she'd tossed the Midnight Blue away less than three minutes after they found it, without a single thought of Sully.

'Look, I am not your sidekick,' he said. 'I'm not Tonto, or Robin. Stop treating me like I am.'

241

'I'm *not*.' She brushed stray braids out of her face. 'I'm just trying to do the right thing. Do you understand how high the stakes are? If I can get the Midnight Blues from Holliday, there are going to be so many marbles that people like Holliday won't be special any more. There'll be big marbles that do epic things. I don't know what those things are, so don't ask.'

Naman opened the car door for Hunter, looking perplexed.

They drove off in silence. Sully stared out of the window, still fuming. Yes, tons of new spheres that made it so people like Holliday couldn't hog all the best ones sounded good to him, but he wasn't sure he agreed with Hunter's tactics. And what if she was wrong about what the Midnight Blues did?

'I warned you,' Hunter said.

'About what?'

'That I wasn't girlfriend material.'

'This isn't about that, though. It's about our business relationship.'

Hunter shifted to face him. 'No, it isn't. I asked you to trust me and come here so I could do what I needed to do. This trip was never about money and business.'

She had a point. They'd never talked about selling the Midnight Blue if they found it. Sully reached over and took Hunter's hand. 'All I ask is that we talk things out, make these decisions together.'

'I'll try.' She squeezed his hand.

Sully wiped his sweaty forehead with the back of his sleeve. His head was spinning. If Hunter was right about the Midnight Blues, what would the world look like if they managed to get both?

CHAPTER 31

Sully pulled into the car park of Yonkers High in his brand-new red Corvette Stingray, riding right on the bumper of Dom's black one. It was a showboat move, a giant brag badge, but, damn, did it feel great.

Everyone in sight stopped to watch. Kids poured out through the main doors, drawn by the snarling, rumbling din of the car engines. Sully could see Mr Looney, the principal, trying to herd kids back inside while simultaneously watching the Corvettes himself, but kids kept scooting away, wanting to see who the hell was inside those brand-new $65,000 sports cars.

Sully opened his door, stepped out and waited for Dom.

Side by side, they headed for the building.

'Sully, Dom, *what the hell*?' Mike Lea caught up, grinning.

'We found another marble,' Sully said. 'A Mustard.' Eventually it would all come out, but for now that was the story. If anyone knew Hunter could find spheres at will, people would follow them everywhere they went.

'*Again?*' Mike said. 'You lucky, lucky bastard. How much did you get for it?'

'A whole hell of a lot,' Dom said. He was grinning so hard it was like his mouth was inside a set of parentheses. 'Like, a dump truck full of money.'

'So when are you taking all your friends shopping?' Mike asked.

'Soon.' Sully pointed at him. 'That's a promise.' He knew Mike was joking, but Sully had plans to spread the wealth to his Garden Apartments peeps, and eventually much further, to all the little Hunters out there freezing under bridges.

The crowd made way as Sully and Dom passed, some kids calling out questions, like the press shouting to a couple of rock stars. Sully felt like a rock star, which made it a little strange to be heading to Mr Caruso's chem class.

He was so tempted to drop out, maybe hire a tutor and get his GED once things settled down. He wanted to be out hunting. Even more, he wanted to be with Hunter.

But once again: Mom. She wanted this, and he was determined to keep her happy.

Dom, on the other hand, was just here for the glory. He was planning to drop out as soon as he got tired, in his words, of acting like a big shot.

It was pizza day at Yonkers High, so no bag lunch for Sully. He was still a little sweaty from gym class the previous period. It was an unseasonably warm April day, so they'd played a little softball. Sully had hit two long home runs. Mr Gregory had encouraged him to try out for the baseball team. Chem class had made more sense than it ever had before, even though he'd missed two weeks of school. Same with trig.

As Sully set his tray down beside Dom's, his phone rang. A Manhattan number. This time he knew exactly who it was. He gave Dom a look, then headed into the hallway to answer.

He put on his best smarmy-asshole voice. 'Alex, buddy. How you doing?'

'David Sullivan.' For once, Holliday didn't sound in the mood for banter. 'There's a car waiting outside. Your associate is already inside, so, if you wouldn't mind.'

Sully looked out through the glass wall of the hallway. A white SUV was parked out front. He couldn't believe Hunter had just climbed into it on Holliday's invite. She'd been cautious to the point of paranoia up to now, and suddenly she was putting herself in Alex Holliday's hands? If Hunter was already in the vehicle, though, Sully didn't have much choice.

'See you in a while.' He tried to keep his tone light, but it was hard with that SUV waiting. The last time he'd seen Alex Holliday, his bodyguard had been pointing a gun at Sully and his friends, and Holliday had told them they were all dead.

Just to be sure, he texted Hunter.

AH says ur in this SUV? True?

Her reply came immediately.

Ya. Come on.

'Holliday?' Dom was heading towards him.

Sully pointed at the SUV. 'Hunter's already inside. He wants to meet.'

'This is a bad idea, Sully.'

'We'll be fine.' He wasn't at all sure of that, but what choice did he have? 'If Holliday was planning to hurt us, he wouldn't call me on his private phone and send a car to pick me up. He's not exactly trying to hide his trail.'

Dom shook his head, not convinced. 'I don't agree with Mandy, that the marbles are bad and all that, but some of what she says makes a lot of sense. Hunter's playing with fire, but she's too in love with the marbles to see it.' He shrugged. 'Hell, how do we know that Gold doesn't have some sort of hold on her?'

Feeling a rising resentment, Sully asked, 'What do you mean?'

Dom scowled. 'Come on. You know what I mean. Her skin is gold. There's something inside "talking" to her. It's in her head, in her brain.' He hesitated, because he saw Sully was getting pissed off. 'For all we know, it's controlling her.'

'It's *Hunter*. Is she a little different from before? Sure. You would be too, if you'd been through what she's been through. But it's still *her*. She's the same funny, intense, occasionally frustrating girl she was the day I met her.'

Dom heaved a big, fat sigh. '*Occasionally* frustrating. Yeah.' He gestured towards the exit. 'Fine. Let's go.'

'What? Where?'

Dom crossed his eyes. 'Where do you think? You think I'm not coming with you? I'm guessing Mandy will want us to swing by and get her, too.'

Sully shouldn't have been surprised. Hunter was their golden goose; of course they'd want to watch over her.

As Sully slipped into the back of the SUV, Hunter gave him a kiss. She seemed wary but excited.

Sully wiped his sweaty palms on his thighs. He had no idea what to expect from Holliday. One thing he was sure of was that Holliday wasn't going to let Hunter have the Midnight Blues just because he couldn't burn them himself. Best-case scenario, they'd have to build up a mountain of spheres to trade. Sully didn't want to think about the worst-case scenario.

'Can you explain again what's going to happen if you burn the Midnight Blues?' Sully asked Hunter.

Hunter took one of his hands and held it in her slender golden ones. She never wore gloves any more. Her hands finally felt warm.

'The third wave will come. More spheres. Some of them bigger – much bigger. I'm thinking maybe they can cure diseases, maybe we'll live longer, but I'm not sure.'

'And they all lived happily ever after,' Mandy said. 'This doesn't strike you as too good to be true?'

It did. But, then again, spheres were too good to be true.

'Where are these things from? Can they tell you?' Mandy asked.

Hunter closed her eyes. 'I get glimpses of it sometimes, from the Golds' memory. There's no ground, no up or down. Colours everywhere, shooting around, sometimes spraying like a rainstorm. Sometimes patches of night sky with stars open up, so it's out in space, I guess.'

Sully had never taken an astronomy class, but in physics Mr Cracovia had taught them about some weird stuff out there – black holes, dark matter, hypervelocity stars. Maybe the spheres evolved in one of those places.

The driver took them to the Holliday's flagship store in Manhattan, where Cosette waited to escort them to an elevator around the back. She told Dom and Mandy they'd have to wait outside. After a good deal of bitching and moaning on Dom's part, he relented.

Cosette led them through the huge lobby and into Holliday's office. Hunter went right to Holliday with her hand extended, maybe to show him she was not intimidated. For his part, Holliday barely flinched at Hunter's appearance. He seemed somewhere between impatient and enraged as they shook hands.

'What is it you want?' Holliday asked. No pleasantries, no offer of a drink or even a seat.

Hunter shrugged. 'I want the Midnight Blues. One of them is mine already.'

'Is that right?'

Hunter nodded. 'I was just loaning it to you, in case that wasn't clear. How much do you want for the other?'

Holliday looked at Sully, as if expecting him to weigh in.

When Sully said nothing, Holliday turned away and paced across his office. 'It's not for sale.'

Hunter's eyes narrowed. 'You already know it's not any use to you. I'll give you a fair price.'

Holliday glanced sidelong at her as he paced. 'Oh, will you? Why are you so sure you can burn them when I can't?'

Hunter put her hands on her hips. 'There's only one way to find out, isn't there?'

Anxious as Sully was, he enjoyed seeing Alex Holliday off-balance. They had him. Besides the Golds, the Midnight Blues were the only spheres in the world Holliday hadn't burned, and they always would be.

'What do they do?' The way Holliday paced, he looked like he was imprisoned in his own office.

'Don't you already know?' Sully said. 'I thought you knew everything about the spheres.'

'They'll bring a third wave,' Hunter said. 'New marbles with new powers. I'm not sure what powers.'

From what little Sully understood, everyone would get the new powers when third-wave spheres were burned, or something like that. It was smart of Hunter to leave out that detail. If Holliday thought the Midnight Blues would bring new, rare spheres that would give him powers that no one else had, he might bite.

Holliday combed his fingers through his hair. 'All right. I'll give you the Midnight Blues. In exchange, you agree to hunt for me, exclusively, for a period of five years.'

'No!' Sully shouted.

'Deal,' Hunter said.

Sully grasped her shoulders. 'Hunter, *no*. That's millions and millions of dollars.'

She turned and kissed Sully softly. 'It's not just you and me in this. If I can burn the Midnight Blues, I have to do it, even if I don't like the price.'

'*No*. Hunter, no. It's *way* too much.'

Holliday looked like he was trying not to smile. 'I'll have my lawyers draw up a contract. In the meantime, can I get you two something to drink? Have you had lunch?'

Sully shook his head. Holliday was back to wearing his smug, charming expression, which made Sully even more certain that Hunter was getting screwed.

'What about Dom and Mandy? They should have a say in this. We still owe them way more than they've got.'

Hunter squeezed her eyes shut. 'Please don't make this any harder on me. I have to do this.'

Sully pulled out his phone. All he could think to do was call Dom and tell him what was happening. Not that Holliday was going to allow Dom and Mandy to storm into his office and stop the deal.

'Don't you understand?' Sully said, not even trying to keep his voice down. 'He'll *own* you. You'll spend the next five years flying around the world so he can scoop up every last marble, the new ones as well as the old, and sell them in his damned stores. He'll run the competition out of business.'

Hunter only gave the tiniest shake of her head.

Sully took a big, huffing, frustrated breath. 'What if the Gold isn't telling the truth, or you're misunderstanding?'

'You said it yourself. Sometimes you have to take a leap of faith.'

The door whisked open, and a woman in a teal jumpsuit and silk scarf breezed in. She handed a sheaf of papers to Holliday and left without a word.

'Here we go.' Holliday spread the papers on a marble desk built into the wall. 'Hunter?' He curled one finger and gestured her over, already getting accustomed to treating her like one of his employees. Sully was certain the contract had been prepared days ago, and was airtight.

'Hold on,' Sully said. 'You can't sign until we have a lawyer look the papers over. The contract could say anything.'

Hunter accepted a gold pen from Holliday that all but disappeared in her hand.

Sully was gasping, breathless. How could she do this, knowing what had happened when Sully signed a Holliday contract? He grasped her elbow. 'I want to talk to you outside, in private.'

Hunter turned to Holliday. 'I'll be right back.' She followed Sully into the lobby.

The door clicked closed behind them. They were alone in the huge, glass-ceilinged space.

'We *always* do it your way. From the Forest Green deal to who keeps the Gold to going after the Midnight Blue, you always get your way.'

As Sully glared, Hunter took his hand and squeezed it. 'Sully, this is bigger than you and me —'

'It sure is. Dom and Mandy risked their lives right beside us to find that Gold. They should have a say in what goes down now.'

'No, that's not what I'm saying, and you know it. It's bigger than all of us. The *Gold* wants this. I'm not doing this for myself, I'm doing it for the Gold.' She gestured at the door. 'You think I *want* to be that jerk's gopher for the next five years? The only way he's going to give up the other Midnight Blue is on his terms. You know it, and I know it. He has to feel like he won, or he's not going to play the game.'

Sully folded his arms, shook his head. They didn't need the second Midnight Blue that badly. Hunter was so stubborn. He was seeing that, *really* seeing it, for the first time.

'Don't we owe the Gold this, with all it's done for us?' Hunter asked.

'We don't owe it *anything*. You said it yourself, we give

251

them a place to live, and they give us something to pay the rent. That's the deal.'

Hunter put a hand on top of her head and exhaled in frustration. She was still holding the gold pen. 'We're so close. Just trust me one last—'

'*No.*' Sully closed his eyes, trying to calm down. 'No. I'm sorry. I'm not trusting you one last time.'

Hunter swallowed. Her hands were shaking. 'We can't stop now, Sully. We've come too far.'

Sully didn't answer.

'Please, Sully. We have to do this.'

'You mean *you* have to do this.'

They faced each other, silent. Sully had said everything he wanted to say. And so, evidently, had Hunter.

'I'm sorry,' she whispered. 'I hope you can forgive me for this.'

Hunter turned and went back into Holliday's office.

'Excuse me, Mr Sullivan.' Cosette whisked past him carrying the Midnight Blues, one in each hand. She disappeared into Holliday's office as well.

Sully headed outside.

Dom and Mandy were on Fifth Avenue, waiting in the SUV. When they spotted Sully, they jumped out.

'What happened?' Dom asked.

'They made a deal.'

'What kind of deal?'

Sully had trouble looking Dom in the eye. He didn't want to tell them.

'What kind of deal?' Dom repeated.

'She agreed to hunt for Holliday exclusively. For five years.'

They gaped at Sully, dumbfounded.

'I tried to stop her.'

'*Sully.*' It was Hunter, running towards them. She was carrying both Midnight Blues.

People on the street immediately began to notice the Midnight Blues in Hunter's hands, or maybe it was Hunter herself who had them staring.

Sully turned his back on her, but Hunter came round and forced him to look at her.

'I don't blame you if you hate me. You're right – I've been a selfish asshole. You've been nothing but good to me, and I took advantage. But can't you see I'm not doing this for me? It's for the kids out there with no homes to go to, for the moms who've gone crazy. For the old people in hospitals dying of Alzheimer's.' She held out the Midnight Blues, one in each hand. 'I don't know if this will help them all. I don't know what it'll do. But can't you see I have to try? I'm giving up everything, giving up my freedom, to do the right thing.'

Dom and Mandy were watching, their faces stony.

Sully believed her, though. It didn't make it OK, but he believed her. Burning the Golds had almost driven her out of her mind, and here she was, ready to burn the Midnight Blues, with no guarantee it wouldn't be even worse for her.

There'd been that day at the flea market, the second or third time he'd seen her, when Sully had thought, *This girl could make a big score one day*. If only he'd known.

She was right: this was bigger than him and his hurt

feelings. Things didn't get any bigger than this.

Sully looked into her golden eyes and said, 'What's it going to be, Bronx? You going to burn them, or what?'

Hunter looked down at the spheres. 'That's the plan. Only my hands are shaking so bad, I'm not sure I can.'

Sully took the Midnight Blues from her. Out of the corner of his eye, he could see Dom glowering, but Dom didn't try to stop him, even though Sully was about to burn a hundred million dollars' worth of marbles. Maybe Dom saw it as well: they'd gone too far to turn back now.

What would the world be like in a few seconds? Sully wondered.

Different. That much was certain.

He lifted the Midnight Blues and touched them to Hunter's temples.

They looked around.

When the second wave had come, at least one or two spheres had been visible just about anywhere you happened to be, but this time nothing had changed that Sully could see.

The Midnight Blues began to fade, becoming glassy, chalk-coloured.

'So where are they?' Dom asked.

In the distance, someone screamed.

Another scream, closer. Higher pitched.

A moon rose silently over the buildings. It was Forest Green, and blotted out half the sky.

'Oh, my God,' Hunter cried. 'There it is.'

When Hunter had said the spheres would be bigger, Sully had expected them to be the size of bowling balls. This was a small moon, soaring just over the rooftops.

As it passed out of sight, Sully spotted another – a Lemon Yellow, higher up, like a balloon carried on the wind. His heart was tripping wildly. Did people realize what they were? Were they making the connection?

'What is *that*?' Dom asked, pointing down Fifth Avenue.

A few blocks away, in the direction of the Empire State Building, something was sliding along the ground. It was ink black and eel-like, with dozens of yellow-tipped tentacles jutting from what must have been its head.

'What *is* it?' Sully asked Hunter.

She squinted, frowning. 'I don't know. Neither does the Gold.'

The thing had no eyes or nose that Sully could see, nothing like a face, but it looked alive.

People were running from it, wide-eyed and screaming.

'There's another!' someone shouted.

It slid round the corner half a block away, sideswiped a pick-up truck, and ploughed into the back of a double-parked car before moving round the vehicle. It was huge – like a giant, bloated eel – and was covered in oily spines that rippled in the breeze. The tips of this one's tentacles were pink instead of yellow. It moved quickly, eagerly, winding this way and that as if searching for something, yet it was oddly clumsy as it bumped its way along.

A young woman came bolting round the same corner. She jolted to a stop when she saw the thing, then turned to flee back the way she'd come.

The creature was lightning fast. A tentacle snapped out, wrapped round the woman's leg and yanked her to the ground. She shrieked, thrashing, trying to break free as more tentacles snared her waist, then her arm. They dragged her towards the thing.

A mouth opened among the tentacles, strands of saliva stretching and snapping as it opened wider and wider. The woman clawed at the tarmac as first one leg was dragged into the mouth, then the other. She reached down, tried to push against it with her free hand, tried to stop it from pulling her in, but it was too powerful. For an instant nothing was visible but her screaming face, then she was gone. The mouth snapped shut.

As the creature moved away, Sully could hear the woman's muffled screams from inside it.

Hunter clapped her hands over her ears. 'Oh, my God.'

Another creature, this one with tentacles blood-red at the tips, was heading towards them. Sully wrapped an arm round Hunter and steered her towards the front doors of Holliday's, with Dom and Mandy on their heels.

'What did I do? God, what did I do?' Hunter said as they merged into a crowd of hundreds who were staring out of the store's window. Her eyes were wild with shock.

'Shhh. Keep your voice down,' Mandy said.

'We need to get out of here.' Sully spotted Alex Holliday being whisked towards the back of the building by a bodyguard. Any minute, Holliday was going to snap out of his initial shock and realize Hunter was the key to this, and he'd send people for her. They had to get out of there, but they didn't have a vehicle.

Sully was still clutching the spent Midnight Blues. He dropped them and tried to call Mom, but reached a recording saying all circuits were busy. Everyone in the city was trying to call someone.

Or was it everyone in the world?

The roar of jet engines rose outside. The people closest to the window looked up. Sully and his friends drew closer so they could see.

Three fighter jets in formation flew right at an Aquamarine moon. They fired missiles that left contrails, and the jets pulled off sharply as the missiles struck the moon with a cracking, booming explosion that reached Sully's ears a half second after he saw the flash.

When the smoke cleared, the moon looked no different. It wasn't even singed.

Sully yelped as one of the creatures slammed into the window, tentacles splaying across the glass. It turned in a wide arc, pushing a car out of its way and bending a lamp post before finding a path between them. It was fast and powerful, but clumsy as hell.

It circled back round as the crowd surged away from the window. People screamed, panicking. Someone stepped on Sully's foot, stumbled and fell against him, bringing them both to the floor. Boots and sneakers landed around his face as people rushed past. A foot landed on his fingers, and lancing pain shot through them.

'Sully?' Hunter shouted, trying to reach him.

The man on top of him managed to roll off and get to his feet as the crowd fled deeper into the store.

Hunter grabbed Sully's arm and helped him up. His fingers were throbbing, already swelling.

He spotted Dom pushing against the surging crowd. Dom shouted, 'We gotta get out of here!'

Sully tried to think. They needed a plan; they couldn't just run blindly from these things until they were exhausted.

The storefront window broke with a crash. The creature burst into the store and came right at them.

Hunter yanked Sully's hand, pulling him towards the long service counter. Sully sprinted after her; they dived over the counter and landed on the floor. An instant later, Dom and Mandy appeared, further down the counter. The creature would be too big to reach them in such a narrow space, but its tentacles could. They needed to find better cover.

When the creature didn't immediately appear above them, Sully ventured a peek over the counter.

It was gone. It had moved on.

Deeper inside the building, someone screamed.

'Why didn't it come after us?' Sully asked. It seemed important to understand, if they were going to survive.

'We're not Lemon Yellow,' Hunter said under her breath.

'What?'

'That's what the Gold thinks. The creature's tips were Lemon Yellow, so it's attracted to Lemon Yellow.'

Sully gaped at her. He had no idea what she was talking about. The thing wasn't going after Lemon Yellows, it was going after *people* . . .

Then it registered. 'You're saying they sense the spheres that people burned?'

Hunter swallowed, nodded. 'It's all about colours to them. Remember how I see them? The parents – the big marbles in the sky – they're like that. They can't see or hear or smell, so we're invisible without the colours. These things work the same way. That's why they're so clumsy: all they sense is the colours – the marbles people have burned.'

What the Gold was saying lined up with what Sully had seen of the creatures – they were running into things as if blind and deaf, but went after people as if they knew right where they were. Before Christmas, Sully hadn't burned a single set of spheres. Neither had Hunter. Now, if the Gold was right, Sully could be eaten by creatures that had tentacles tipped with Mustard, Cream, Aquamarine, Chocolate, Periwinkle, Turquoise, Olive or Seafoam Green.

'Does the thing inside you know how to make this stop?' Mandy asked.

Hunter shook her head. 'It doesn't understand what's going on. They're just children. They –' Her eyes widened as she stared at something outside.

It was a minivan chased by a creature with Army Green tentacles. The minivan flew round the corner and slammed into the back of a UPS truck parked in the middle of the road. The front of the van crumpled.

The creature paused at the driver's-side door of the van, then moved on.

'We have to get out of here,' Dom repeated.

Sully eyed the UPS truck that the minivan had crashed into. When the driver took off, would he have bothered to take the keys?

No way.

In fact, exhaust was spewing from the tailpipe. The truck was still running.

Sully pointed out the truck to the others. They looked up and down Fifth Avenue: two creatures were in sight, both a few blocks away. One was Vermillion, so theoretically they had nothing to worry about. The other was Turquoise, which they'd all burned except Mandy.

'Let's go. Fast as we can,' Sully said.

They ran. All of them but Mandy had also burned Seafoam Greens in the past week, so they were fast. Not as fast as one of the creatures, if that was what it came down to, but fast.

Sully jumped into the driver's seat, Hunter the passenger's. As soon as Dom jumped in behind Mandy, Sully threw the truck into drive and gunned it, heading for the West Side Highway.

'Sully, I'm so sorry,' Hunter said. 'I was so sure.' She covered her eyes. 'They're the only thing I ever believed in. I'm so stupid. I am so stupid.'

'Don't.'

He checked a passing street sign, saw they were on Fifty-First Street. The on-ramp to the West Side was on Fifty-Seventh.

Barely slowing, Sully hung a right and headed uptown, trying not to look at what was happening outside the windows.

'*Look out!*' Mandy screamed.

Sully swerved, just missing a grey-haired man running across the street. A Forest Green creature was closing on him.

On the next block, a trio of cops was hammering one of the creatures with automatic rifle fire. It wasn't bleeding, but it jerked and twisted as hunks of it were shot off by the high-calibre bullets.

As they flew past, Dom turned to keep watching.

'Did they get it?' Sully asked.

'It's in pieces, but it's still moving.'

Sully hung a left on to Fifty-Seventh Street. He stabbed at

the power button on the radio. A newscaster's voice came on at deafening volume, speaking rapidly, breathlessly.

Hunter turned the volume down.

It was happening everywhere. The newscaster, at least, hadn't connected the attack to the spheres yet.

A creature snaked from behind a parked truck, right into their path. Sully slammed the brakes, instinctively raising one arm to protect his face.

The impact hurled him forward; his chest slammed into the steering wheel, the crown of his head cracked against the windshield. The truck rolled to a stop.

'Sully?' Hunter, who'd slammed into the dashboard, reached for him. 'Are you all right?'

Sully took a couple of breaths to clear his head. 'Yeah. I think so. Dom? Mandy? You OK?' Mandy's lip was bleeding.

The driver's-side window shattered.

Sully shouted, gripped the steering wheel and gunned the accelerator as tentacles surged through the broken window.

One of the tentacles landed on his shoulder before the truck's momentum tore it away. It sliced his skin as if the tentacle was covered in fishhooks. The tips were barbed.

As they sped off, Sully's torn shoulder burning with pain, he realized the tips had been Turquoise. He'd burned a pair of Turquoise spheres. Enhanced hearing. Rarity four.

'It's chasing us.' Mandy was watching out of the window.

Sully glanced in his side mirror, saw the creature slithering after them with remarkable speed.

Ahead, the ramp to the West Side Highway was jammed with traffic. Four or five of the creatures glided around the cars. Sully hung a right, heading uptown. They'd have to take the avenues.

He was surprised traffic wasn't worse. Maybe that was understandable, though: most people's instinct would be to retreat to inner rooms or basements, where the creatures couldn't reach them. That's what the people in Holliday's had seemed to be doing. The only people in vehicles were probably the ones who'd been there when the creatures struck.

He checked the mirror: the Turquoise creature was falling behind. It wasn't as fast as a truck, thank goodness.

As Mandy and Dom pulled out their phones, Sully dialled his mom with one hand.

'Sully? Are you all right? Where are you?' Sully's chest tightened at the sound of her voice. She was safe, at least; she'd wanted nothing to do with burning spheres after seeing what the Gold did to Hunter.

'We're on our way. We're OK. Mom, we screwed up. We screwed up so bad.'

'Just don't let those things get you. Don't come here, head into the country. They're saying there aren't as many in the country.'

'I'll call you when we're out there. Stay inside, Mom.'

As he hung up, he saw he had missed a call from Holliday. Maybe they'd be safer with him. He had bodyguards with guns.

Sully hit redial.

'Where are you?' Holliday asked.

'In a truck, on Eleventh Avenue.'

'You see how stupid you are? Do you see what you've done?' Holliday sounded unhinged.

'What do you mean?' Sully said. '*You* tried to burn them, too. We didn't know this would happen.'

'I hope they get you. I hope one of them eats you, and you're inside that belly screaming your lungs out and crapping your pants.'

'Same to you!' Sully shouted into the phone. 'And every single one of them is after you, so good luck with that!' He disconnected.

'Let me guess who that was,' Hunter said. Out of the corner of his eye, Sully saw her wiping tears from her cheeks.

'My mom said there aren't as many out in the country, so that's where we're headed.'

'I don't want one of those things to eat me,' Hunter said. 'I know I deserve it, but I don't want to die like that.'

'You don't deserve it,' Sully said. 'You did this because you thought it was going to help people. You weren't doing it for yourself.'

Dom and Mandy didn't chime in, but maybe they were too preoccupied watching for monsters.

Mandy leaned forward, looked up through the windshield. '*Look at that. Oh, my God, look at that.*'

Sully followed her gaze. One of the creatures, a Cranberry, was snaking through the air as if gravity was nothing, heading towards a Cranberry moon. The sight made Sully want to crawl under the seat.

Hunter's sharp intake of breath made him start. 'The Gold is getting it now. It understands.'

'Well, we don't,' Dom said. 'You think you can enlighten us?'

'They're harvesting people and delivering them to the parents. The spheres are markers, like dye in our blood, so the harvesters can find us. They're bait. Nothing but bait.' Hunter folded, her head sinking to her knees. 'The Gold can't believe it. They thought they were children, but they're nothing. They were dropped here for us to burn so these things would be able to locate us.'

At the moment, Sully couldn't muster much sympathy for the spheres, but he kept his mouth shut. He didn't have one of them inside his head.

'At least we understand what's happening,' Sully said. 'Sort of.'

'Because, why wouldn't we believe the aliens? They haven't steered us wrong yet,' Mandy said.

'Mandy, come on,' Sully said. 'We're in this together.'

Mandy gestured at the windshield. 'Do you see what's going on out there? I *warned* you. Don't tell me to come on and get with the team.'

'You had to push it,' Dom said to Hunter. 'You just had to push it.'

A booming explosion overhead rocked the truck.

Dom looked up through the windshield. 'Jets attacked a moon with something bigger.' He kept watching. 'It doesn't look like it did anything.'

'If they're made of the same stuff as the spheres, nothing is going to damage them,' Sully said.

'We have to call someone,' Dom said. 'The police. The FBI. We have to tell them what we know.'

'How does that help anything?' Sully asked. 'They're hitting them with everything but nukes.' If they called the authorities, they'd surely all be thrown in prison. Hunter would probably be sent to some top-secret military prison.

'I don't know how that helps anything!' Dom shouted. 'I don't know anything. At this point I don't even know if your girlfriend is human.'

'Dom,' Mandy said, 'hold on.'

'No. This is bullshit. I'm calling the police.' He lifted his phone.

Sully stabbed a finger in Dom's direction. 'If you make that call, you're walking. And I don't think you want to walk right now.'

'Pull over!' Dom shouted. 'Go ahead and pull over.'

'*Shut up!*' Mandy shouted over him. 'Everyone shut up. Maybe we do need to call the authorities, but let's think this through. We don't have to do it right this minute.'

Out of the window, Sully saw an Army Green creature swallowing a kid. A kid.

'I don't blame you for wondering about me,' Hunter said to Dom. 'For a while *I* wasn't sure I was still me. But I am. The Gold's inside me, but it's separate.' She pointed an emphatic finger at Dom. 'Just like all the things inside *you* are separate from you.'

Dom didn't reply. Sully had almost forgotten that, in a very real way, they were in the same boat when it came to housing aliens. The only difference was Hunter could talk to hers.

'My parents are freaking out,' Mandy said, looking down at her phone. 'They want to come and get me.'

'Do you want me to drop you at home?' Sully asked.

'*No*. We're safer in the boonies. I convinced them to head up the interstate, that we would meet up later.'

The thick forest on either side of the highway was reassuring. They hadn't seen one of the creatures — the harvesters, the Gold called them — for almost ten minutes. Mom had been right; there were fewer in the country, just as there were fewer spheres hidden in the country. Sully had also noticed that more harvesters seemed to be the colour of common spheres — Army Green, Rose, Lavender, Lemon Yellow. If that was true, it was good news, because Sully, Hunter and Dom had mostly burned rare, high-end spheres. Theoretically, the harvesters couldn't sense Mandy at all, although Sully didn't blame her for not wanting to bet her life on that.

He was glad he'd got a chance to talk to Mom before the phones went out. According to the radio, everything was going out — phone, electricity, Internet. No one was hanging around to keep services running.

'Does the Gold know what the moons are doing with the people the harvesters bring them?' Sully asked. He spoke quietly, because Dom and Mandy were asleep in the back, among undelivered packages.

After a pause in which, Sully assumed, Hunter consulted the Gold, she said, 'It has something to do with us being intelligent. That's why the spheres are hidden and have to be burned in pairs — it's so you have to be intelligent to burn them.'

And only intelligent species could ultimately figure out how to open the gate and let the harvesters in. They'd triggered an elaborate alarm, or maybe a dinner bell, although Sully didn't think the moons were actually eating the people the harvesters delivered. Although, what did he know? Maybe they were.

'They do the same thing on other worlds,' Sully said. It wasn't a question. Of course they did. They were setting traps on billions of worlds, wiping out intelligent species all over the universe. Maybe there was some chemical in the brains of intelligent species they fed on, or they used the beings they captured as slaves. Maybe it was simpler than that: this could be an invasion. They could be taking over.

It occurred to Sully that the damned Mustard spheres he'd burned were probably allowing him to make these connections. Would the old Sully have been able to spin theories about what was happening so quickly? He hadn't been a dummy before, but there was no denying his mind was nimbler now. Insights came effortlessly; before he had to sweat to make things click.

As they approached the next exit, Sully checked the gas gauge.

'We're below empty; if we drive for much longer we're going to run out of gas.'

'OK,' Hunter said.

Sully put on his signal.

Maybe the gas stations out here still had gas, but he doubted it. The news said at most of the stations the pumps were either tapped out from people trying to outrun the harvesters, or they weren't working because the power was out.

At the end of the exit ramp, a sign indicated that Rhinebeck was to the left. Sully turned right, drove for a mile, and pulled into a dirt lot in front of a small concrete building, the office of Lomeli Sand and Gravel. There were piles of stone and gravel all over the grounds.

Mandy climbed into the front, looking alert, as if she hadn't actually been sleeping. 'You think we're safe spending the night in the truck? Maybe we should break into that office?' It was getting dark. Soon it would be harder to see harvesters coming. The office had small windows, so a harvester might not be able to get inside. It would also be more comfortable than spending the night in the truck.

Sully wasn't sure what they were going to do in the morning. Find food, water, and a gassed-up vehicle and head deeper into the country, maybe? Keep driving until they reached complete wilderness?

'Let's go inside,' Dom said from the back. No one argued.

They broke out a window and boosted Mandy through, and she unlocked the front door.

It wasn't much of an office, just a room with wood panelling and a concrete floor, two steel desks, filing cabinets with a TV and portable stereo on top, a coffeemaker, piles of papers. No food.

The stereo had a radio, so they listened to the news for a while. No one knew exactly how many harvesters there were, but there were millions. They could be stopped if you shot them up badly enough, or doused them with gasoline and burned them, or dropped a bomb on them. If you had nothing but a handgun, the newscaster said not to waste your time emptying the clip into them. Just run. She pointed out that not only was shooting a handgun at a harvester useless but also there might be people inside it. Sully hadn't even thought of that.

The news report also confirmed that harvesters were preying only on people who'd burned spheres that matched the colour of the tips of their tentacles. They'd figured that much out, at least.

'You were right all along, Mandy,' Dom said. 'Burning marbles gives you worse than cancer. Smart girl.'

'You could go home, if you wanted to,' Sully said. He gestured out the window. 'There's nothing out there that can hurt you.'

Mandy was sitting cross-legged on the carpet. 'I'll stick around. If it's safe for me to go out there, I can get food and supplies. Plus we still haven't decided whether to tell the authorities about our part in this.'

'Can we decide in the morning?' Sully asked.

No one objected.

Sully volunteered to take the first watch. He pulled one of the rolling desk chairs to the window with the best view of the road.

As it grew dark, Sully eyed the mountains of gravel blocking his view to the left. A harvester could sneak up behind one of those piles and they wouldn't see it until it was on top of them. Then he remembered that harvesters couldn't see piles of gravel, and he doubted they thought in terms of sneaking up.

He didn't want to get eaten by one of those things. Somehow it made it worse that they didn't seem to actually kill you, that they brought you to a 'parent' alive. He didn't ever want to find out what happened when you got there. His imagination summoned vague, unspeakable possibilities that stayed on the edges of his mind, just out of reach.

Dom appeared behind Sully. Arms folded, he watched out of the window.

'I can't imagine why you're having trouble sleeping,' Sully said softly.

Dom laughed through his nose. 'Right.'

They stared at the road, barely visible now in the fading light. Sully felt uneasy, not sure what to say. They'd never had an argument like the one in the truck. Not even close. Not even when they were kids.

'I know you don't want to hear it, but I don't trust her. I don't think the marbles were duped. That's way too convenient. It's a story the marbles dreamed up out of self-preservation, to keep us from hurting them until those harvesters can get us.'

Sully glanced at Hunter, curled on her side on the floor. Mandy was on the other side of the office, lying behind one of the desks. 'You're saying Hunter is in on this? That she's secretly happy about all these people dying?'

'I'm saying I don't think she's Hunter any more.'

Sully absorbed this, feeling the distance between him and his best friend growing. 'That's some messed-up thinking.'

'This is a messed-up situation.'

Sully sat up straight, raised his hand. 'You hear that?' He leaned towards the window. A muffled honking came from outside.

Dom turned an ear to the window. 'What?'

Dom hadn't burned Turquoise, so he wouldn't hear the honking, given how soft it was. The sound was familiar, but Sully couldn't put his finger on what it was. He went to the window on the opposite side of the office, looked left and right.

Nothing.

Dom's nose was pressed almost to the window as he squinted into the darkness.

Suddenly, he lurched away. *Everybody up. There's one out there.*

Hunter and Mandy sprang to their feet.

'What colour is it?' Sully asked, his heart hammering.

'I can't tell. It's too dark.'

The humming was louder; now Sully knew what the sound was.

'It can't fit through those windows,' Mandy said.

The door crashed open. The harvester surged in, its mouth open wide. Tentacles whipped around both of Hunter's thighs and yanked her off her feet.

Sully lunged, grabbed Hunter under both arms, and locked his hands behind her as more tentacles snared her right arm, her waist, her ankle. Dom grabbed her left wrist, batted away a tentacle coiled like a cobra about to strike.

'Don't let it get me. Please don't let it get me.' Blood soaked Hunter's jeans where the barbs had sunk into her thighs. It poured down her right arm in streams.

Sully squeezed Hunter tight as he scrabbled to stay on his feet. The sound he'd heard earlier wasn't the harvester itself: it was the screams of the people inside it. He heard them clearly now.

Mandy got hold of Hunter's other arm. The harvester was incredibly strong; Sully was pulling with all his might just to keep it from dragging Hunter outside.

It lunged forward suddenly, swallowing Hunter almost to her waist. Sully lifted one foot and pushed against the edge of the thing's mouth for leverage.

The harvester was Tangerine. Hunter had burned that pair

of Tangerines on a lark, a silly whim just to give them a laugh by imitating Dom.

Without warning it whipped its head from side to side, trying to shake them loose. Mandy was thrown across the room. She slammed into the desk and flipped, landing hard on the floor, as Sully and Dom struggled to hang on.

'Shit! *Mandy!*' Dom shouted.

Mandy was writhing on the floor. She looked badly hurt, but Sully couldn't let go of Hunter.

The harvester lunged again, swallowed Hunter up to her armpits. Sully's hands were in the thing's wet, hot mouth. He was going to lose her if he didn't do something. His arms were tired and rubbery; the harvester didn't seem to be tiring at all.

Hunter was the only one who'd burned Tangerine, so the harvester couldn't hurt Sully. If he had a chain saw he could cut the tentacles, or go outside and cut the damned thing to pieces while Dom held on to Hunter. He glanced around, looking for a weapon, or something to wedge open its mouth. There was nothing but papers, framed photos, coffee mugs. He needed something big. Had he seen anything outside? Steel pipes, two-by-fours?

He looked out, saw the UPS truck in the driveway.

He didn't have a chain saw, but he had a truck.

The problem was, either he or Dom would have to let go of Hunter to reach it. They were both strong after absorbing the Chocolates, but Dom was still stronger. If one of them could hang on to Hunter on his own, it was him.

'Dom. Come here. Hold her.'

Dom shifted, wrapped his arms around Hunter, and locked his hands behind her back.

'Don't let go,' Sully said. 'Whatever you do, don't let her go.'

'Don't leave me.' Hunter's eyes were wide, her breath coming in gasps. 'Sully, don't leave me.'

'Trust me,' he said.

'I love you, Sully,' Hunter called after him. 'Know I love you.'

Sully raced for the truck. He turned the ignition before his ass hit the seat, threw the truck into drive, and gunned the accelerator.

Most of the harvester was outside, tensing and relaxing as it fought to pull Hunter from Dom's grasp. Sully steered right for the middle of it, building speed.

As he bore down, he thought of the people screaming inside it. He might kill some of them.

He swallowed it down. They were going to die anyway if he didn't stop the harvester.

The truck ploughed into it. Sully pressed down on the gas and kept going, driving the harvester right into the concrete building.

Sully hurled forward.

Everything went black.

CHAPTER 32

'Sully? Please be OK. Please be OK.'

Sully struggled to open his eyes. His head was a bright, hot ball of agony. It felt as if it was cracked wide open.

Hunter pressed her cool palm to his cheek. 'There you are. You're going to be OK. The Aquamarines will fix you up. Don't forget your Olives.'

Olives. He could numb the pain. He'd forgotten about the Olives. Sully closed his eyes, concentrated on his head.

It was like moving a dial, slowly dimming the throbbing until it was just a whisper.

Hunter helped him sit up.

They were in a cement mixer. Dom was driving. Mandy was on the floor, gasping, her eyes open but face slack, like she might be in shock.

Keeping his eyes on the road, Dom said, 'We need to find a doctor. A hospital.'

Sully studied Mandy, trying to figure out what was wrong with her, but there was no outward sign of injury, no blood. 'Mandy, what hurts?'

Mandy's wide eyes rolled to look at him. 'I think my hip is broken, or my leg up high.'

'It would take a few hours and a lot of driving around, but I could find a pair of Aquamarines to help speed up healing, Olives for the pain—'

'*No*,' Mandy said. 'Are you *kidding me*?'

She had a point. It was a double-edged sword, though; Sully and Dom had probably been able to hang on to the harvester and avoid getting injured because of the additional strength the Chocolates provided.

Hunter lifted her pack, fumbled in a pocket, pulled out a bottle of Tylenol. 'Here.' She shook three into her hand and gave them to Mandy, who dry-swallowed them.

There was no one out to ask directions from, no Internet to check. Heading towards Rhinebeck, they spotted a blue hospital sign and followed it.

'There were people inside that harvester. I could hear them screaming,' Sully said as they drove. 'Could you still hear them after I hit it?'

Eyes narrowed, Dom tried to recall. 'I don't remember. They may have still been screaming. The thing was thrashing to get free of the truck, I was carrying Mandy on my back . . . I just don't know.'

Sully looked at Hunter, who shook her head. 'I was so focused on you. I thought you were dead. I'm sorry, I don't know.'

So Sully may or may not have killed people, and he probably would never know for sure. He'd done his best to hit the harvester up high, near its head. Hopefully, he'd missed the people inside it. Of course if the harvester freed itself and carried them into the sky, it didn't matter.

Two harvesters circled the hospital. The windows at the front of the emergency room were shattered.

Cursing, Dom swung a U-turn, driving the mixer up over the kerb. He headed back on to a country highway. 'What now? We can't keep driving around until those things pick us off. Man, I hate those things. They're like something out of my nightmares.'

A police car passed, lights flashing, heading in the other direction.

'Find weapons,' Mandy said. 'Axes. Maybe something you can use as a spear to ram down their throats.'

'The first thing we have to do is get you to a doctor,' Sully said.

'My parents are doctors,' Mandy said. 'I'm supposed to meet them at the Saugerties exit. Exit nineteen.'

That seemed like a great idea to Sully, provided the harvesters hadn't got to Mandy's parents. Unlike Mandy, her parents apparently had no qualms about burning spheres.

Hunter pointed out the windshield. 'Up ahead.'

A harvester was in the road. Dom slowed the cement mixer.

'Can anyone see what colour it is?' Sully asked. He hadn't bothered to burn Magentas for night vision. He didn't think any of them had.

'Red,' Mandy said. 'I think it's red.'

Sully's stomach did a flip. 'Rose?'

Hunter squinted hard. 'Ruby. I think.'

Sully relaxed. Ruby was white, even teeth. He hadn't bothered with that one, either. He was glad he practised good dental hygiene.

'Ruby Red?' Dom said. 'Anyone?'

When no one spoke up, Dom stamped the mixer's accelerator, his elbows locked, both hands clutching the steering wheel.

'Wait,' Sully said. 'There could be people inside it.'

'Shoot, I forgot.' Dom veered to the left, on to the shoulder, and steered for the harvester's head. The mixer's cab jolted, then rocked furiously as they hit the harvester's head and knocked it out of the road.

Dom whooped as they roared off.

Hunter turned in her seat. 'It looks sort of twisted and broken, but it's back on the road and moving already.'

What good would an axe or spear be if you couldn't kill a harvester by hitting it with a cement mixer?

'Where am I going? How do I get to the interstate?' Dom asked.

Sully hadn't been paying attention as they followed the hospital signs. He leaned forward, opened the truck's glove compartment. Wedged between receipts and maintenance reports, he found a map of New York.

'You're good,' he said, tracing their route with his finger. 'A couple of miles, then left on to Route 9G.'

The cement mixer slowly built speed as Dom shifted gears. 'We need a plan.'

'I have a plan,' Hunter said. She'd been quiet for a while. 'The Gold and the Midnight Blue don't think it will work, but they're willing to try. They're devastated by what's happening. They care about us, in their way. They do. And we're in this together — if the parents get us, the spheres die, too.'

'What's the plan?' Sully didn't like the flatness in her eyes as she turned to him.

'The plan is, I die.'

'No,' Sully said immediately. 'What are you talking about? No.'

Hunter put one hand over his. 'If the Midnight Blue is dead, maybe the gate will close. They don't think it will, but I have to try. Billions of people could die if I don't.'

'What good does it do to close the gate? They're here already.'

Hunter shook her head. 'The parents have one hand here, in our sky, but mostly they're still home. Wherever that is. If I can close the gate, it will cut off the hand.'

The idea boggled Sully's mind. These giant moons were like an arm stuck through a wormhole or something?

'So what the Midnight Blues opened up was like a window. It wasn't a door they stepped all the way through.'

'Yes, I guess.'

Still, if the spheres didn't think it would do any good, Sully couldn't let Hunter sacrifice herself out of sheer desperation.

'You're our only link to the spheres.' Sully was more worried about losing Hunter than losing the link, but he knew that wasn't going to change her mind. 'If you're gone and the gate doesn't close, we have no way of knowing what they're thinking. Then we really have no chance.'

Hunter shook her head. 'Unless we can close the gate, it doesn't matter. Help me –' She choked up, took a few breaths to get herself under control. 'Help me think of a way that won't hurt.'

'The spheres don't think this will work?' Dom asked.

'Now that the gate's open, they don't see how the Midnight Blue dying would close it, but they don't know anything for sure. They were told so many lies.'

'It's off the table.' Dom made a chopping motion with one hand. 'If it's not going to fix anything, it's off the table.'

'Even if it's only a small chance, it's a chance,' Hunter said.

'It's off the table,' Dom said. 'Despite what you seem to think, this isn't a dictatorship. We all decide what goes down.'

'That's right,' Mandy said. 'Nobody's dying.'

Sully turned his hand over, squeezed Hunter's. 'Three to one.'

'*No*,' Hunter said, sitting up. 'We don't vote on this. I *have* to try.'

It occurred to Sully that Hunter felt she deserved to die after what she'd done. Maybe she was right, and maybe Sully deserved to die for going along with her as far as he had. But their deaths wouldn't solve anything.

'Could the army bomb the gate closed, if they knew about it?' Sully didn't relish being shoved into a squad car, but Dom might be right. Maybe it was time to tell the authorities what they knew.

'It's not one gate,' Hunter said. 'It's a million gates. Every parent came through a gate.'

'The Midnight Blue opened them all, but it doesn't know how to close them?' Sully said.

'It doesn't know how it opened them.'

Through the closed window, and over the rumble of the cement mixer's engine, Sully could hear crickets singing in the tall grass along the road. He tried to ignore them; he needed to think. What would reverse the process? Sully pressed his fists

279

against his eyes, trying to think. There had to be something that would . . .

Sully froze. Reverse the process. Could they? Was burning a sphere exactly like a birth, or could the Midnight Blue revert back to its sphere form? He was afraid to ask, afraid of having this sliver of hope dashed.

'Hunter, can they go back into the spheres?'

'What?'

'Can the Midnight Blue go back into the Midnight Blue spheres? Can it undo itself?'

'Undo itself?' She said it softly, not so much a question as an echo of Sully's words. 'It has no idea.'

'Would that close the gate?' Dom asked.

Hunter was silent for a long moment. 'They're not sure. But they have trouble imagining the gate open and the Midnight Blue spheres intact, both at the same time.'

'Maybe because it's not possible for them to go back into the spheres,' Sully said.

Mandy grabbed Sully's ankle. 'You can try it on other spheres.'

Yes. If the regular spheres could do it, the Midnight Blues could do it.

'Hunter, are there two matching spheres anywhere close?' Sully asked.

'Yes.' She pointed towards the passenger door. 'That way. Slate Grey.'

Dom slammed the brakes; the mixer skidded to stop.

'I'll wait here with Mandy,' Dom said.

Hunter led Sully into an apple orchard at a jog. She pulled a Slate Grey from beneath a rotting straw basket in the weeds, then hurried over a stone wall, squeezed through a barbed-wire fence, and pushed into the dark forest.

Sully ran, branches snapping against his outstretched hands and occasionally his face, until they reached a brook. In the darkness he could see the barest outlines of a makeshift bridge – planks laid across the water. Clearly the work of kids.

Hunter squatted, tipped one of the planks, and plunged her hand into the stream. She pulled out another Slate Grey.

With water still dribbling from the sphere, Hunter touched the pair to her temples. She lowered the spheres, closed her eyes.

'Well?' Sully asked.

'The Slate Grey was just born. The Gold says it's excited – it can't wait for me to sing. It'll take a minute for the Gold to break the news and explain what the Slate Grey has to try to do, and why.'

Sully eyed the Slate Grey spheres. It was so dark they were nothing but dark circles surrounded by more darkness. 'Let's head back to the mixer. We're going to need its headlights to see anything.'

As they left the woods, four different moons were visible in the sky, their colours disguised by the darkness. The real moon was a barely visible glow behind heavy clouds.

As they stepped in front of the mixer, Dom flicked on the headlights.

The Slate Greys were pale and mottled, clearly spent.

'OK,' Hunter said. 'Here we go.' She closed her eyes, pressed them to her temples.

Sully watched her face, waiting to see either joy or disappointment bloom. Her brow stayed pinched in concentration.

'Well?' Dom said, his head poked out of the window.

'It's trying. It doesn't know what to do. The Gold and Midnight Blue are coaxing, but they're not sure, either.'

Headlights appeared down the road. Still holding the spheres to her temples, Hunter stepped to the side, where the cement mixer would block the driver's view of her.

Red lights flashed. A police car – probably the one that had passed earlier. The window lowered as the cruiser pulled to a stop beside them.

'You need to get inside.' The police officer, who had a thick white moustache, glanced up at the cement mixer. 'What the hell are you doing?'

'One of them almost got our friend,' Sully said. 'We drove a truck into it and pinned it to the wall of the gravel office, then used this cement mixer to get away.'

The officer nodded. 'Good for you. But you need to get inside. The high school's set up as a shelter. What are you doing out here? Did you run out of gas or something?'

'*Oh, my God.*' Hunter stepped from behind the mixer holding out the Slate Greys. 'It worked. Oh, my God, it worked.'

Sully gaped at the Slate Greys. Their deep, rich colour was restored.

'And you know what? I can't sing worth a damn.' Hunter belted out a few lines of a song Sully didn't recognize. She was right, she wasn't very good. 'It's like I never burned them.'

The police cruiser's door slammed. 'What the hell is

going on here?' The officer approached Hunter, frowning. 'What happened to you? Are you the one who was almost eaten? Did it infect you or something?'

'It's make-up for a school play,' Dom blurted.

The officer reached out to Hunter, swept his finger across her cheek, examined his finger. 'That's not make-up.'

'It's waterproof. Spray-on,' Dom said.

The officer studied Hunter. The name badge pinned over his shirt pocket said WILKES.

As if she could care less about the police officer, Hunter turned to Sully. 'Where are the spent Midnight Blues? We have to get them.'

She was right. That was all that mattered now. If they went to the shelter, Mandy might be able to get medical attention, but people were dying, and they might be able to stop it.

Sully tried to remember where the Midnight Blues were. He'd been holding them when the gate opened. Had he dropped them right away?

'Come on,' Officer Wilkes said. 'I'm going to take you somewhere safe, or as safe as we've got, and you can explain what you're doing out here and why this girl looks the way she does.'

'Look,' Dom said. He stepped close to Wilkes. 'We need your help. We may know how to stop this, if you can get us to the city.'

'Stop what?' Wilkes asked.

'All of this.' Dom swept a hand at the sky. 'All the dying.'

Scowling, Wilkes studied each of them in turn. 'Are you all high?'

'No, we're not *high*.' Dom took a deep breath, clearly trying to control the wild sense of urgency he felt. 'We know how this whole thing got started, and we may know how to stop it —'

'The whole invasion? You may know how to stop the invasion of Earth?'

'*Look out.*' Hunter pointed down the road at the harvester coming their way. Its neck was crooked, its face bent to the right. Ruby Red.

Sully looked at Officer Wilkes's teeth. They were impressive. White and straight. 'I'm pretty sure it's coming for you.'

Wilkes looked at Sully like Sully had lost his mind. Then he ran for his cruiser. They needed that cruiser, but stopping Wilkes would be the same as killing him, so Sully watched as he made a frantic U-turn and peeled out.

The wounded harvester slithered past without slowing. For a moment, Sully watched — it blended into the tarmac so well it almost looked as if the road itself was moving. It slammed into the nose of the cement mixer, shifted course, and slithered around it. When harvesters were moving slowly, Sully had seen them use their tentacles to avoid obstacles. But they were rarely moving slowly.

'Let's go!' Dom shouted from the cement mixer. 'We have to find a faster vehicle. We can drop Mandy with her parents on the way.'

As they climbed inside, Mandy said, 'I'm staying right here.'

'No you're not,' Dom said. 'You're hurt. You could be bleeding internally or something.'

'Oh, there's a cheery thought.'

Sully thought she looked a little better. She was clearly in pain, but the glassy sheen was gone from her eyes.

'I'm not leaving you guys,' Mandy said. 'A few more hours won't matter. Just get us back to the city.'

CHAPTER 33

On the radio, a breathless announcer was assuring people who'd never burned spheres that they were safe and should report to their local police station to help with the crisis. Sully tried to remember what percentage of the US population had never burned spheres, not even the common ones you could buy for a hundred bucks. Was it even ten per cent? Certainly no more than that. In poorer countries, where a lot of found spheres were exported to the US and Europe, they'd face better odds.

Dom slowed the Volvo station wagon they'd taken after kicking down the front door of a dark house and locating the key. In the trunk were an axe and some two-by-fours they'd found in the garage.

'Shit. There's another,' Dom said. 'What colour is that?'

Sully studied the harvester heading towards them, right down the centre lane of I-87.

'*Indigo,*' Sully said. Better eyesight. They'd all burned Indigo, except Mandy.

Dom leaned forward, gripped the wheel with both hands

and accelerated. The whine of the engine grew higher as Dom steered right at the harvester, as if they were playing a game of chicken.

The harvester kept coming; it might have sped up in its eagerness to reach them, but it was hard to tell.

'Wait till the very last second,' Sully said.

'I know, I know.' If Dom signalled his move too early, the harvester would move to block him.

Hunter clutched Sully's leg; Sully wrapped his arms round her, unable to look away as the harvester bore down on them, looming . . .

Dom jerked the wheel left, then straightened as the Volvo fishtailed.

Sully looked back. The harvester was turning to give chase, but it had no chance of catching them.

If they broke down, they were dead. The harvesters were getting thicker by the mile as they headed towards the city, and they were seeing more of the rarer colours, the ones they'd burned. They'd spotted a Chocolate twenty minutes earlier. Sully had no idea how they were going to make it back into Holliday's to retrieve the spent Midnight Blues. They'd need a tank to keep the harvesters away.

It occurred to Sully that they didn't have to be the ones who personally retrieved the Midnight Blues. It could be someone else, someone who hadn't burned any spheres, who wasn't in danger of being swallowed. Such as his friends at the Garden Apartments. Mike hadn't burned any spheres as far as Sully knew. Laurie had burned Army Greens. He wasn't sure about the others.

'I think I have an idea,' Sully said.

As soon as they left the interstate, a Periwinkle harvester slithered from behind Walmart and headed towards them. Dom took off, but it was harder to build up speed on the surface roads. Other drivers were on the road to avoid harvesters, weaving among abandoned vehicles, most of which had one broken window where a harvester had extracted the occupants.

The Periwinkle harvester was a few hundred yards behind when Hunter shouted, 'Another!'

A Cream glided out of a crossing road.

Cursing, Dom hung a right. 'This was a mistake. Even if we make it to the apartments, how are we going to stop long enough to pick someone up?'

Sully hadn't thought that part through. Their phones hadn't worked since before they reached the gravel office in Rhinebeck, so he couldn't call his friends.

'All right,' Sully said. 'Let's head back to the interstate. We'll have to get the Midnight Blues ourselves.' He didn't know how they were going to do that. There were even more harvesters in the city. There'd been so many people for the harvesters to prey on at first that they'd been able to slip through the cracks at the outset, but that wouldn't be the case now.

Dom turned right, barely slowing. The turn was wide; the Volvo jumped partway over the kerb and on to the grass before Dom straightened it out. The Cream harvester loomed in the rear window, its tentacles brushing their bumper. Dom swerved round a truck stranded in the left lane and gunned it.

A half mile on, they hit the on-ramp for the interstate, and the harvesters fell behind.

Hunter lifted Sully's hand and kissed it. 'I'm sorry. I should have listened to you. I was so sure I knew what I was doing.'

'We were all fooled,' Sully said. 'The whole world.'

Still squeezing Sully's hand, Hunter looked out of the window. 'I thought the marbles were the best thing. It turns out you're the best thing.'

Sully brushed her golden braids, kissed her temple.

Outside, moons filled the sky with brilliant colours. Here and there, harvesters rose like giant black eels.

A bulldozer was keeping the Tappan Zee Bridge clear, dozing empty vehicles over the railings and into the Hudson. Dom honked thanks as he passed. The bulldozer operator must have been one of the volunteers who hadn't burned any spheres.

As they pulled off the West Side Highway, Sully spotted twenty or thirty harvesters surrounding a school with boarded-up windows. Automatic rifle fire lit the air; one of the harvesters shuddered as bullets ripped into it. The school must be a refugee centre.

'Should we make a run for the place?' Dom said. 'We could get soldiers with rifles and flamethrowers to help us.'

'They look barricaded in,' Hunter said. 'What if they're full, and they don't open the doors when we get there?'

'*If* we get there,' Mandy muttered from the back.

The area around the school was thick with harvesters. Sully hoped Holliday's wasn't, because Holliday's should be empty.

They reached Fifth Avenue. The street was deserted, at least of people. A Seafoam Green harvester was pressed

289

against the wall of an apartment building, its tentacles inside an apartment three stories up. Its back twitched and fluttered as it pushed deeper inside, going after someone. Another was chasing a woman on a motorcycle.

'Get low,' Dom said as Holliday's appeared on their right. Dom jerked the wheel, accelerated right for the building.

Sully ducked into the seat beside Hunter, as low as the seat belt would allow, and squeezed his eyes shut.

The car hit the kerb. An instant later, it crashed through whatever glass and steel was still intact in Holliday's big front window.

When Sully opened his eyes, the Volvo was idling on the showroom floor. He immediately heard the muffled wails that meant a harvester fat with victims was nearby. From the number of screaming voices it sounded like more than one harvester, but he couldn't tell how many.

'Harvesters.' He turned to Hunter. 'You hear that?'

Hunter nodded.

'Here, take this.' Mandy pushed the axe at him.

Sully grabbed it, leaped out, scanned the floor for the Midnight Blues.

They were nowhere in sight.

'Where did you drop them?' Hunter asked.

Sully pointed. 'Right there.' He'd been at the back of the crowd watching what was going on outside. He remembered looking down at the Midnight Blues and realizing he didn't need them, so he'd tossed them to the floor.

A thunk echoed from deeper inside the building.

Another.

A harvester, slamming into steel.

'Where could they be?' Dom asked.

Sully had trouble imagining anyone bothering to pick up used spheres with everything that was happening.

Anyone, that is, except someone who recognized how important they were. 'Holliday.'

The thunk came again.

'*Harvester.*' Dom pointed.

It was slithering down the wall from the second level, heading towards them.

Sully followed Hunter to a door marked STAIRS and rushed inside. Dom came last, pulling the door closed behind him. They'd left Mandy lying in the back of the Volvo with a broken leg, or hip, or something. God, Sully hoped she'd be all right.

As they climbed the stairs, Sully pictured the space outside Holliday's office. It was wide open, with high glass ceilings. More than big enough for harvesters.

Even with the Chocolates and Creams Sully had burned, he was gasping for air by the time they reached the tenth floor. They huddled around the door as Dom cracked it open.

The lobby was packed with harvesters. They were climbing all over each other: Army Green and Mint, Violet and Peach; it looked as if every colour was there. A Cranberry slammed into the door to Holliday's office. The door was partially caved in, its top hinge snapped. There was a three- or four-inch breach through which Sully could see the ceiling inside Holliday's office.

The stairwell door slammed closed with a tremendous bang, throwing Dom backwards. A harvester had slammed into it.

The full weight of their situation hit Sully. They were

trapped in the stairwell, with harvesters waiting at both ends. They didn't know for sure that Holliday had the Midnight Blues and, even if he did, they had no way to get to them.

His friends looked as hopeless as he felt. Dom was staring, dead-eyed, down the stairwell.

A harvester hammered the door again. Sully heard one slam into Holliday's door as if in answer.

Sully pushed the door open a few inches and shouted, 'Holliday!'

'*Sullivan?*' Alex Holliday shouted back.

'Do you have the Midnight Blues? We think we know how to stop them.'

Holliday gave a harsh laugh. 'Oh, really? Sure, I've got them. Come on over, I'd be happy to let you have them.'

The door slammed shut as another harvester hit it. Sully opened it again.

Gunshots rang out. Sully flinched, sure that Holliday or one of his men was shooting at him, but the shots were aimed at a Forest Green harvester. It moved away, seemingly unharmed. Sully wondered if Holliday even cared that there were people inside some of these things.

'We have to figure this out!' Sully called. 'We're talking about a billion lives.'

'One of those lives happens to be mine, and I'm quite fond of it!' Holliday shouted back. 'I'll tell you what, though.' His face appeared in the breach in the door, and was quickly replaced by his hand, clutching a Midnight Blue sphere.

He flung the Midnight Blue through the gap. It bounced once, rolled halfway to Sully.

The other followed, rolling to a stop a little further, maybe thirty feet away.

'I hope you burned some Seafoams,' Holliday said.

Sully felt a hand on his shoulder. 'I'll get them.' It was Dom.

Sully shook his head. 'I'll do it. Just help Hunter stay safe.'

The door slammed shut again. There was a distinct crunch this time as a crease formed towards the top.

'What if we find some rope and rig a line with some kind of rake on the end to drag the spheres to us?' Hunter said.

That sounded great to Sully. Only, where could they find rope? Sully looked down the stairwell for a box with a fire hose folded up in it. The walls were bare as far down as he could see. Somewhere in the store they must have had ribbon for gift wrapping, though.

On the other side of the door, there was a bang, and the screech of twisting metal. Holliday shouted in alarm. Gunshots rang out.

'*Sullivan!*' Holliday screamed. '*David!*'

Sully opened the door and peered out. The centre hinge on the door to Holliday's office had torn free; the door itself was partially folded and stuffed through the doorway. A Copper harvester hit it. It shuddered, bent a few inches further.

'Come on, David. Get the Midnight Blues.'

'You get them!' Dom shouted. 'Come on, you're safer over here anyway.'

A Cranberry harvester surged into the breach in Holliday's door. Gunshots rang out as it wedged itself into the space. The back half of it thrashed, straining to push through the gap. If it remained stuck, Holliday was in luck — it would block the rest of the harvesters from reaching him.

The Cranberry harvester jerked forward a few feet before getting stuck again.

Then it broke free, disappearing inside Holliday's office.

'Sullivan!' More gunshots.

Then silence.

A harvester hit the stairwell door; the crease in the centre grew deeper and more ragged. This door wasn't nearly as strong as the one to Holliday's office.

Another harvester hit the door almost immediately. A sliver of daylight appeared between the door and the moulding. The harvesters didn't have Holliday to distract them any longer; they were all focused on Sully and his friends.

'I gotta go now,' Dom said, pulling Sully away from the door. 'Close it behind me, but be ready to open it when I yell so I don't have to slow down.'

Another harvester hit the door.

'You warned me not to mess with the Midnight Blues,' Hunter said. 'It makes no sense for you to go. I'll go.'

'*I'll* go,' Sully said. 'We need to keep you safe, Hunter.'

Dom grabbed Sully by the collar and shoved him, hard. 'Just be ready to let me back in, goddammit.' He opened the door a foot, looked around and took off.

Half the harvesters in sight turned and surged towards Dom as he sprinted for the Midnight Blues.

'Oh, God. Dom,' Hunter said as Dom bent and scooped up the closer one, then scrambled to the other, sliding on one knee and sweeping the sphere up.

As he turned towards the door, a harvester snared him round the neck. Dom reached up, tried to tear the barbed appendage off. Two more tentacles snared him, round the waist and one calf.

As he was dragged towards the harvester's mouth, Dom underhanded the Midnight Blues towards the door.

Sully burst out and scrambled for the Midnight Blues, with Hunter right behind him. He grabbed one and shoved it at Hunter, who already had the other. Then he raced towards Dom, axe in hand, as the last of Dom — his booted foot — disappeared inside the harvester.

'*No.*' Sully swung the axe; it sank into the harvester to the hilt, spraying a clear, oily liquid. Wrenching the axe free, Sully swung again and hit the harvester in the same spot.

He felt the sting of a harvester's tentacle as it whipped round his knee and yanked. Sully dropped the axe as he hit the floor. He dug at the tiles, trying to pull away as the harvester dragged him towards its waiting mouth.

Hunter screamed his name as he grabbed for the edges of the thing's mouth, trying to find some weak spot he could pull or tear. Its mouth was slick, coated in slime; it squeezed the breath out of Sully, clamping down on his waist, then his chest as he kicked at its insides, trying to hurt it. There had to be some way to hurt it.

He could hear individual voices inside it now, crying for help, praying.

The mouth seemed like a cavern as it opened wide and snapped shut.

Sully was inside it, in darkness.

He shouted in disgust as a ring of muscle convulsed above his head and rippled downward, driving him deeper inside.

He struggled to get back up and out, fought the panic

choking him as his feet touched something. He jerked them up instinctively before realizing it wasn't part of the harvester. It was a victim.

Fingers grasped his foot.

He wished it was Dom, but he knew Dom had been taken by a different harvester.

Sully clawed at the slick insides of the harvester, trying to reach the mouth. He felt the thing begin to rise, maybe heading to one of the moons to drop off its catch.

He tried not to imagine what might happen up there. Instead he focused on Hunter. Had a harvester got her?

He felt like he couldn't breathe, but that couldn't be right, because there were people in there with him who were still alive.

Was it Holliday? Had he been swallowed by the same harvester as Holliday?

For a moment Sully felt certain he had. Then he remembered Holliday had been taken by a Cranberry. This one was a Mustard. He'd been taken by a rarer harvester than Holliday, at least.

Sully cackled at the absurdity of the thought, when the harvester suddenly lurched.

Sully recognized the fluttering feeling in his gut as free fall just as the harvester hit the ground, knocking the wind out of him.

The harvester lay still as Sully gasped, drew in a tight squeal of air, then inhaled again, deeper.

Outside, Hunter called his name.

Sully clawed his way towards the mouth. He pushed his hand through the narrow slit. Blood lubricated the opening.

He drove with his legs until he forced his face through, out into light and fresh air.

'*Sully*.' Hunter knelt in front of the harvester, grasped his hand, and pulled, dragging him out, into her arms. 'I didn't know which one you were in.'

'There are more people in there,' he managed to say as he clung to her.

Hunter pulled the harvester's dead mouth open wider. Reluctantly, Sully stuck his head back inside, reached out, and brushed a flailing hand. He grabbed hold of it and pulled.

A middle-aged woman came out. She rose to her hands and knees and vomited on the tiled floor.

Soon after, Sully gripped another hand, a teenage boy's.

The floor was littered with dead harvesters, draped across each other in a spiny rainbow of colours. Sully glanced around, seeking the one that had got Dom.

Instead, he spotted Dom himself, head down, hands on his knees, looking dazed.

'*Dom*.'

'*Sully*.' Dom raised his head.

They came together in a hug, joined a moment later by Hunter.

'That was, by far, the worst three minutes of my life,' Dom said, still breathless.

'I feel like I just rose from the dead,' Sully said.

A rumbling outside shook the floor, rattled the walls. They headed for the windows.

The moons were bursting. There was no other way to describe it. To their left, a Lime moon was there one moment, nothing but an expanding circle of particles the next. In the distance, seven or eight candy-coloured moons went off in quick succession.

Sully thought of all the people inside. So many people had died, all because he'd raised those spheres to Hunter's temples.

'Look at that.' Dom pointed straight up, through the glass ceiling. A Hot Pink moon was directly overhead, not a thousand feet up.

It exploded, bursting into hot-pink confetti.

Everyone broke into cheers.

'Bye-bye,' Dom said.

The hot-pink confetti fell. As it approached the roof it began to look less like confetti, more like solid debris. When it hit the roof, the glass would come crashing down and cut them to pieces.

Sully grabbed Hunter and Dom. *'Run.'* As they raced for the stairwell, he shouted, *'Look out!'* loud enough for everyone in the room to hear.

The ceiling shattered with a deafening crash as they pushed into the stairwell. They made room for a half-dozen others who ducked in as Hot Pink spheres rained down, hitting the tile floor and ricocheting madly.

Sully spotted a guy running for Holliday's office. He must have realized what was happening too late. Spheres pelted his head and shoulders and he dropped. Sully turned away, not wanting to see.

They kept coming – a hard, thundering hot-pink rain, the spheres piling up, creating small hills as they carpeted the vast lobby. Sully watched, mesmerized. He imagined this happening all over the world.

It seemed to go on for a long time, but probably lasted

only half a minute. When the last sphere finally dropped and clattered to a stop, there was silence.

Sully stepped into the lobby, picked up one of the spheres. It was nothing but a Hot Pink sphere, no different from the one he and Hunter had found in Doodletown. He marvelled at the pink dunes. How many spheres were in this lobby alone? Tens of thousands, at least.

'I'm going to check on Mandy,' Dom said.

Sully nodded. He kept thinking of the dead man buried somewhere under the Hot Pinks. A lot of people must have suffered the same fate, although most people would have been hiding from the harvesters, safely indoors, unless they happened to have a glass roof.

He wondered what happened now. If Hunter hadn't burned the Golds, someone else would have. That was what you did with spheres. That's what everyone did. But he and Hunter were the ones who'd actually done it. Were they heroes for stopping the harvest, or criminals for setting it in motion? Sully imagined that would get sorted out soon enough. Right now he was just glad to be alive, glad Hunter and his friends were alive.

What about Holliday? Sully looked around. A dozen or more refugees from the harvesters were standing around the edges of the lobby, ankle-deep in Hot Pinks. There was no sign of Holliday.

He couldn't remember if he'd seen the Cranberry harvester leave Holliday's office.

'I'll be right back,' he told Hunter.

Walking on the spheres was a challenge; they were slick, and Sully was exhausted. He had to get down on hands and knees to cross a rolling dune, as spheres kicked out beneath his feet and rolled.

When he reached the mangled door, he gripped the frame and stepped through, leaving a smear of blood behind. His wounded hand was throbbing, but he was too preoccupied to numb it. Let it throb; it reminded him he was alive.

He found Holliday in the far corner of the office. There was a handgun lying a few feet from his body, a halo of blood blooming around his head. Holliday hadn't wanted the harvester to get him, so he'd saved the last bullet for himself.

Sully squeezed his eyes shut and turned away.

CHAPTER 34

Across the Hudson, an avalanche of Sky Blue spheres blocked the winding highway that hugged the steep hills. Anyone who couldn't get to work could always pull over, burn a couple of Sky Blues and better appreciate the humour of their situation. Maybe Sully should burn some Sky Blues; he thought he had a decent sense of humour, but who couldn't use a little more laughter in their life?

He wouldn't, though. He was through burning spheres after what had happened. It was hard for him to sort out his feelings about the spheres. The Midnight Blue had undone itself to save them all, and while Sully still struggled to think of a sphere's life the way he did a human life, what the Midnight Blue had done showed that they really did mean well, just like Hunter had said. They cared about their hosts. Maybe, in their own way, they even loved them.

It was interesting how, in the weeks after the parents exploded and the harvesters died, people were repulsed by the spheres lying all over. They didn't want to touch them, let alone burn them. Five months later, people were dipping their toes back into the water. It was hard to resist something that made you better than you were, with no effort on your part. People who'd burned spheres before the invasion seemed especially willing, because, what the hell, if the parents somehow figured out a way to return, they were already screwed. Why not be stronger, faster, smarter and funnier until then?

Sully could see the logic in that, but the scars on his hands and feet were still red and angry, the memory of being inside that harvester still fresh. He imagined it always would be.

Could the parents come back with new harvesters, without someone burning the Midnight Blues and reopening the gate? Every day that went by, Sully breathed a little easier on that front. If they had another way of opening the gate, or some sort of back door, what were they waiting for?

Hunter reached over, took Sully's hand. Sully turned, and as he gazed into her eyes he felt a rush of pleasure, a moment of disbelief that she was here with him, that they were alive.

In the front seat, Mandy laughed. 'They're making a movie about us.'

'Oh, yeah?' Dom said. 'Who's playing me?'

Mandy scrolled down. 'They haven't cast any of us yet.'

Dom pulled into the Bear Mountain lot, parked right around the same spot Sully had parked the last time he'd been there. The black SUV containing their Secret Service contingent had parked about ten spaces away.

As he hopped out, Sully grabbed the plastic sack of Subway sandwiches they'd picked up. Hunter got Mandy's crutches out of the back as Dom helped her out of the car.

'Hopefully, whoever plays you won't scream like a mama's boy when the harvester eats his head,' Sully said.

'I didn't *scream*. I shouted. There's a difference.'

Sully heard hushed voices behind them; he could hear every word without straining.

'That's not her. That's make-up.' Over the past few months it had become the thing among school-age girls to colour their skin gold.

'I'm telling you, that's *them*. There's *Cucuzza*.'

Dom turned at the sound of his name, smiled and waved.

'We have to make sure this doesn't go to our heads.' Mandy was scooting along briskly. She'd got her cast off last week; the steel rod in her femur would be with her forever. 'I hate self-important celebrities. I don't want to end up becoming one.'

'I do,' Dom said, laughing. 'I want to become a self-important jerk.'

'Can we have your autographs?' shouted one of the kids following them, as if on cue.

They stopped and waited for two young girls and a mom to catch up.

'I'll get two of the eight-by-tens from the car,' Dom said. He was beaming. He loved this.

'He'd play himself in the movie, if they'd let him,' Sully said.

'There's gonna be a movie?' one of the girls asked.

Sully was still surprised that everyone so easily overlooked the part about them starting the whole mess in the first place, instead focusing on how they saved the world. CNN, MSNBC, Fox News, all called burning the Midnight Blues 'inevitable'. That four seventeen-year-olds had figured out how to stop the invasion once it was set into motion was, in the words of *The*

New York Times, 'astonishing'. In a speech watched by pretty much everyone, the president called it 'an act of bravery that will never be forgotten, so long as humans walk the earth'.

Sully was just glad it was over.

Dom returned with the photos. When Hunter passed them to him, Sully signed as neatly as his crappy handwriting would allow, thinking about that day not long ago – yet also a thousand years ago – when he'd worried he would always be remembered as the kid who lost the Cherry Red. If he'd only known.

As the family went on their way, Sully put his arm round Hunter, and they headed towards the lake. It was a beautiful fall day, perfect for a picnic.

Hunter laughed.

'What?' Sully asked.

'There's a Plum, hidden right over there.' She pointed in the direction of the Bear Mountain lodge. 'If we'd stayed longer that day we came here hunting, we could have found a rarity six as well.'

'They're all rarity one now,' Sully said.

He wasn't sure if that was good or bad. After what had happened, a lot of people had decided it was bad and wanted the spheres hauled away and dumped deep in the ocean, or buried like nuclear waste. That would be some project, because there were billions of them.

On the plus side, there were no more brag badges. Anyone who wanted to be a little taller, more athletic, or better-looking could just pick up a couple of spheres, if they were willing to take the chance.

ACKNOWLEDGEMENTS

My agent, Seth Fishman, played an especially huge role in this book, guiding me into the realm of young adult fiction and providing copious feedback as I wrote. Sincere thanks, my friend.

I'm grateful to Ian Creasey, whose feedback on the first draft of this novel transformed it, as his critiques often do, and to James Pugh, who was always there with solutions when I got stuck. His ability to generate brilliant ideas in a matter of seconds leaves me dumbfounded.

Special thanks to my niece, Sarah Berghela, who was my coolness consultant. She helped make sure my characters spoke and acted like modern seventeen-year-olds. I now know that high fives are no longer cool.

Thanks to fellow writer Tina Connolly, who posted some kind and very timely words on the Codex Writers Group website that gave me the idea to write a novel based on a short story I'd all but forgotten about.

Sincere thanks to Sheila Williams, who bought 'Midnight Blue', the short story that was the genesis of *Burning Midnight*, for *Asimov's Science Fiction*.

Many, many thanks to Kate Sullivan, my editor at Delacorte Press, for believing in this novel, and for her incredibly insightful feedback and guidance.

Finally, love and gratitude to my wife, Alison Scott, for her support, especially during the times I struggled with doubts as I wrote this one.

ABOUT THE AUTHOR

Will McIntosh is the author of several adult speculative fiction novels and a frequent short-story writer. His first novel, *Soft Apocalypse*, was a finalist for the Locus Award. 'Bridesicle', a short story published in *Asimov's Science Fiction*, won a Hugo Award for Best Short Story and was later expanded into his second novel, *Love Minus Eighty*, which was an ALA RUSA Reading List selection for science fiction. His newest novel for adults, *Defenders*, has been optioned for film by Warner Bros. *Burning Midnight* is his first novel for young adults. Will lives with his family in Williamsburg, Virginia, where he is working on his next young-adult novel.